D1328574

The Princess
of Las Pulgas

This book is dedicated to two teachers from whom I was fortunate to learn.

Mrs. Stockton, thank you for all those afternoons when you read stories to your third-grade class at Columbia Elementary. Thank you for creating a classroom where children learned and loved the experience. Thank you for all that time you spent with us outside of class.

Mr. Ridgley, your sense of humor and your belief in me were largely responsible for getting me through a rough senior year at Live Oak High.

The Princess
of Las Pulgas

C. Lee McKenzie

WestSide Books ®
Lodi, New Jersey

Published by WestSide Books
60 Industrial Road
Lodi, NJ 07644
973-458-0485
Fax: 973-458-5289

This is a work of fiction. All characters, places, and events
described are imaginary. Any resemblance to real people,
places, and events is entirely coincidental.

Library of Congress Cataloging-in-Publication Data

McKenzie, C. Lee.
  The princess of Las Pulgas / C. Lee McKenzie. -- 1st ed.
    p. cm.
  ISBN 978-1-934813-44-7
  [1. Grief--Fiction. 2. Loss (Psychology)--Fiction. 3. Interpersonal relations--Fiction. 4.
Moving, Household--Fiction. 5. High schools--Fiction. 6. Schools--Fiction.] I. Title.
  PZ7.M4786758Pri 2010
  [Fic]--dc22

2010031119

International Standard Book Number: 978-1-934813-44-7
School ISBN: 978-1-934813-46-1
Cover design by David Lemanowicz
Interior design by David Lemanowicz

Printed in the United States of America
10 9 8 7 6 5 4 3 2 1

First Edition

The Princess
of Las Pulgas

1

Last night I pleaded with Death, but he turned a bony back to me, pushed Hope into the corridor and shut the door.

Now we're waiting, all of us. Mom in the chair next to Dad's bed, holding his hand as if she can keep him with us as long as she doesn't let go. Keith asleep on the rollaway bed a nurse wheeled in earlier. He's on his side, his long runners' legs drawn to his chest and his head resting on his arm. I'm scrunched down into a chair at the foot of Dad's bed. I no longer feel like I have a body. I'm not even tired, just numb. Then there's Death. He's backed into the darkest corner.

I twist my Sweet Sixteen bracelet around and around, counting the tiny links. Mom and Dad gave it to me in June, before I learned how hospitals smelled at two a.m., or how I preferred nightmares to being awake.

I hate being here.

I hate what's happening.

I want it over.

I close my eyes and let my head fall back against the vinyl chair.

No. I don't mean that.

Two a.m.: The hands of the wall clock go around and around. Slow. Steady. Doling out the hours, one second at a time.

Three a.m. I must have slept, but I don't remember dozing and I still feel tired.

Three-ten a.m. Something's different, and the shift is as sudden as it is subtle—a missed tick of a clock, an un-explained space in the air, a suspended drip over a sink.

A steady, high-pitched sound shrieks through the room. A flat line of green streaks across the monitor and that darkest corner of the room is suddenly empty.

Keith sits up on the edge of the rollaway, staring at the floor. Mom rests her head against Dad's still chest. Around me the room seems to curl up at the edges like a late autumn leaf and I'm sure everything will soon crumble into tiny bits.

∞

My dad was an important man in Channing. His in-vestment counseling business had survived despite the economy and all of his clients were presidents or board chairpersons. Dad had held just about every office on the city council, too, and was the financial advisor to the mayor, so the memorial service is long with speeches and the church crowded with VIPs.

Mom hired the caterer that her best friend, Maureen Fogger, always uses; that meant white-jacketed strangers armed with trays of perfect small food are threading their way among the black-or gray-clothed guests. Our home fills with the hum of voices.

The mayor proposes a toast; the arts commissioner proposes a toast; three board members of Dad's company propose toasts. By four p.m., people who were silent and sad-faced earlier are now talking too loudly, smiling, and telling jokes. Maureen Fogger has one of Dad's young partners cornered. She's leaning in a little too close and the guy's face is flushed, with his eyes darting around the room. Nobody notices his silent cry for help except me.

An hour ago, Keith retreated upstairs. Mom stationed herself in the chair by the fireplace like a lonely planet, and the guests orbit her, taking her hand, touching her shoulder. I haven't seen her cry since that night at the hospital, but I've heard her through her bedroom door. Now I think her whole body must be filling with tears while she waits for the reception to end and for everyone to leave.

Dad was always inviting people home. "Come for dinner, for the weekend, for Labor Day," he'd say. He insisted on balloons and confetti for special celebrations. Confetti still turns up in the carpet from last New Year's Eve. He had the barbeque ready hours before my end-of-year beach parties started, hours before Mom had a chance to tell him whether he was cooking hot dogs or hamburgers. We called him our party animal. If Dad were here, he'd be moving from group to group, telling a joke, gently guiding Maureen away and letting his young partner escape. Dad would have loved this "party."

I'm not in the mood to love anything about what's happening, so as soon as possible I slip away to hide in my room, where my cat Quicken is curled up on my pillow in a tight, purring ball. Even with the door closed, I'm not far enough away to avoid the noise of people chattering downstairs. I slide open the window facing the beach, inviting the drum of ocean waves to enter. Their steady rhythm has always rocked me when I was uneasy, but today, the crashing waves are angry, not soothing.

Closing the window, I fall across the bed with my arms spread wide. Quicken arches her back, stretches, and then brushes back and forth along my side before curling up against me. In seconds her purr rumbles deep in her throat.

Disappearing inside my head, imagining a happy ending, saw me through those months of Dad's cancer, so I need for it to get me through tonight and tomorrow and the next day.

"Carlie, love. This is tough, but you'll be just fine. I know it."

Dad used to say that whenever I'd bring him a crisis. Then he'd brush my cheek with his fingers and kiss the tears.

I'm not so sure this time, Dad.

2

This is the first year since I learned about Jack-O'-Lanterns that we don't have one for Halloween. Snaggle-toothed grins were Dad's specialty. Mom turns out the walkway lights at dusk. We don't answer the door for the goblins and witches.

Only one ghost is allowed here now.

3

Mom's friend, Maureen Fogger, invites us for Thanksgiving dinner.

We go.

We eat.

We leave early.

I fall asleep to Mom's crying. It's become as much a part of the background noise as the sound of the ocean outside our windows.

4

I drive Keith to the Christmas tree farm like Dad used to do. We saw down a six-foot fir and tie it onto the top of the car. At home we carry it as far as the front door, look at each other and set it down in front of the bay window.

That's where it stays.

5

Mom goes to Maureen Fogger's New Year's Eve fundraiser. I think Keith's at Mitch's house. I cancel babysitting for the Franklins and stay home. It's just the TV and me, with Quicken curled on my lap, purring.

6

"Ten. Nine. Eight." The chorus of Time Square voices beat out the final seconds of the year. As the ball plunges to the count of one, paper bits flurry across the TV screen—a sudden end and a sudden beginning. I choke back tears at that thought—the one I've had since I watched my dad die—the moment when the world grew one breath smaller.

When I switch off the television the house goes silent. Tonight's the first time since the memorial service that I've been here after dark without Mom or Keith someplace close by, and now loneliness crowds the room.

I twist my Sweet Sixteen bracelet around and around, fingering the tiny links.

Setting Quicken down, I stretch up from the couch. "Come on, fur person."

Leaving on a few downstairs lights for Mom and Keith, I pad up the steps behind my cat. She leaps to her cushion at the foot of my bed and curls into a tight circle.

I wish I could fall into a steady purring sleep like she does. I wish Mom would come home. I even wish Keith would shuffle down the hall to his mole hole of a room.

On my desk, my journal lies open to the almost blank sheet of paper with a date across the top. I trace my finger over "October 22." The rest of the page is blotched with old tears.

Maybe because I can't stand to reread about the darkness inside me, I've avoided writing anything since that day. I feel like I'm wrapped in a cocoon of grief.

"Carlie love, you've been shut away long enough. It's time to rejoin the world."

My dad's talking to me like he used to, only now his words come like whispers inside my heart.

The journal was his idea. After I won Channing's Scribe contest my freshman year, he handed me a small package. Inside was this blank book embossed with C. E. On the inside cover he'd written, "For Carlie Edmund, one girl who has the imagination to write wonderful stories. Put some of those ideas down and use them later, when you need them."

Since October 22nd, there's nothing this One Girl has to write that anyone would want to read, especially me.

"You have all kinds of good ideas, Carlie love."

"I only have one idea, and it's so not a good one."

"Good or bad, you have to start sometime."

I turn to a blank page and take up my pen. "Sometimes bad things happen . . . even in Channing."

The first bad thing that springs into my head is spelled c-a-n-c-e-r, then comes the vision of that hospital room, the hours plodding forward. More memories creep forward like tiny monsters and sit hunched, waiting for me to notice them.

I drop my pen onto the journal page, tasting rather than hearing the low sound just behind my lips; not quite a cry, not quite a moan, just something sharp-edged. Something I'd like to keep hidden.

When I read what I just wrote, some letters aren't clear. Even though I've turned to a new page, the tears have made the surface rough, so October 22nd has bled through to a new day.

What can I write that won't tear at me every time I read it? What can I write that won't crush my heart and send me back to that awful day when life changed forever?

The answer—*nothing*.

"I'm sorry, Dad," I say softly, then I listen to the silence. I don't know what's worse, when he talks to me or when he doesn't.

From outside comes the sound of a car pulling into the driveway, then the garage door slides open. Mom's home.

I change into my pajamas and robe, brush my hair and pull it into a long dark ponytail that hangs to my shoulders. I got the thick black mane from my mom's side of the family. Keith inherited Dad's sandy color and the spatter of freckles across his cheeks. We don't look like we're related, except for our eyes, and those are all Dad—sand-pebble gray.

Mom will make cocoa before she goes to bed, just like she did when Dad was here. Cocoa is still a bedtime ritual, but it's not the happy one it used to be. Now she sits alone at the table, studying real estate books, or, as she says, "sorting out the finances." After being by myself most of the night I need company, so cocoa and Mom to talk to sound good.

17

"Hi, Mom. How'd the fundraiser go?" She's already pouring milk into a saucepan when I come into the kitchen.

"Let's see." She sets the saucepan on the cooktop, and stirs in cocoa. "I made a hundred bucks, plus a fifty-dollar bonus from the caterer at Maureen Fogger's annual charity event—proceeds going to Bangladesh or Milwaukee, depending on which place needs it more this year."

Mom's attempt at keeping it light doesn't fool me. She was embarrassed over having to work with the catering crew at a party she should have been enjoying as a guest.

"Oh, and I saw Eric Peterson. He was parking cars."

"Wonderful. Now I suppose he'll spread the word about our money problems."

"I don't think so. I gave him an excuse about volunteering and escaped to the back entrance." She turns the flame under the pan to low and sits at the table. "It was only a small uncomfortable moment." Mom's humor fizzles again.

For years, she helped Mrs. Fogger organize her charity party. She hired the caterers. She walked in the front door with the guests. From the way Mom looks and sounds, tonight's been an embarrassing ordeal, more like hell than just uncomfortable.

"You didn't go out? No party at Lena's this year?"

I shake my head. *There was a party. I just didn't go.*

We jump at the sudden sound of the front door slamming. Keith's familiar shuffling starts at the entry and crosses the dining room toward the kitchen. He pauses at the kitchen door.

"How was the movie?" Mom's voice gives her away,

at least to me. She wants Keith to stick around and talk to us. She knows he won't.

"Didn't go. Stayed at Mitch's." His jaw is tight, like it's been for months, and I've forgotten when he looked at either one of us as if we were really there.

"Do you want some co—?" But Keith has already started upstairs. When his bedroom door closes, not exactly with a bang, but close, Mom slumps in her chair and rubs her eyes.

Thanks to my mole of a brother, she looks more exhausted than when I came in. Slowly she straightens her back as if every muscle aches, then she goes to the stove and pours cocoa for each of us.

We sip from our mugs, staring into the steamy liquid and letting the quiet hang in the air between us. We have more to think about than we have to talk about.

"I do have some good news for the start of the new year." Her words should sound hopeful. They would if she said them that way. "When I finally opened last week's mail, I found out that I scored a ninety on my first Realtor's exam."

"Great, Mom." I try to mean it, but everything that has to do with her real estate course reminds me how different our lives are now.

"It's only a practice test, but I feel a lot more confident after taking it."

We fall into more silence. I have no good news, except that Lena called to tell me that *the* Nicolas Benz might be asking me to the Spring Fling. It's not a sure thing, so it's only semi-good news and it's just not so important as it would have been last year.

"Carlie. . . I—," Mom clears her throat and looks up at the ceiling. She does this when she has something to tell us that isn't good. When Dad was first diagnosed with cancer, she studied the ceiling for a long time, letting the tears trickle into her hairline before she looked Keith and me in the eyes and told us about the reports.

I can't take too much more of her staring-at-the-ceiling news.

"I made a decision." Now her eyes are on me, and the way the word *decision* sounds sets off an alarm in my head.

"I wasn't going to say anything yet, but . . . . Well, there's never going to be a good time to tell you. It's not something I decided tonight either, and it's something—" Mom sits back in her chair. "We need to sell this house."

"Sell?" I sound like all the air is leaking out from between my ribs.

Mom puts her hand over mine, but I snatch mine back.

"We can't make it otherwise. I have to free up some capital and the house is the only asset that'll get us out of this mess. The health insurance company isn't coming up with any more money to cover the last of the hospital bills unless we sue them, and I can't face that right now. Not ever." She sighs. "All I want is some peace for a while."

"But Mom! It's the middle of my junior year!"

"I know, Carlie. It'll very hard for you and Keith, but no matter how I add up the figures, I come up way too short. Even if I finish the real estate course and start working by the summer, we'll end up losing everything. I can't even promise you college right now." Mom gazes into her mug as if she's looking for answers. "We can't afford to live in Channing anymore."

"No!"

"I borrowed money on the house and now the payments—" She presses her hand against her lips as if she doesn't want the words to escape. "They're so much bigger than I'd thought. I made a mistake when I figured out how much I'd have to pay each month, but I wasn't thinking clearly. I knew I needed money, so I got it the quickest way I could."

I push away from the table and get to my feet. "You can't do this. There has to be some other way—"

"It's late. We'll talk tomorrow. Let's keep this between us until we have a family meeting, okay? Your brother's so edgy that I need to choose one of his good moments to tell him."

I hurry out of the kitchen.

"Wait." She catches me at the stairs. "I need you to understand." There's pleading in her voice, something I've never heard before when she's talked to me.

I yank my arm free and run up the stairs.

"I wouldn't do this if I didn't have—"

Slamming my door, I lean against it, squeezing my eyes shut and tasting the salt tears at the corner of my mouth. Quicken jumps from my bed and rubs against my legs until I pick her up and cry into her short gray fur. She nuzzles her Siamese understanding and sympathy under my chin.

With her tucked close to me, I open my window, and the sound of the Pacific floods my room. When I set the cat onto the windowsill, she wraps her tail tightly around her haunches and stares across our beachfront. Like me, she's never lived anywhere else but here. The steady rhythm of waves has always rocked me to sleep, and I've never thought about how important that sound was until right now. I get one of those heart-shock moments. *What if there's no ocean where we end up living?*

I lift Quicken and close the window, leaning my forehead against the pane, wondering where we'll wind up and what the next bad event will be that we'll have to face.

The shelf over my desk holds a paperweight I won in the eighth-grade poetry contest. Two Channing Yearbooks lie stacked next to it, and on top of those sits my broken Jack-in-the-Box. When I crank the handle of the metal toy, it swings around freely, not catching the tiny gears. The puppet's trapped inside.

Cradling Jack's small prison, I lie curled around it on my bed. *I hate you for dying, Dad.* I can't bury my face any deeper in the pillow. *I hate everybody in this stupid world.*

"Carlie love, this is tough, but you'll be just fine. I know it."

No, Dad! This will not be just fine.

7

The house sells in less than three weeks. Prime location, top-notch school district. The buyers need to move in ASAP, and they're willing to pay our moving expenses if Mom agrees to be out before the end of February. The day they came for a walk-through I kept my fingers in my ears and tried to block that Realtor's voice. She clicked her way through the rooms on stiletto-heels with a clipboard in hand, calling Mom Sarah as if they've known each other a long time.

She sweeps in Sunday morning after the sale, before even my early-bird Mom dresses or any of us eats breakfast. She waves the papers that, once signed, will turn our house over to a couple from Arizona with a teenage daughter.

I can't watch while Mom signs away our family home. I grab Quicken and take the stairs two at a time. In my room I put her on her cushion and throw myself face-down across my bed. I can't cry, but my heart feels bloated and heavy. It's holding all the tears I can no longer shed.

Who's getting my room? That snotty redheaded sophomore with the tight jeans and too much mascara, that's who.

"Missy will be a sophomore at Channing. I'm so happy that she'll already have someone she knows there." That's what the girl's mom said the day they came to see the house.

I wanted to scream "Get out" as Prissy Missy swaggered her way through the rooms, fingering my bedspread, peering into my closet.

Rolling over I cover my eyes with one arm.

So she arrives in Channing and, what, takes my place? My house that's right on the beach? The house everyone wants to come to for the end-of-the-school-year party?

Why did you have to leave us in this mess, Dad?

I'd hurl myself out the window, but I'm smart enough to know I'll probably only break a leg. Instead, I hurl a pillow at the door. Quicken does a cat stretch, then curls up again. I dive under the covers.

⌇

The next day at school I write a short essay in French class, but after I hand it in, I can't even remember what it's about. I stumble through chemistry, and one of Mr. Mancy's pop quizzes in English. Listening to my teachers' voices, studying the faces of my friends, and capturing the sounds and images of the school take on a kind of frenzy. Each desk I sit at becomes important. Each conversation about homework or Mancy's quizzes becomes precious, something to be tucked into a scrapbook. On the English bulletin board, the deadline for the Scribe's yearly nonfiction contest is posted as April 20th—a lifetime away, and a contest that might happen without me.

A phantom hand clenches my stomach at the thought that I might not be at Channing for much longer. Mom kept saying she'd try to keep us in the school district, but she couldn't promise anything. And then yesterday, when I brought up the subject, she suddenly had somewhere to go.

As I pile my books into my backpack, Lena catches my arm. "You haven't answered my emails. How come?"

"I've been sort of *busy*. You know—"

She squeezes my hand. *Busy* has become my code for "crying in my bedroom."

As we make our way to the hall, Lena says, "What I wrote was that Nicolas is definitely asking you to the Spring Fling." I must not look so happy as she expects. "What? You don't want a date with Nicolas Benz?"

"No. I mean, yes."

She shakes her head. "Well, there's more. You've got to check out Sean Wright, the new French tutor."

"I don't need a tutor." I learn French almost the same way I learned to walk. It's the one class I can ace with almost no effort.

"You need one now." She flutters her eyelashes, performing her coy act, and then she grabs my arm. "It's him. Don't look." She tightens her grip. "Okay. Now!"

He's closing his locker when I glance back. Then he walks past us and our eyes lock onto his dark hair that's swept behind each ear, and his deep-set blue eyes. *Where did he get that tan in January?* He must need glasses because he doesn't even notice the two of us gaping.

"I'm signing up for French and dropping study hall."

I roll my eyes. "You hate French."

"I've changed my mind." She looks over my shoulder. "Eric's coming," she says, then whispers in my ear. "Now do you need a tutor?"

"No." I thread my arms through the straps of my backpack.

"So are we meeting for lunch?"

"Sure. See you after chemistry."

Eric steps around me and hangs his arm over Lena's shoulders and they nuzzle their way to their next class. At the end of the hall, Lena glances back, mouthing *au revoir*.

Before I tackle lunch with Lena, I need to figure out how to tell my best friend I'm moving and may not finish my junior year here, so I cut chemistry. It's one class I shouldn't cut, but it's also one class at Channing that I wouldn't miss.

The wide sweep of lawn leading to the grove of eucalyptus trees at the edge of the campus offers a quiet hideout. I slide my back down the peeling bark and draw my knees under my chin. If I could, I'd stay here until the end of the day.

"Carlie love, hiding doesn't make what's scary go away."

You don't understand, Dad. Once I tell Lena what's happening, it becomes true.

"You're brave enough to handle the truth."

I hope he hears my sigh. It's brimming with messages about how brave I feel.

☞

Heading into the cafeteria, I spot Nicolas in the Bistro section. I haven't hung around school or gone to Sam's

Shack in months, so even if he did want to ask me to the dance, he hasn't had the chance. I haven't given *anybody* a chance to ask me *anything*. I've avoided talking to most of my friends by making excuses about needing to study, needing to help Mom, even needing to clean my room. Dad's right. Hiding won't change what's about to happen, but he's wrong about my being brave.

Before I can duck out the door, Nicolas spots me, waves and comes straight toward me in that slow stroll that makes every girl stop what she's doing and gape. He leaves a wake of huddled chatter and longing down the center of the room. *No wonder he has an ego the size of Planet Earth.*

"Hey, Carlie. How's it going? Haven't seen you at the Shack lately." He sweeps the drape of golden hair from his forehead.

"I've been *busy* with things at home."

"Yeah. Sorry." He comes close and, in what Lena calls his velvet voice, says, "I know it's been rough. I mean about your dad." He clears his throat. "Is it okay to call you now? Thought I'd ask. You know, in case—"

"That's . . . fine. Yes."

He brushes my arm with his hand, then makes his way back to the Bistro section, ruffling the sea of lust again. A few girls cast envious glances my direction, showing me that at least one thing is still the way it should be. I'm still Carlie Edmund, the girl who has Nicolas Benz's attention. For just a second, I'm excited about the Spring Fling. Then it's gone. In its place is the question, *How am I going to buy a dress?*

I should have kept that babysitting job New Year's Eve

*with the Franklins. If I could wheedle Mrs. Franklin into
hiring me again and her social life picks up, I might be able
to make two hundred dollars in time for the dance. Then I
could get a dress.*

Lena waves at me across the noisy room, her bouncy
ponytail held high by a pale blue ribbon.

I weave through the crowded tables and sit across from
her.

"I waited outside chemistry for you, and you, like, vanished." She sounds pouty.

"I took a break." I remove the top slice of bread from
my sandwich and fold the bottom slice over the lettuce and
cheese.

"Are you still on a diet?"

Lena knows *way* too much about me. "I'm just not that
hungry."

"I saw you with Nicolas. So did he—?"

"Not yet."

She places her bowl of soup on the table and pushes
the tray aside. "Were you, like, sick Sunday? You didn't answer your cell, and when I called your home phone, your
mom said you were in bed."

"I was tired." I bite into my half sandwich.

She dips her spoon into the soup and stirs up rice and
peas from the bottom. "So what's up with you? I mean you
seemed to be getting . . . well, better a few weeks ago, and
now . . . Do I have to dig for what's going on, or are you
going to clue me in sometime, maybe before the world
ends? Aren't we still BFFs?" Lena spoons soup into her
mouth and fixes her eyes on me.

"Of course we are. It's just that . . .We're moving."
Those two words have been festering inside my head for
over a month and now they've finally burst out.

Lena's spoon halts halfway to her mouth, soup dripping back into the bowl. "You can't move! Where will we
have the end-of-the-year beach party?"

I crush the sandwich bag and hope the wetness in my
eyes will evaporate.

"I'm sorry, Carlie. Really. That didn't come out right.
I was so . . . Will you have to leave Channing?"

"To be determined. Listen—I have to go." I grab my
backpack and walk out the cafeteria door as quickly as I
can without running. My life's unraveling and I want the
threads to come apart in private, not in front of the entire
student body.

∽

By the next week it's all been determined. Keith and I
will have to change schools.

At dinner, Mom sits at the end of the dining room table
where Dad used to sit. I hadn't noticed until now that
she'd moved from her end of the table to his, and how Keith
had slid the extra chair on his side to the wall, and that I'd
started sitting across from him. The three of us are all clus-
tered together—the incredible shrinking family.

"The only place I can find on such sort notice is in Las
Pulgas." Mom's face says what remains unspoken: *I'm
sorry we have to move. I'm sorry it's Las Pulgas. I'm sorry.*

"Las Pulgas is the worst place in the world," I say.
"Flea Town's a joke. Why would any place want to be
named after disgusting bugs?"

"Carlie," Mom frowns. "The rent's affordable, it'll let me pay off our bills and still have something to tuck away until I can get my Realtor's license and start making a decent salary." Behind her, boxes are stacked three high against the dining room wall. She's already taken down the family pictures and packed them. "Besides, at least they'll allow one cat."

I push my salad around with my fork. "When do we have to go?"

"I put down the cleaning deposit and the first and last months' rent today." Mom's eyes water, but she stabs a last bite of chicken and says a little too loudly, "We can move in by the fifteenth."

My fork clatters onto my plate.

Keith reaches for another roll and slathers it with butter. "How come we can't finish the year here?"

"For one, you're not going to be living in the Channing district anymore." Mom shoves her chair back, stands quickly and carries her plate into the kitchen. "For another, we'll be down to one car, so commuting here's out of the question."

Keith and I exchange looks. "One car?" We sound like a mini-chorus.

"Now's the time to come up with one of your bright ideas, Carlie. Save our cars," Keith says.

"I've spoken to your counselors," Mom says over the sound of running water. "They'll help with the transfer paperwork and setting up your classes at Las Pulgas."

"Las Pulgas's track team sucks." Keith says.

"I hate that word, Keith," Mom calls from the kitchen.

30

"Yeah? Well, I hate Las Pulgas's track team." Keith shoves his chair away from the table and disappears into the TV room.

Mom returns to sit across from me. "So what do *you* hate?"

I want to say *you* but I can't, not when Mom looks at me like that. I can't say out loud that I hate Dad for getting sick and dying. *How about the universe and all the rotten, stinking stuff it offers up? What do I hate?* Instead, all I say is, "My life."

Mom cradles her head between both hands. "Tell me about it."

I close my eyes, letting a shadow pass between us; then, even though I know it's my imagination, fingers soft as down brush my cheek.

8

At breakfast that next Saturday morning, Mom springs her surprise for how I'm going to spend the day, ruining any plans I might have made. Not that I had any, but I would have made one if I'd known what she had in mind for us.

"Carlie, I don't want to argue with you. You and Keith are going with me to see the apartment." Mom stacks the dishes in the dishwasher and returns to the table. "It's the only way you're going to be able to decide what to take and what to . . . get rid of."

I mash my back against my chair and cross my arms. "Do I even get a closet?"

"Of course. It's just smaller. We're all going to be living in a smaller space, but you'll each have your own room."

Keith grunts and stares at his empty plate.

"Be ready in half an hour, and, Keith, take that Christmas tree from the front of the house." She doesn't give either of us time to say anything else; she's out of the kitchen and up the stairs to her room.

An hour later we're inside the Las Pulgas apartment,

but I'm seeing nothing but catacombs. The dark rooms with a narrow connecting hall remind me of pictures in a *National Geographic* article about the early Christian burial site. When I open the door to my room, I half expect to find bones stacked in crevices.

From my window I look out onto other windows the same as mine. We're in a complex that forms a rectangular courtyard, with two stories of identical doors facing across a central cement space. *Catacombs on the inside, San Quentin on the outside.*

Our apartment is on the second floor so we have *the view*. Below and to the right is a kidney-shaped pool the size of the hot tub at Dad's club. One soon-to-be-dead palm droops in the corner where I guess it used to shade some plastic lounge chairs. Dead palm next to collapsed chairs. *This must be a Las Pulgas still life.*

I walk off the distance from the window wall to the closet, then do the same between the other two walls. *Things to get rid of: bed, dresser, chair, desk. Not enough room for most of it.*

When I look up Keith's leaning against my door jamb. "Mine's smaller," he says.

"That's impossible."

"Want to hear the really good news?"

Keith wouldn't be talking to me like a normal human being if he didn't have something evil planned. He wants to see my reaction to his "good" news. I brace myself.

"Maybe you should see this for yourself." He points down the hall and walks in that direction, motioning for me to follow him.

33

Whatever you do, Carlie, do not give him the satisfaction of showing how you feel . . . no matter how terrible . . . no matter how—

He's stopped a few feet from my bedroom, waiting with a smug look.

"Okay, what is it?"

"Our bathroom."

I peer inside at a shower stall, a single sink with one cabinet underneath, and a medicine chest above. I have to look behind the door to find the toilet. Along one side, linoleum peels back at the edge of the floor, and there's no window. I flip the switch and a fan churns, clicking loudly every few seconds. And then it hits me.

"Did you say, *our?*" Too late to stop myself, I've reacted exactly the way Keith knew I would.

He does his evil laugh, the one that microwaves my blood to an instant boil, then shuffles back toward the depressing living room.

"Mom!" I hurry into the kitchen where she's counting shelves. "I can't share a bathroom with Keith."

She writes in her notebook, then she fixes me with her patient expression, which means she'll try to reason with me before she tells me to get over it.

"Never mind. I've seen enough. I'll meet you at the car." I pound my way back to where we parked and slouch in the passenger seat. I'm deep into thoughts of running away to live with an isolated Indian tribe when my cell chimes Beethoven's Fifth, Mrs. Franklin's special ring tone.

"Carlie, I desperately need a sitter for tonight. Are you free?"

34

"Hold on—let me check my calendar." I put the phone to my chest. *Think Fling dress.*

I put the phone back to my ear. "I'll make some changes so I can help you out, Mrs. Franklin. I know I kind of let you down on New Year's Eve."

She agrees, and as I put my phone back into my pocket, Mom and Keith come down the street. Keith's walking ahead, with his hands stuffed in his jeans, his head down. Mom's behind, letting the space between them grow with every step.

9

That night, helped with a small bribe of yogurt and chocolate sprinkles smuggled in under Mrs. Franklin's vegan nose, I tuck the Franklin kids into bed by eight and settle into Mr. Franklin's office. I finish my French assignment in less than half an hour and I'd love to get online, but no matter how clever I try to be, I can't unlock Mr. Franklin's super-secret passwords. There's no TV. That was banished when their son, Kip, turned six. I have three hours left with nothing to do but stare at the walls.

I haven't looked at my journal since New Year's Eve, so I pull it from my backpack and let it fall open to my last entry.

"Sometimes bad things happen . . . even in Channing."

Something else should be on this page, something about life turning around or how you have to hit bottom before you bounce up. One happy cliché.

I snatch up my pen and draw a line through what I wrote that last night of the year, then slip my journal back into my backpack. I'm about to stretch out on the couch when a scraping sound comes from outside the house.

The Pacific low tide tumbles onto the sand, washes out and returns—nothing unusual. *Still, there was something. A creaking board?* Pushing up from the office chair, I go to the window and peer around the curtain.

Outside on the deck, the spa lights glow under circulating blue water of the hot tub and steam rises into the air. In the background the surface of the ocean shimmers in the moonlight. A gust of wind snaps the flag that's mounted on the railing.

"Just the flag," I whisper out loud as I roll my neck to loosen my shoulders.

I'm about to return to the desk when a male figure darts across the deck.

"OMIGOD!" The words are smothered at the back of my throat and I press against the wall, shaking.

Risk another peek. Be sure you're not making something sinister out of ordinary nighttime shadows. As I ease the curtain back, the man ducks behind the topiaries that edge the steps. Then he creeps toward the back door.

Every part of me stands on end, like fur on a cornered cat. *Is the kitchen door locked?* I didn't check this time like I usually do when I babysit for the Franklins. I'd been too bent on getting the kids to bed so I could get my homework done. *Where's my cell?* I feel for it in my pocket, then search under my notes on the desk.

Where did I leave it?

On the kitchen counter next to the refrigerator.

Idiot!

I lift the receiver on the desk phone, punch Talk and hold it to my ear. There's . . . no . . . dial . . . tone. An icicle plunges from my head to my stomach and I fight to keep from screaming.

Get to Kip's room. He'll have his cell.

With a shaky hand I open the office door and listen— no sound. I tiptoe across the oak floor of the living room, into the carpeted hallway, and upstairs to Kip's bedroom door. Grabbing the handle, I start to turn it and push.

Glass shatters downstairs.

My skin tightens across my forehead.

He's inside.

I duck into Kip's room. The light next to his bed is on, his iPod's plugged into his ears. Leaning close, I press my fingers on his lips.

His eyes open and fix me with a glazed, half-asleep look. He seems so much younger than ten with his hair tousled over his forehead.

"Where's your cell?"

He points to his desk on the opposite side of the room, his eyes wide. He can tell I'm scared and I sense his panic rising to match mine.

"Someone's," I gulp air, "broken into the house." My whisper stretches to its breaking point. *Keep your head. Hide yourself and the kids.* "Let's get Jessie." I try to moisten the inside of my mouth. "Be really quiet, okay?"

He nods, fully awake now.

Grabbing the cell phone, I slip out the door first. Kip holds onto the back of my sweater and follows.

Fump. The refrigerator door opens and I halt mid-step. Mrs. Franklin hides jewelry in the freezer trays. Burglars know people do that; even I know that. *Maybe he'll take the jewels and leave*. With Kip clinging to me, I creep forward.

At Jessie's door, I twist the knob carefully. This door squeaks and I've woken Jessie a couple of times trying to sneak out of her room after reading her to sleep. The trick is to push it fast. Jessie's Little Mermaid nightlight casts an orange glow across the rug and Kip enters on tiptoes. I *whoosh* the door shut behind us, stopping an inch short of the jamb. Then lifting slightly, I shut it and go to press the—

But there's no lock. Now I remember about those stupid safety precautions. The Franklins removed the locks from the kids' bedroom and bathroom doors so they wouldn't be able to lock themselves in, intentionally or otherwise.

Kip and I huddle at the end of Jessie's bed, washed in the glow of the Little Mermaid. Jessie's snuggled under her blankets, her breath regular and untroubled, a sharp contrast to my shallow panting.

Kneeling, I whisper into Kip's ear. "Do you know a good hiding place?"

He points to Jessie's closet.

I shake my head. "Too obvious."

Kip is already sliding the door open. Inside is a stepladder that Jessie uses to reach toys on her top shelf. He pulls it to the center of the closet and climbs the four steps. "Carlie, in here," he whispers.

Sticking my head inside, I look up. In the ceiling is a square wooden panel. "Where does that go?"

"It's kind of an attic. You can't stand, but you can sit."

"You go ahead. I'll help Jessie."

As Kip crawls up inside the opening, I tiptoe to the bed and lift his sister.

"Carlie, read more story," Jessie murmurs. Her eyes flutter open, then close again.

"We're going into a special secret place to read, so be very quiet, okay?" I climb the ladder and hoist Jessie through the hole in the ceiling. Kip grabs his sister under her arms and lifts her all the way inside. I pull myself up. Once I'm in the crawl space, I reach down and draw the ceiling panel into place with a click.

I catch my breath I open Kip's cell phone. BATTERY LOW flashes three times.

Then the phone dies.

10

My illuminated watch reads almost midnight. We've been here for nearly two hours. I'm a Popsicle in the Franklins' unheated crawl space. Kip's teeth chatter, and he's wound himself into a ball so he looks like a spaniel on a cold night. Jessie groans, but then snuggles against me, never opening her eyes. I smooth her forehead. *Please don't cry out, Jessie.* I stroke her hair and sway with her in my arms until her breath is steady.

How are we going to get out of here? What if I promise to change? Really. I'll make an early New Year's Resolution to start being nicer to my family—really show Mom I love her, talk to my brother like he's a human being, feed Quicken before she begs.

"When can we get down?" Kip whispers.

"Soon," I whisper back. *But how? Any ideas, Carlie?*

"Not yet," I sigh.

"What?" Kip grips my sweater.

"Nothing." I put my free arm around him and hold him against me. He doesn't resist like he usually does, or complain that he's no baby.

41

"Are you okay?" Kip whispers from the shadows next to me.

I nod, but that's not true. I'm scared and working on not being terrified.

"Carlie," Kip tugs at my sweater. "What time is it?"

"After twelve."

"I hafta pee."

"It won't be long."

As he sinks back against me a dull sound comes from below the crawl space.

Kip grabs my arm and squeezes.

The intruder's in Jessie's room.

The murmur of people talking over each other comes from below. Easing Jessie off my lap and putting one ear to the floor, I hear two male voices. Then Mrs. Franklin cries out. *What's happening to her?*

If only I could see into Jessie's room. Mrs. Franklin's sobs have become noisy enough to cover the sound of the magnetic latch, so I press and release the door, opening it a crack.

Mr. and Mrs. Franklin stand next to Jessie's bed, facing my direction. Mr. Franklin's arms are wrapped around her shoulders and she's sobbing. Across from them, his back to me, stands someone in a sweater and jeans. I stifle a gasp. He has to be the one who broke into the house. Does he have a gun leveled at them?

Kip taps my arm. He's sidled next to me, also peering through the crack. I signal him to get back.

"When did you come in?" That's Mr. Franklin.

"It must have been around nine," the guy in the sweater answers.

It was nine you . . . you creep. I'd love to drop kick you to the North Pole. Let you get chummy with some cold.

Kip tugs on my sweater. I swat him away, but he tugs again, harder.

"Sean," he whispers.

"Huh?"

"He's my cousin," Kip says.

"Your cousin?" I've let my voice rise above a whisper and before I can register what Kip has said, the trap door is wrenched from my hand.

Mr. Franklin stares up at me. "What—?"

Mrs. Franklin, who is still shaky but no longer crying, joins him. "Carlie!

I reach for Jessie and hand her down. Then Kip lowers himself into his father's arms. "Carlie made us stay up there for hours. I've got icicles on my feet," he whines.

If there were another exit I'd sneak out that way, but there isn't, so down I go.

"What's this about?" Mr. Franklin's eyebrows form two upside-down V's. He looks a touch angry, yet relieved, and really puzzled.

"I heard him break the window on the back door." I point a shaky accusing finger at—*Sean Wright, the French tutor? Where did he come from?*

"I didn't break any window." Sean looks at me like I'm nuts. Then he turns to Mrs. Franklin. "Oh, right. Sorry, Aunt Corky, I accidentally knocked over a vase on the kitchen counter."

"A vase?" Anger rises like a tide from my chest to my head.

Sean faces me. "Hey, sorry. I didn't mean to scare anybody."

He's staring at me with those deep-set blue eyes that have Channing females crowding French classes, and I feel embarrassment flare in my face. My throat clogs when I try to say something, and instead I make a hacking sound like I'm coughing up a hair-ball.

"You were creeping around! Why didn't you knock, walk in the door like a . . . a real nephew?"

"I didn't see many lights so I thought my aunt and uncle were gone with the kids. They hide the key on the back deck, so I decided to come inside and hang out until they got home."

I need to let these people know I'm not an idiot. "I tried to call 911 when I saw him sneaking to the back door, but the phone was dead."

"It was fine before we went out. I'll go check." Mr. Franklin leaves the room.

Mrs. Franklin tucks Jessie into bed and marches Kip out the door. I follow Sean into the hall and down the stairs to the entry. I don't want to be alone with him, and even if I have a lot to say, none of it's fit for the Franklins' house. Besides he's very distracting—tall, handsome—a poster boy for "Come to the Bahamas."

I look down at the floor, then scan the pictures on the wall. Twisting my bracelet around, I pretend to be fascinated by my wrist and concentrate on staying mad. *I have every right to be mad. Even if he didn't mean to terrorize me, he deserves some kind of punishment.*

He clears his throat, but I'm not noticing him. *No way.*

"Sorry I gave you such a scare."

What a lame apology.

Mr. Franklin comes from the office, my jacket over his arm and his phone in the other. "We need a new handset. The pads are wearing out, but the phone works, Carlie. You were upset and probably didn't press the TALK button hard enough." He places the phone on the entry table. "Come on. I'll walk you home."

"Let me do that." Sean steps next to me. "I think I still need to apologize some more."

"Thanks, Sean," Mr. Franklin says. "It's been a long night and I'm tired."

I don't want him to walk me home. I can go home on my own. But the tightness around my head is there—that last bit of cold fear hasn't quite vanished. I slip into my jacket, grateful for its warmth.

Mrs. Franklin comes downstairs from Kip's room holding the empty yogurt dish, remnants of the illegal chocolate bits clinging to the edge. She shoots me a "you-know-better" look. Maybe the health food diva won't call me again to babysit. That'd be just fine.

Still, I need money for that dress. I'll call tomorrow and apologize. For what? The bedtime yogurt snack? For keeping her kids safe from an intruder, even if he did turn out to be a relative? Even so, I'm the one who deserves the apology.

At the front door, Mr. Franklin hands me the scrumptious sum of twenty-five dollars. Then he opens his wallet again. "Here." He hands me another ten. "You did some quick thinking tonight to keep the kids safe. That was a great job. I'm sorry I didn't say so earlier, but, well, finding you gone and the kids' beds empty was quite a shock."

They'll call me again.

11

Sean and I walk alongside each other, letting the sound of the ocean fill in for the lack of conversation.

"How far is it to your place?" he asks.

I point to the two-story house across the street, home for as long as I can remember. The wide path winds to the main entrance and the leaded glass panels in the door glow from the hall lights Mom leaves on until we're all home. Inside, the vaulted ceilings cast soft shadows in the living room, and at the back of the house I see someone, probably Mom, in the kitchen.

"That's the Edmund place, isn't it?"

I'm still not talking to him.

"You're Carlie, Madame Lenoir's star pupil in French 3." He fills the uneasy silence between us by staring at my house. "You've taken down your Christmas tree already."

I'd like to punch Sean Wright in the jaw. I'm in no mood for chitchat with this guy. I don't bother to tell him we never took the tree inside, that it's likely to turn brown where it stands next to the front door because my dimwit brother still hasn't hauled it to the curb for pickup. My hands are still shaking, even though I've stuffed them inside my jacket pockets.

"Look—I'm really sorry," he says, as if repeating his apology is going to erase tonight.

"Sorry? What kind of lame word is that for making me think we were all about to die?" I stayed calm as possible hiding in that crawl space and on this *stroll* home. Now I'm having a hard time not yelling. "And what were you doing all that time you were in the house? Playing video games?" *You should be hung by your very beautiful, tanned neck!*

"*Désolé de vous avoir donné une telle frayeur!*"

"Oh." The sound I make is so small, I'm not sure it even got out into the night air. *Sorry I gave you such a scare* sounds so much more sincere in French.

"I mean it—really."

I know he means it, but I can't get the words out to tell him.

When I don't answer, he backs away, palms up, silently pleading: *What more can I say?* "I'd better get back to my aunt's" are his parting words.

I watch him leave from the driveway. "*Désolé.*" I repeat and savor Sean's word, letting it linger on my tongue.

He strides away, his sleek black hair glinting under the streetlights, and I can almost see the word *luscious* on a page of my journal. Maybe I should pay attention to what my dad's telling me. Maybe it's time to come out of that cocoon. This is the first time since October that I even feel like it might be possible.

I walk past the dead Christmas tree and brush my hand

against the needles. They prickle and some scatter to the ground. If Keith doesn't carry it away, maybe we can light it as farewell bonfire when we move.

"Is that you, Carlie?" Mom calls as I close the front door and toss my jacket on the entry table.

"*C'est moi.*" I'm in a French mood now and want to stay that way.

"I'm in the kitchen. How did the babysitting at the Franklins go?"

"It was, um, fine." Last year I would've rushed in to tell Mom what had happened, especially the part about Sean. I want to, but life's so different now. She gets edgy if I have a headache these days, and I don't need a lecture about keeping my imagination under control—not tonight. I run my fingers through my hair as I glance at the hall mirror, making sure I don't show any signs of what happened at the Franklins. "You're up late," I say.

"I needed to get an hour of studying in." I don't hear her yawn and the sigh that follows it, but I know they're there, just like I know that later, when I'm almost asleep, I'll hear her crying on her way past my door.

I walk through the dining room and into the kitchen, where Mom faces the stove, her head bowed, a spoon resting on the edge of the saucepan. We've been at each other for weeks, so now I remember the promise I made to show Mom I love her.

I wrap my arms around her waist from behind, then press my cheek against her familiar deep-blue cashmere. "Can I have some cocoa?"

With a quick swipe across her eyes, she pours the

steamy liquid into two mugs, gives me one and sits at the kitchen table. "So tell me about your night," she says.

"No, you first," I tell her. I need time to get my story right so I sit across from her, both hands wrapped around the mug.

"We'll take turns." Mom used to love this game, when we'd all manage to be around the dinner table at the same time. First Dad, then me, then Keith, and last Mom—each sharing a small piece of what we'd done that day. She sighs. "Let's see. My night—" She holds up her real estate books as if they tell the whole story. "Okay, your turn."

I'm not getting out of telling her something about tonight. But what? If Mrs. Franklin calls to complain to Mom about what happened, she'll hear a version of the story I probably won't like. That would so be like that cranky vegan. Mom's in a pretty mellow mood—playing her take-turns game. If I tell the Sean story, keep it light—

"A really strange thing happened at the Franklins." My laugh sounds forced, but she doesn't tense up. I tell her about Sean the burglar, only I don't use that word, choosing "suspected intruder," "hidden safely," and a "little nervous" to explain what happened.

"Carlie!" She lunges for my hand as if she's saving me from falling off a cliff. She's been so protective of Keith and me that we can't go outside to get the newspaper without her asking where we're going.

"I just overreacted, Mom. Really. And it ended . . . fine. Sean—"

"I'm calling the Franklins. Don't they have an alarm system?"

"Yes, but I told you. It was a nephew who had a key. I just didn't know and he wasn't expected. It wasn't a big deal."

She still hasn't let go of my hand and now she grips it even more tightly. "It's a big deal to me. If anything happened—"

"But nothing *did*. It was my imagination." I want to say, "You have no idea how unimaginative this version is," but instead I stroke the back of her hand. "Okay. Your turn."

She rubs her forehead with both hands, taking her time before starting. I've seen her do this a lot, as if she's constructing interior dams to hold back a flash flood—sometimes tears, sometimes fear. Sometimes I think it's anger. It's as if she'll be washed away if she doesn't control every emotion as it rises inside her.

"I arranged for the moving company today."

I'd almost forgotten about Las Pulgas. I come down from my Sean high so fast that I swear my ears pop. Now tonight's scare is nothing, compared to that move on the fifteenth.

12

Sunday morning I stumble into the kitchen far earlier than usual. I'm sure I haven't slept more than an hour, and then I dreamed about catacombs. My stomach growls, reminding me I've eaten nothing since half a burrito before babysitting and a handful of celery sticks from the Franklins' refrigerator.

Keith sits at the kitchen counter with a tall glass of milk, his hands wrapped around a microwaved waffle. His teeth sink into the steamy dough, butter and syrup dripping through his fingers onto the plate.

He grunts, closes his eyes and chews.

"Good morning to you, too." My books and homework assignments are spread out at the end of the kitchen table where I left them before making my way to the Franklins' last night. I push the books aside. "Did you leave anything in the refrigerator besides the shelves?"

"No."

I yank open the refrigerator door and peer inside. "Ah, two hard-boiled eggs. You're a perfect start for the day," I say to them. "Then there's you," I hold up a limp slice of pizza in plastic wrap and slap it back on the shelf. I grab the milk carton and shake it. "And you've almost got enough for half a cup of cereal."

Quicken purrs her way into the room and winds between my legs. "Didn't anyone feed you, fur-person?" I fill her bowl and give her a scratch behind her silky black ears.

"Do you talk to everything?" Keith mumbles, then dumps his plate into the sink and, dragging his feet across the tiled floor, heads toward the TV room. "The fridge is lonely. Say something to it."

"Yeah, Yeah, Yeah." It feels good to make faces behind his back. I've poured the last of the milk into a bowl of Cap'n Crunch and spooned in one bite when the phone rings. It can't be for me. My friends only call my cell and never this early on Saturday. I take another spoonful and chew.

"Carlie?" Mom calls from upstairs. "It's for you."

When I lift the receiver to my ear and say hello, I don't recognize the voice.

"Hi. Glad you're an early bird, too."

This is definitely not a friend. My *friends* know "early bird" is not in my vocabulary. Mom didn't pass on that morning gene to either of her children. I prop my head up with one hand and dip my spoon into the Cap'n Crunch. "Who *is* this?"

"Sean. I'm calling to make up for scaring you last night, and I'd like to take you someplace today. Anywhere you want to go."

I yawn, then double blink. "Sean?"

"That would be me," he breathes into my ear.

53

I chew more cereal, trying to wake up enough to say something that makes sense.

"I think there's something wrong with your phone," he says. "Lots of static."

I stop chewing and push the remaining cereal into one cheek.

"I'll pick you up about ten."

"No. I'm—" I swallow—"busy."

"You're still mad about last night."

"Ya think?"

"I really want to make it up to you. Please let me do something."

I picture his smooth, tanned face and perfect lips. Before thinking about what I'm doing, I spoon the last of the cereal into my mouth.

"So ten, okay?"

"Temm. Rrit."

"Think about where you want to go. Bye."

The click comes before I can swallow. "Mm. Bye." I'm left staring into the receiver; then I click the END button. Is this guy nuts? Who goes on a date at ten a.m. on a Saturday?

Now that my brain has come online, I smile to myself. This is a great chance to get even with Aunt Corky's nephew for last night. Not one guy I know likes shopping at the mall, and that's exactly where I want to go. Satisfaction settles nicely inside me as I go to my room, grab my cell and click on Lena's number. This is the first good news I could share in months.

Lena doesn't pick up so I leave a message. "You— will—*not* believe what I have to tell you! Call me."

My journal lies open on top of *Introduction to Chemistry* and for once I think of writing something wonderful to myself—. Something about today and Sean. But when I pick it up, it's only to set it aside. Homework wins out over those beckoning blank pages.

By nine-thirty I've done one chemistry assignment, showered, blown my hair dry, and stepped on and off the scale—twice. Even when I force out all the air possible, the dial stops way past the mark I made with nail polish. That "Passionate Purple" line has been my goal since last summer and I'm still six pounds away. "Rats!"

I put on my halter-top and low-rider jeans, then stand in front of the bathroom mirror.

"No."

The halter lands on the bed as I reach for the tieback top in the closet. "No. No. No."

The tieback top lands next to the halter. There *has* to be something. I look in the top dresser drawer, and *Ah ha.* My V-neck hoodie. *Why am I so worried about looking good for Sean?* I get my answer from the girl in the mirror. "Like Lena said, he's hot, that's why."

That idea sends me back to the closet.

The doorbell rings at ten a.m. sharp. Mom's at her desk studying, so I stick my head inside her room. "Bye. Going to the mall." I don't give her time to turn around before I duck out.

By the time I reach the bottom step, Keith stands at the front door with Sean.

"Hi." I'm trying to sound pleased but not eager.

"Hi, yourself. You look . . . awesome."

Keith grunts and shambles back to his TV-room hideout.

"Your brother's nice," Sean says.

He's got to be kidding. "Sometimes."

Mom leans over the balcony. "Carlie? Who're you going with?"

"This is Sean. Uh, the Franklins' nephew. I told you about him last night."

At first I think she might run down the stairs and throw herself between us, but Sean waves and says, "Pleasure to meet you, Mrs. Edmund."

That scores a point. She nods at him. "What time are you coming home?"

"Is two all right?" he asks.

Score two.

Mom nods again. "That's fine. Enjoy yourselves."

Sean opens the front door. "So where *are* we going?"

"The mall." I expect him to cringe, but he sweeps ahead of me down the stone walkway to the car and opens the passenger door in one fluid movement.

"Milady."

I stifle a "huh?" I've never been called My Lady before. And no one except Mom or Dad has ever opened the car door for me, and that only happened before I could open it myself, so it didn't count.

This is definitely shaping up into a "different" kind of date.

13

The mall is fifteen minutes from the house. During the drive, I've already managed two "Is that rights?" and one "Un-huh," while Sean tells me about Aunt Corky and Uncle Mike, and their conversation following the bizarre situation last night. I can't concentrate on what he says, even when I try, because I'm thinking about his blue eyes and how I feel when they're focused on me. Then there's his dark hair and Bahamas-tanned skin that only make those eyes into deeper blue seas.

"What?" He said something while I was off visiting my imagination. "What did you say?"

"Just that you seem to be somewhere else."

"Just thinking."

Do something if you can't say anything. Try smiling. Another glance at the visor mirror. *The scarf isn't right. The hoodie might have been better after all. Maybe the red sweater would have been more interesting than the black. Why is this guy so disturbing?*

I've been on dates before—well at chaperoned dances. Dad was such a guard dog. Maybe that's what's making me so twitchy; no guard dog anymore. I feel that catch at the back of my throat and dig my nails into both palms to distribute the pain. I can't start crying now, not today.

Sean parks and I manage to open my own door before he reaches the passenger side. "So where do you like to shop?" he asks.

"I just look these days. I'm so broke I can't afford to buy anything." Why'd I say that? I don't know him at all. I really don't want Aunt Corky to find out the Edmunds are out of money. Once she knows, everyone in Channing will, too. "That's between us, okay?"

"Of course." He seals his lips with his fingers. "I'll tell my aunt to give you a raise. Come on. I have a place I'd like to check out. Do you mind?" He takes long steps across the shiny mall floor and I hurry to keep up.

I'm expecting an hour of wandering through Electronics Inc., but he stops in front of the Cornucopia of Toys.

"I love this place!" I tell him.

"Toy junkie?" He smiles at me.

"I liked getting toys when I was little. Now all I get are socks and gift cards."

"What was your favorite toy present?" he asks me.

"You'll think I'm nuts," I say.

He crosses his heart. "Nope."

The automatic door to the toy store *swooshes* open and we walk inside where bins overflow with stuffed animals.

"It's a Jack-in-the-Box . . . my . . . dad gave me when I was four. I'd push the jester down thousands of times, and every time it popped up, I'd scream and my dad would hold me and—" My eyes burn. "It's broken now." I turn away from Sean to hide the tears welling, then pick up a stuffed rabbit to give myself something to do.

"Sorry about your dad, Carlie. Aunt Corky told me." Sean slips his hand into mine, sending a tingly sensation through me. "Let's go find something to play with."

His hand feels firm around mine as he leads me to the escalator.

On the second floor, a brightly colored hopscotch board with a "Try Me" sign brings us to a quick stop. We wait in line behind a little boy and two bigger girls who look down at him from the age of about eight. When our turn comes, Sean hops to the end and returns with his arms out in a *Ta-Dah* ending.

I'm next. I make it to the end and hop onto the bright red 7 and 8, but when I turn to come back, my right shoe sticks and I land on my butt.

The twittering eight-year-olds cut me no slack.

But Sean helps me up. "Come on. All that exercise has given me an appetite." He takes my hand again and we ride the escalator down to the main gallery. Our choice is the Teriyaki Bowl and Sean hands me chopsticks. "I bet you're better using these than your feet."

"I slipped!"

He picks up the tray and surveys the noisy room. "Table at three o'clock." We jockey our way through the crowded Food Court until we reach an empty table along the wall.

"Before I forget." I open my bag and hand him five dollars for my lunch.

"This is part of my apology. I'll buy lunch, since my

impression of a French guy didn't work all that well last night."

Au contraire. It worked way too well. *Désolé.* The memory of that word, his voice saying it—I've never had such a soppy feeling—but with Sean sitting across from me, his dark hair swept back from his face, I'm wrapped inside something beautiful, the first in a long time.

Later, when we're on our way to my house, Sean tells me he left his mom in New York—with her new husband. "There was bad chemistry between us from day one, so I moved here to live with Dad. I'll enroll at Elmhurst College after I graduate."

By the time we pull to a stop in front of my house, I don't want this day to end.

When I look up, he's already opened my door. *Is this pampering? I really like it.*

On the way up the path I think, *Awkward moment on the horizon. When we get to my door, what then? Do we shake hands? Stay three feet apart, while each of us searches for the good-bye that's just right?*

Before I'm in a total bunch, he says, "I had a great time. Hope I've made up for the other night."

No handshake, no hug. Nothing.

He's back to his car and inside, waving as he drives off.

Did he have somewhere else to go? Maybe he didn't like me so much as I thought. Maybe . . . Stop imagining yourself into a snit, Carlie. He spent the whole morning with you. He said he had fun and told you a lot about himself. He likes you.

Having him in my life has to be some kind of sign, a signal that there's a change coming, one that'll make my life better than it is now.

I can't help the happiness that starts inside and spreads across my face. Carlie Edmund may be moving away, but she might be taking along the one senior at Channing that every girl craves.

As I open the front door, my cell phone chimes "Jingle Bells"—Lena. Mental note: change those Christmas tones, sometime before summer. "Hi, Lena. I've got so much—"

"Mom caved. I can take the car my uncle offered after all. And you will not believe this! Gene Connell made a pass at me. I was at The Shack and he, like, sits down right next to me and gives me the look."

"That's . . . interesting. I've—"

"I've decided to teach Eric a lesson for flirting with that French exchange student. Maybe I'll just break our date for the Spring Fling. He'll go green when I show up at the dance with Gene." She takes a short breath. "Where have you been all day? I tried to call you on your cell a couple of times. You want to go to the mall, maybe see that new movie? What? Oh—never mind. I have to go. Mom's calling. Gotta keep on her good side until the car's officially mine. Ciao."

I close my phone and suddenly that bubbly feeling vanishes. Pop! One bubble. Pop! Another. *Thanks for all your good news, Lena. Thanks for not wanting to hear any of mine. Thanks for reminding me that today was probably the single good one for the rest of my life—which I mostly live in the toilet these days.*

Keith passes me in the entrance hall.

"Going out?" I ask him. I'm trying to keep that promise again, making eye contact. Not growling.

"No, I'm walking backwards. Didn't you notice?" Keith snarls and slams the door hard behind him.

He makes keeping my promise impossible. When I start toward the stairs, Mom stands on the bottom step, her eyes red. "We had . . . another argument." She turns and runs up the stairs, then slams her bedroom door.

At least I have company in the toilet.

14

The week before we move goes almost too fast to re-member. No other time in my life has disappeared this fast, and only one other time has been so steeped in gloom.

I sit in the middle of my bedroom floor, surrounded by boxes. *How many decisions can I make in a single day without a brain-collapse?* Choices surround me like a brush fire, closing in, sucking the oxygen from the air.

There are all sorts of categories, like Returns—things to give back to friends I probably won't ever see again. Treasures—I can't leave behind anything in this stack. Then there's the dreaded Undecided—way too much stuff to fit into a single packing box, which is all I'm allowed. I have until tomorrow morning at eight, when three men from Shamrock Movers show up to haul off the furniture and the boxes that'll be too big for the car.

From the Undecided pile, I pluck a rhinestone-studded box. Lena and I made these at Christmas last year to raise money for the homeless. We sold all but one, so I bought it myself. I used to be charitable; now I need some of that charity myself. The box lands with a thud between Undecided and Treasures, where I've stacked my journal.

Keith shuffles past my open door. This is his fourth trip in an hour, his arms loaded each time. Slung over his shoulder are four tennis shoes tied together by their laces. He's tucked his freshman yearbook under his left arm and hugs his basketball against his right side. That mole hole of a room should be empty by now.

"How come no boxes?"

"I don't need boxes." He looks at my floor. "What's that?"

"I'm culling. No sense in taking everything I own to Las Pulgas. You saw my new bedroom; it's about this big." I hold my thumb and index finger an inch apart.

"Where's Mom?" he asks.

"I guess she's still in Dad's office." I stretch and get to my feet. I'd decided it was better for me and Mom to stay in our separate places. We've been growling at each other all week.

Keith shakes his head, then bounces down the stairs two at a time, tennis shoes slapping at his back.

I should ask Mom if she wants some cocoa. *Just don't say anything rotten, Carlie.*

Dad's office is down the hall at the back of the house. On the door used to be a small brass plaque, our Christmas present to him from three years ago that read MR. RICHARD EDMUND. Now only two small screw-holes remain. Mom's taken the plaque off. If she's sorting possessions into piles, I wonder where that plaque goes?

64

I lean my forehead against the wooden panel, trying to remember what his room looks like. I haven't been inside since last summer. I'm about to knock when the sound of something shattering against a wall stops me. "Mom?"

She doesn't answer, so I press my ear to the door. Mom's crying. I back away.

∽

In the morning, Leo, Jake, and Tom enter wearing Shamrock green uniforms with their names stitched above their hearts. When they step into the living room, Quicken hisses, cat-leaps up the stairs and crouches at the back of my closet. Even her favorite catnip crunchies can't coax her from the corner where she sits, growling.

"I'll get the cat carrier," Keith says. "There's no way she's mellowing out before we go and I'm not getting shredded."

Later, as the moving truck pulls away from the curb, I stand in the center of the empty living room. The only sound is the steady hum of the Sub Zero refrigerator Mom sold along with the house. There's no room for the luxury-sized appliance in Apartment 148 in Las Pulgas.

When I walk to the stairs, my footsteps ring hollow. Sitting on the bottom step, I watch Mom move through the house like she's lost, slipping into the empty dining room, staring down at the rug, glancing at the walls where sunlight has etched the impressions of picture frames onto the wallpaper. The depressions in the rug where the table and chair legs have been for so long are all that remain of the dining room set. She sold it at the auction, along with the living room sectional and king bed with matching dresser.

Mom starts into the kitchen but stops at the doorway. With a quick turn she walks back to the fireplace and sweeps her hand along the mantel. When she glances over her shoulder, I'm looking into a face I've known forever, but one that I suddenly don't recognize. Living here, I've watched storms gather over the Pacific and I know their midsummer lightning is most likely to ignite the dry California grasses. Right now, her face is that storm.

She opens the front door, and without turning to look back, she steps outside. "Let's go." Not closing the door behind her, she walks toward the car, her head down, as if she's looking for something she lost.

I remember Mom when she'd be in one of her thoughtful moods, sitting with her knees pulled up to her chest, watching Dad and Keith huddled over a board game. Dad called her Mona then.

"Who's Mona?" I remember asking when I was eight.

"The woman with the most beautiful, mysterious smile in the world—that is, before your mother came along," Dad said. "Now Mona Lisa is only second best."

"Not anymore," I say to the empty room. Mona has no competition from Mom now.

I stand with my hand on the well-used door handle but its smoothly curved brass feels cold. When I was three, I had to reach above my head and press on the latch with both hands to open it. Now it feels small and low, and yet it holds memories of all the times I've opened and closed it. For one last time, I pull the handle toward me, hear the click that always said *Welcome* or *See you later*. I rest my forehead on the familiar leaded glass door panels and whisper, "*Adieu.*"

Our "new" car waits at the curb—a black Tercel, only slightly dented on the driver's door panel, only a little dinged and pitted on the hood, with a clock that always reads two forty-five. It's only been driven 200,000 miles by a grandmother the salesman knew personally. This is Mom's first solo car purchase, and Keith and I have an un-spoken agreement: we will never say anything to her about that car.

As we climb into the Tercel, Keith sets the cat carrier behind the passenger seat and Quicken howls when Mom starts the car.

"Stifle it. You're not going to the vet," Keith says and taps the top of the carrier, but Quicken only howls louder.

I dig my fingernails into my palms and keep my eyes straight ahead.

Mom drives with both hands clutching the wheel, her knuckles white. The one sound in the car besides the motor is Quicken. She's howling for all of us.

It's only a twenty-minute drive to the apartment in Las Pulgas, but while the time is insignificant, the difference it makes in my life is huge. Mom turns into the narrow drive-way and winds through the backside of the complex, where Dumpsters line up against a chain-link fence, and cardboard boxes and black plastic garbage bags poke out from under the heavy metal lids. On the opposite side is a flat-roof car-port. Some of the bunker-like spaces shelter trucks or cars that no longer need to be smog-checked because they're so

67

old. Moving boxes, broken furniture, and freezer chests are the most common items stacked along the walls of those spaces.

When we come to space 148, Mom parks. Even Quicken quiets down and we all sit there in silence.

My cell suddenly rings and breaks the spell. As Mom and Keith get out of the car, I flick open my phone and a number I don't recognize appears on the screen.

"Moving day, right? Aunt Corky knows all." Sean's voice sends shock waves through my chest.

"Right, " I say, and climb out.

"What's your new address?"

I'm in the bowels of Las Pulgas, and Sean Wright wants to know where I live? Is there no justice in this world?

"Um, I don't even know the address yet. Can you call me later? I'll give it to you then." Then I remember—I'll only have my cell phone for one more week. I glare at Mom's retreating back. She's taking everything away. Without explaining that all I'll have is a home phone, I give Sean our new number and my email address.

As I snap my phone closed, my thoughts churn. *How am I going to keep my friends at Channing from seeing where I live? And what about Lena?* I've deliberately missed three calls from my best friend already, and she emailed about coming over to see my new "house." I can't tell her I'll be living in a crappy Las Pulgas apartment, and I have no intention of ever letting her see this dump with the dented refrigerator and the stove Mom calls vintage Ark. I'm wearing out the chain on my Sweet Sixteen bracelet by twisting it so much—almost all the time now—counting the links, where they begin, where they end, and pushing away the reason that makes me ache so much inside.

I follow Mom and Keith, who pick their way toward the gate that separates the carport from a kidney-shaped pool. Quicken is curled into a silent, fetal ball in the cage that Keith holds against his chest. They push open the gate and walk through the pool area, where tables are littered with overflowing ashtrays. Keith kicks aside a dented beer can and, following Mom, climbs the steps. With one hand I grasp the iron railing and it wobbles. *A lot of good this thing is going to do to keep anyone from falling.* Then I make my way across the creaky balcony to the apartment.

∽

Night brings a whole different character to our palace. What starts as an afternoon kids' hide-and-seek game by the pool turns into a weekend keg party and the music's booming by eleven. The windows vibrate so hard to the beat that I'm sure they're going to pop right out of their flimsy aluminum frames.

When Mom yanks the front window curtain closed in frustration over the noise, it falls off the hooks and right onto her head. She hurls the curtain across the room, sending years of dust exploding all around us.

Keith disappears down the hall, leaving Mom and me about ten paces apart—dueling range.

"Don't say a word, young lady. Do you hear me?" She snatches the phone from her purse, flips it open and stabs her finger on her keypad.

"This is Mrs. Edmund. 148. Can't you put a stop to that loud party?"

While she's talking I coax Quicken out of her carrier, where she's gone to try and escape from the noise, and then I slip away to my bedroom, shutting the door without turning on the lights. It's better not to show that world outside where I'm hiding. Tomorrow I'll borrow one of Keith's black sheets to hang over my window.

Later the police arrive, and for a while red swirling lights chase each other around the walls of my room. Bull horns shout the command to clear the pool area. One more glass bottle shatters on the sidewalk; then slowly the sound and light show winds down, leaving only the hum of the pool pump and the yellow glow of bug lights beside each apartment door.

The quiet doesn't last long. Something crashes against my wall and a woman's angry voice shouts words that would get her bleeped off the air by the FCC. I hear a man's voice mumble something I can't make out; then a door slams; now the pool pump is the only noise once again. I crack open my door to the hall like I did when I was little. Somehow that makes my room less scary and it reduces the faint smell of cigarette smoke that's seeping through my wall.

I don't hear Quicken, but I know she's in the back corner of my closet, crouched and staring out. Getting on my hands and knees, I look inside. "Quicken, come here, fur person."

But she hisses and when I reach for her, she slinks along the wall, then disappears into a dark space behind my desk.

I lie down and roll inside my comforter, not bothering to make my bed. Right now I want to vanish, and not just for tonight, but forever.

Soon another sound begins, one that's become as familiar a part of the night as the surf used to be. Mom tries to muffle her sobs as she passes my door, but she can't hide her pain. And tonight, in this desolate place, hearing her hurts me so much more than it ever did in Channing.

15

"Quicken? Here kitty-kitty."

Mom's voice startles me from a dream that's left a sour lemon taste in my mouth. I jump up from my bed, letting the comforter fall to the floor, and look around the room cluttered with boxes. I've come back from a dream and into a nightmare. I keep listening to hear the familiar sounds of ocean, expecting the traffic noises to fade once I get my bearings. I wish this was the dream instead of my waking reality.

My door is slightly ajar and Mom sticks her head inside. "Honey, is Quicken in here?"

I shake my head; my mouth won't open. My eyes feel like slits and if I look in the mirror I know what I'll see: the new Carlie Edmund, puffy-eyed Las Pulgas dweller.

"Get dressed. We'll have to go and look for her. She must've run out when I went to the store this morning." Mom closes my door and continues calling, "Quicken? Here kitty-kitty-kitty."

After we search every crevice in the apartment and still can't find the cat, I go outside to scout the area. When I knock on the door to Apartment 147, the door pops open the width of a security-chained crack and a woman squints at me.

"What?" she says. I recognize the voice, but at least she doesn't scream at me.

"We've lost a Siamese cat."

The woman slips the chain free and opens the door. "What, is it, like, joined at the hip or something?"

At first I don't get it, but then when I do, I don't appreciate the joke much. "Her name's Quicken and she's silver with a black face," I tell the woman.

She steps outside and says, "Sounds interesting, but she's not here." She eyes me and lights a cigarette. "You the new neighbor next door?"

I nod.

The woman flicks her ashes over the balcony.

"Who is it?" A gravelly voice asks from inside her apartment, then a man pokes his head out and fixes me with heavy-lidded eyes and asks, "Whaddya want?" His jowls jiggle when he talks.

"Butt out, Gerald." She sounds as if she's giving commands to a particularly stupid dog. She flicks ashes at his feet and he ducks inside, leaving the door open. The woman follows him, but before closing the door she reassures me, saying, "Cats come home when they get hungry."

I try a couple more doors but nobody answers. At Apartment 152, the door jerks open when I knock and a man in an orange prisoner-style jumpsuit stands there staring at me. Looking over his shoulder is a lanky teen boy with short dark hair and intense eyes that travel up and down my body, making me feel like meat on a hook.

"Whatta ya want?" the man asks. "Whatever it is, we don't need it."

The boy's eyes make another quick sweep over me.

"I'm looking for a Siamese cat. Have you seen her? She's wearing a —"

"I ain't seen no cat," the man says, then shuts the door so fast I still have my mouth open.

That's enough of meeting the neighbors. "Jerk," I mutter under my breath and go to the pool area. There I check behind the barbeque pit and under plastic lounge chairs, but there's no sign of Quicken anywhere.

Keith walks down the short path from the carport and lets himself in through the gate. He kneels at the edge of the pool and tests the water with his hand, then asks, "I wonder what the percentage of pee is."

"That's gross."

"Any luck?" He says as he flicks the water from his hand.

"Quicken's the only sane one in this family. That's why she's escaped." I test one of the plastic chaise lounges to see if it collapses. When it doesn't, I sit down with my legs stretched out.

Keith joins me on the next one, his arms on his knees and staring at his feet. "This place totally sucks." The silence hangs between us, until he says, "I'm dropping track."

"Track is all you ever wanted to do."

"Not in Las Pulgas."

I know why he feels that way. He doesn't want to com-

74

pete against his old teammates at Channing High. He knows Las Pulgas will lose because Channing has top-notch runners.

This is the first time in ages that we've been alone and talked instead of sniping at each other. He hasn't gotten a haircut in two months, and the way his hair falls across his forehead reminds me of Dad. Now that's something I can work with; it'll let me talk to my brother like he's human.

Keith plucks at his Channing Track shirt as if he wants to rip it to pieces.

I get that, too. He's as ashamed of where we've landed as I am. "Come on. Let's blow this dump and see if we can follow Quicken's escape route," I say.

We walk the perimeter of the complex, calling to Quicken. When we come to the street, we turn toward the center of town. Bits of black plastic flutter tangled in spiky weeds along the sidewalk and the curb is littered with used paper cups, candy wrappers, and other trash I don't want to identify. At the stoplight, we turn back, discouraged. If Quicken crossed into town, we'll never find her.

When we reach the driveway leading into the complex, I stop to look more closely under the bushes. I now notice that the sidewalk on the left side of the driveway becomes a dirt road. It's like whoever paved around the apartments ran out of concrete.

"Let's look down there," I say to my brother, pointing.

Keith starts off in that direction, saying, "Quicken might have gone exploring."

"Wait," I say, pointing to a sign that's partly covered by a low-hanging limb. "It says, 'No Trespassing.' "

"But we're not trespassing," he says. "We're looking for a lost cat. Come on."

The road slopes away and becomes overgrown. The traffic sounds from Las Pulgas blend into a distant hum as birds flush from the undergrowth and small critters scurry behind rocks as we approach. With each step, I have this feeling that we're walking into another time, before open spaces disappeared under asphalt and apartment houses.

We continue around a sweeping turn and come to a gate with a rope looped around a post. Keith ignores the second "No Trespassing" sign and slips the rope free. We enter a silent grove of trees, their gnarled trunks lined up on either side of us. Somewhere behind all these leaves is the Las Pulgas of today, but it looks like the developers forgot about this place. At the end of the road we see a two-story house with a wide front porch. The curtains are drawn, but it's obvious someone lives here. On the porch, plants in hanging baskets are sprouting their first green leaves and wooden rockers sit empty, waiting for the warm weather.

"What are these?" Keith asks, touching the bark of a tree.

I shrug. "Trees?"

"Very funny. What kind?"

"They're apple trees." The voice comes from behind us and I spin around. I'm face to face with a man holding a long-barreled gun across his forearms. "Seems you don't know your trees anymore than you know how to read."

"We—" I choke. "We lost our cat. We wanted to see if she might have come this way." I grab Keith's hand like I used to, back when he was four and I was six. Dad always said I was the big sister and I had to keep Keith safe when we crossed the street. He'd never said what to do when facing a man with a big gun.

His wide-brimmed cowboy hat sits squarely on his head, casting a dark shadow over his broad shoulders. He cradles the gun as if it's a part of him, and although I can't see his eyes under his hat brim, I'm sure they're trained on us—steady and unblinking. His skin is tight across his cheekbones, which are bronzed and shiny, and his features are sharp like a hawk's. I can see he works with his hands, but in spite of the scars and leathery skin, his nails are trimmed and clean. He stands easy and balanced on both feet, silently watching us.

"Her name is Quicken." My mouth is dry and my tongue coated with dust. "Our cat, I mean." I squeeze Keith's hand to say let's get out of here, and he returns the pressure.

"Where do you live?" the man asks.

I point in the direction from where I think we've come.

"Las Pulgas Apartments," he says. If words could be on fire, his would have burned down the entire apple orchard. "What a waste of good orchard land."

I glance at the evenly spaced tree trunks to avoid looking at him.

He walks around us and down the path toward the house. "Close the gate on your way out." He turns after a few steps. "Next time, read the signs—and pay attention to them."

"Wait!" Keith shakes free of my grasp and runs after the man. "Look, we're sorry about trespassing, but if you find our cat, would you please let us know?"

I hold my breath. *What is Keith thinking?* This guy's packing a major weapon and he'd probably love an excuse to use it.

The man looks from Keith to me and back, then he climbs the steps to the house. He goes inside, letting the door slam behind him without a word.

"Jeez, Keith, are you trying to get us killed? There are other ways to escape Las Pulgas, okay? I'd like to do it while I'm still alive."

As I place the rope over the post to secure the gate, I look back at the house. He's there at the window, watching us.

16

On Monday, Keith and I file through the security checkpoint at the main entrance to Las Pulgas High. One guard uses a wand; another does random backpack searches. Security cameras perch high along each side of the hall, their Big Brother eyes scanning and recording everything.

While the guard rummages through my backpack, I concentrate on the cracked plaster behind his head. If anyone needs searching, it's this guy. I hate standing across from him, smelling his stale tobacco odor and seeing his greasy hair. I try to remember the entrance to Channing High but I can't. All I know is that where I am today is more like entering hell than high school.

"You're cleared." As the guard shoves the bag at me, his dirty nails are only inches from my hand. I can't stop the grimace as I avoid touching the canvass where Mr. Icky's hands have been.

After Keith passes through security, we make our way down the congested hall and follow the signs to the counselor's office. Half way down the main corridor, at the first door on the right is the office, but the counselor isn't here today—out sick. The secretary gives us each a map and a class schedule, and Keith peels off into a connecting corridor while I head straight down the main hall to scout for my locker. I work the combination and throw my jacket inside; the halls are so stuffy, I won't need it.

I approach my first classroom, grip the door handle and pray I can slip in unnoticed. When I step inside, my prayer isn't answered.

A cluster of kids near the entrance turn to stare at me but nobody moves to let me through, leaving me wedged between them and the door. One guy wearing a baseball cap with the brim pulled low on his forehead watches me edge my way into the room. I've seen him before, but can't remember where. I hold my hands out and brush against people's backs until I make it to the teacher's desk.

No teacher. So far it looks like the secretary in the office runs the school. When I look around, I'm surrounded by a sea of eyes.

"Bitchin'!" That comes from a boy at the back of the room whose eyes scan me as carefully as that icky guard at security did

"Hey, Chico, I seen her first." It's the guy in the baseball cap. "Hola, bebe."

"Down in front, Anthony."

Suggestive, throaty laughter breaks out around the room.

The classroom door opens behind me and a hand rests briefly on my arm. "Miss Edmund? I'm Mr. Smith, your English teacher."

The class applauds.

What kind of teacher gets applause when he comes into a room? His eyes behind metal-rimmed glasses droop at each corner and are a slightly darker brown than his skin. His smile is broad as he pries the schedule from my hand and heads for his desk.

"Miss Carlie Edmund will be joining us," he announces as he looks out over the room. "There's a front seat in the row by the windows, Miss Edmund."

Grateful to get out of the spotlight, I slip into the desk and face the front of the room. Mr. Smith hands me a book and I hold it like a lifeline. I've plunged into Las Pulgas High, Room 9, and I have to stay afloat for the next forty-five minutes.

Someone taps my shoulder and says, "You got the hot seat."

I swivel around towards a thin-faced boy who leans forward, his chin propped on one hand.

"Hot?"

"You get called on a lot."

Mr. Smith looks in our direction. "Jamal, the final bell rang a while ago. It's my turn to talk now. First, I have an announcement. Our Othello has left school, I'm sorry to say."

From the back of the room comes a loud whisper, from the boy who I now know as Chico. "Kane's out the rest of the year this time. Got hisself—"

"Thank you, Mr. Ramirez," Mr. Smith looks at Chico over the top of his glasses. "So we will take some class time today to select a new leading man."

C. Lee McKenzie

A low chorus of groans ripples around the room.

"Think of that extra credit, gentlemen, and the reputation of the junior class. Let's turn to Act III, Scene iii. That's page forty-three, Miss Edmund." Mr. Smith opens his copy of the play flat across both his hands. "Anthony, Cassio doesn't have much to say in this scene, and Katy, Desdemona makes a short appearance, as does Emilia. Dolores, do you have your script?"

The girl in the desk across from me holds up her copy.

"Good. Pavan, you can continue to relax this morning. Brabantio isn't in this scene."

Across the room a guy jerks his head up from his desk, yawning. "Yessir."

"Chico, give us your best Iago this morning." Mr. Smith looks around the room. "Now for Othello."

Nobody raises a hand. Some slip low in their seats and hide behind the books they prop up on their desks.

"Come, gentlemen. No volunteers?" He pauses. "Think of this as your opportunity to impress the director and win the part of one of Shakespeare's most famous tragic characters." Taking his time to study each down-turned head, he finally looks to the back of the room. "Ah, Mr. Pacheco. I think I saw your hand."

"No way, Mr. Smith. I can't learn all those lines by April." The boy who answers runs his fingers through his thick black hair.

"You are too modest." Mr. Smith leans against the edge of his desk.

Mr. Pacheco smiles. It's a heart-stopping, sideways grin that's a sharp contrast to his deeply tanned features.

82

"Desdemona, please begin." Mr. Smith nods at Katy.

"'Be assur'd good Cassio, I will do All my ab-il-i-ties in [your]—'" She stabs her finger on the page. "What's this mark mean?"

"Good question, Katy. That shows the editor changed a word. We're using an abridged version of the play, with a bit more modern language."

Slouched at her desk, Katy reads Desdemona like a bad rap song, shifting her head from side-to-side, as if she's keeping time to some beat in her head. I rest my chin on one hand, staring at her. I know my face screams disbelief and Mr. Smith catches my eye. He's frowning. *At me?* This is going to be a *very* long forty-five minutes.

"Katy?" Mr. Smith hasn't said, "Stop fooling around," but his voice implies it. When he looks at her, she scoots up in her seat, sweeping the hood of her maroon sweatshirt off so it hangs at her back.

While the actors do their best to ruin Shakespeare, I sneak a quick glance around me. I'm in a room with fifteen other girls and about twenty guys, none dressed like I am. My deep red V-neck sweater, my designer jeans and suede boots stand out among the sweats and tees. There are lots of skulls, and way too many lightning bolts and "interesting" mottos.

"Anthony." Mr. Smith nods at baseball cap boy. "Let's hear that last line before your exit." Anthony's dark eyes find mine before I can look away.

"'Madam, not now. I am very ill at ease, Unfit for [my] own purposes.'"

I focus on the play, trying to ignore Anthony's glances over the top of his script.

"'Well do your dis . . . dis . . . '" Katy-The-Rapper looks up from her book. "What's that word?"

"Discretion." Mr. Smith writes it on the board. "What does it mean? Anybody?"

"Good judgment." I answer, before remembering I already stick out like a neon sign. Katy slowly swivels her head and we lock eyes. I look away before she does. *Where's my discretion?*

"Thank you, Miss Edmund." Mr. Smith signals Chico. "Continue."

"'Ha!'" Chico stops, shakes his head, and then starts again. "Ha? I don't like that."

"Rewriting Shakespeare, are we?"

"I like not that.'" Chico looks up. "That just don't sound good, Mr. Smith."

"Granted, it may sound a bit strange, but humor me and trust Mr. Shakespeare's grammar. We're already taking liberties with this abridged version, so with that line we'll adhere to the original. But now that we've stopped, let's discuss this single line and its importance. Why does Iago say this?" Mr. Smith points to the back of the room at Othello. "Juan."

"He's a jerk, you know? Trying to stir the pot for Desdemona." Juan casts another dazzling smile over the heads of the other students. He gives me a slight nod and I feel my cheeks flush.

"But he doesn't say anything bad about Cassio talking to Desdemona, does he?" Mr. Smith scans the room.

"In-nu-en-do." The girl named Dolores doles out the word in hushed syllables. "You know like hinting and letting the old man make the connections hisself."

"Excellent, Dolores. Now, Chico, read Iago's next line as if you were hinting that, as you say, 'something bad has gone down.'"

Chico reads the line and throws in a sneaky side-glance.

Mr. Smith claps. "Now we're starting to get the drama our playwright intended!"

The rest of the class passes quickly. I'm surprised when Desdemona stops rapping and starts sounding more like the doomed heroine. I close my eyes and listen to the words. As long as I don't see Katy's magenta-tipped hair, it's possible to believe she's the obedient wife of the Moor. Poor jealous Othello plays right into Chico's Iago hands, just as I remember from the time I saw the play with Mom and Dad at Shakespeare in the Park.

At the end of the period, before I can get up to leave, Chico's at my desk, looming over me. "So, where you from?"

I don't have time to answer. "Buzz off, Chico." Anthony shoves Chico and they pretend to sock each other.

"Gentlemen, please take that outside."

The two play-punch their way out of the room.

On my way to the door, Mr. Smith signals me to wait. "You're from Channing," he says. It isn't a question. "You'll like this bunch, once you get to know them."

I don't plan to take the time to "like" them. I'm just a tourist. Yet I sense the implication. "Don't be a Channing snob," he's saying to me, "and you'll get along here." He should play Iago; he's great at innuendo.

"I don't think I'll be here too long. This is, uh, temporary."

"That's too bad. Las Pulgas has much to offer." He stacks Shakespeare on top of Grammar and Composition III, then picks up a folder. "I've learned a great deal since I arrived. I hope you enjoy your time here, for however long it may be."

The rest of today will be way too long. But I just back away, saying only, "Thanks."

Juan Pacheco, the guy who's a toothpaste manufacturer's dream, meets me in the hall. "Hi, Channing."

"What? Do I have Channing tattooed across my forehead?"

"You might as well. Or preppy."

"Why's everybody so uptight about Channing?" I walk around him and he follows me to my locker.

"We're not uptight. Are you?" He smiles at me and I can't look away. It's as if he's captured my gaze with some kind of tractor-beam. My palms grow sweaty until I dig my nails into one of them to break the trance.

"Look. I have to be in this stupid school, but I don't have to like it, and I don't have to talk to the . . . the inmates." I spin my locker combination and slam the door against the next locker.

"You sound kinda uptight—like royalty." He walks away, saying, "See you later, Princess."

It's only February. How am I going to make it to June, let alone next year?

I cram my English book into the locker and go in search of my French class.

17

Tuesday, when I slip into Room 9 for English, it's still fairly empty, with only one clump of students at the back by the bulletin board, and Jamal who's already in his seat— the one behind mine by the windows. Juan's among the group in the back of the room. He sees me come in and walks down the center aisle before I can reach my desk.

"So, Princess. You're back for another day with us."

"I wouldn't be here if I had a choice."

He shakes his head. "No. I guess you wouldn't." He steps out of my way, as if he's allowing me to pass.

A low growl comes from the back of my throat. He is the most irritating person on this planet!

Jamal has his nose in a book, but he looks up when I get to my desk. "Did you hear what happened?"

I'm not sure if he's talking to me, but when I point to my chest and lift my eyebrows into a question, he leans over his desktop. "Katy got herself in another fight. This time it's bad."

I shrug because I care zero that Katy got into any fight. Second, I don't get what he means by bad, but I like seeing

87

her desk empty. Now I won't get any scorching looks if I open my mouth during class.

The first bell clangs and students pile through the door. Mr. Smith walks to his desk and, as the final bell rings, he writes *Desdemona* on the board. "Most of you have heard that our star will not be able to continue in the play, so again we'll be casting a lead role in Othello. This is a perfect opportunity for those extra credits some of you need in this class." He takes a long time to scan the room. The guys don't hide behind their books this time, but the girls do, except for me because, of course. I'm not the Desdemona type, and I don't really need extra credit.

"Our pool of actresses from our class is quite small, as you know." His eyes stop at each of the girls who aren't already in the play or working on the stage crew; it's as if he's remembering why they can't take the role. "Work and family do take priority."

I'm filling the time doing some high-level math in my head, calculating the number of days before the end of the school year when Mr. Smith says, "Miss Edmund. You're new to our school and this would be a wonderful opportunity for you to get acquainted with your classmates. Would you consider taking on this challenging role for us?"

My mouth is open and my face must resemble that painting with the crazed guy screaming.

Jamal pats my shoulder. "Told you. You got the hot seat."

"I can't. Uh, I really can't. I—"

"How come?" Dolores asks with her quiet voice.

"Well, because—"

"You got a job after school?" Jamal asks.

I shake my head no.

"You'd make our class fund-raiser possible, something we can't do without a full cast and we'd have to cancel otherwise. The students and I would very much appreciate your effort." Mr. Smith gives me a "how about it" look and his honey voice flows through my head. "With the money we raise, we can paint the auditorium this year. It's in need of some . . . redecorating. Isn't that right, class?"

A chorus of agreement fills the room. When I glance behind me, Juan grins as if he's just set a foolproof trap. Chico licks his lips. *Arrg.* Anthony looks first at Juan and then at me. I sense a plot to get the Channing transfer.

Jamal pats my shoulder again. "I got two parts and I work the stage crew. Alls you got is one part."

"All . . . right." I close my eyes and let the scream loose inside my head.

∽

The house phone rings Saturday morning before I'm up and dressed. I ignore it at first, until I remember that's the only phone I have now, and the call could be for me.

"So how's the new school?" Sean's voice sounds like home and the promise of something wonderful.

"It's okay." I almost choke on the words. There's nothing about it that's anywhere near okay. "One week under my belt, I'm getting used to it."

I leave out that Mr. Smith coerced me into playing

Desdemona in the spring play, now that Katy's on crutches. I don't tell him I've discovered Katy is really K.T., and those initials are tattooed on the back of her neck—and that she shoves her way past me even when there's plenty of room. I also don't mention that *Othello* is the Las Pulgas junior class fund-raiser, something I'm supposed to tell absolutely every living soul, according to Mr. Smith, so they'll come and support the show. For a second I close my eyes, but instead of Sean, it's Juan Pacheco in his Othello role that I see, his dark eyes looking into mine, his deep voice saying, "'Farewell, my Desdemona. I'll come to thee straight.'" I shake my head, as if I can clear the image.

"Can you talk to my mom about getting used to change?" Sean says. "She's pissed because I'm not moving back to New York after graduation, so she's working on making my life a capitalized miserable. Guess I'll have to visit her and smooth the waters."

"When will you go?"

"Probably before spring break. I can get a good fare if I go before vacation starts." He pauses, then says, "When can I come see you?"

He has to hear the thud of my heart sinking in my chest. First because he won't be here for the dance, so there's no way he'll ask me to go. And second, because I want to see him. I just don't want to see him *here*. I stifle a groan, glad that he can't see my face. "How about I come to Channing? I, uh, have things I need to do there."

"Sure. When?"

"I have to—" I almost say, *ask for the car.* "Check with my mom. I'll call you."

After he hangs up, knots form in my stomach while I look around my room: sultry dark cube with a clever Rorschach carpet design by Stains Galore. Chic black-sheet window treatment, a real mood setter. Air courtesy of my neighbors—Smokers Unlimited.

What will I do when I run out of excuses? If I start dating Sean, I won't be able to keep him away from Las Pulgas forever. But I have to admit those knots have a lot to do with the humungous number of lines Shakespeare wrote for Desdemona, and because Juan Pacheco keeps popping into my head, looking like a smoldering Othello. Another big reason for stomach knots anytime is that I miss Lena, but I can't call her or she'll want to come visit. Then there's Quicken. I picture her starving in a Las Pulgas slum—and that's yet another pain.

I dress and throw the covers back on my bed.

Mom sits at the kitchen table with books and papers, her chin propped on both fists. She looks up as I come in. "Hi, hon. Cocoa? It's hot."

I pour cocoa into a mug and sit across from her. "Can you let me have the car today?"

"Where're you going?"

"I thought I'd drive over to Channing and look for Quicken, just in case she made it back to the house. I don't have play rehearsal until 2:30." Several times last week I'd considered going back home to look for my cat, but each time I changed my mind. Somehow Sean's phone call helped me decide I can see Channing without imploding.

"Ask Keith to go with you." Mom rubs her eyes and yawns. "I'd feel better if you went with someone, and I'm tied up all day." She waves her hand over the books. "The practice test on real estate principles is next Tuesday."

What will happen when Mom gets her license, starts selling real estate, starts making money? Could we go home to Channing? Could we somehow toss that redheaded squatter and her parents out of our house and move back where we belong?

On my way from the kitchen, Mom reaches out and takes me by the hand. "I think I have a job as a cashier at the Las Pulgas Market. That should help us get through this rough patch a little faster." She looks up at me. "What? You look like I just sold you into slavery."

"Cashier? In a market?" *How can she think of doing that? What if my friends find out? Is she trying to completely ruin my life?*

"The job will help with groceries. Things are getting better, like I promised."

"What's better, Mom? Just tell me, okay?"

"Stop it!" She covers her face with both hands, then slams them onto her books. "I don't have a choice, Carlie. Don't you understand?"

I do understand, but she doesn't. Every day we live here, we sink deeper into Las Pulgas. I grit my teeth and flee down the hall. How can I help being a terrible daughter if she strips away the last tiny bit of dignity I have left?

Keith is still in bed, buried under his pillow, when I peek inside his room. No matter where he sleeps, his room turns into a mole hole. At Channing, he painted his walls indigo and kept all the curtains pulled tight. Here he didn't bother to redecorate. He didn't need to. This room started with all the prime qualifications for a mole dwelling.

"I'm going to Channing to look for Quicken. Want to come?"

His foot shoots from under the covers. Then he pushes his pillow aside and opens one eye. "When?" When he's sleepy, my brother looks like a tall ten-year-old instead of the high school sophomore who's out to give his older sister grief.

"Ten minutes," I tell him.

"Make it fifteen and I'm there." He puts the pillow back over his head and his foot disappears under the blankets.

I'm surprised when he walks down the hall and into the living room almost exactly fifteen minutes later. He wants to go home, too.

18

We navigate through the Las Pulgas traffic and head west, toward the coast highway. Once I point the Tercel north and follow the familiar winding road along the oceanfront, I breathe the sea air. I remember how much I love the smell, and how much I miss it, but I didn't expect to ache all over like I'm coming down with the flu.

I pretend I don't notice how Keith shuts his eyes and seals himself away.

When I turn down our old street, my heart pounds so hard I feel it bruising against my rib cage. I pass the Franklin place and pull to the curb across the street from our house without looking at the two-story beach home that I miss like a piece of myself. I imagine walking inside, seeing the fireplace mantle decorated with fresh holly and lights for Christmas, then sitting at the dining room table with one of Mom's lush bouquets and candle flames dancing in the reflection of the polished wood. I remember how it used to be, when Dad swept down the driveway in the evenings and came in shouting, "The king is home!"

"They painted it." Keith's voice shakes me out of my trance and I jerk my head up.

"It's green!" I say and clutch the steering wheel, swallowing the bile that rises in my throat. While I'm staring at the putrid pastel house, the door—my door—flies open and that redheaded witch sashays down the path—my path. I feel rather than hear the growl coming out of my mouth.

"Chill, Carlie." Keith opens his door. "Stay here. I'll go to the back where Quicken used to hang out."

Keith's only gone a few minutes before he jogs back across the lawn empty-handed. We leave in silence, and I take the familiar route toward Sam's Shack, where everyone goes during lunch and after school. On Saturdays, burgers are half-off, so the place is packed. I don't park in the lot, but hide the Tercel in the grove of eucalyptus down the street.

"Are you going in?" Keith asks.

I want to, and I don't. I'd like to pretend today is the way Saturday used to be. I'd like to walk inside Sam's, sit with Lena, make plans for the dance or next week or—

"Well, I'm starved, so I'm heading in." Keith opens his door and gets out.

You can do this, Carlie. Just have your story straight. Keith won't say anything. His mouth will be too full.

I trudge behind my brother, but before Keith pushes Sam's door open, Lena steps out and blocks the way, tapping her foot.

"I'm glad to see you," I say. My voice isn't too convincing.

"Really?" She puts a fist on each hip and sticks out her chin. Lena's a master at playing "hurt."

Keith walks around her, saying, "Later," leaving us face to face as he goes inside.

"I'm sorry. I've been so—you know trying to—" I choke back tears. I'm not ready to talk about how I'm the uptight princess at Las Pulgas High, or about K.T. and her remarkable hair or the tattoos, or Juan or Anthony or Chico. "I've been trying to get used to living—" I can't say it. I can't say living in a dump, living without any friends, living a life I hate. "I'm just sorry."

Lena shifts her weight, then smiles. "Me, too. Really sorry."

She steps in close and we hug. For the first time in weeks, I feel like myself. I'm with someone I've known forever, someone who doesn't have initials tattooed on her neck. "I've really missed you, Lena."

"I've missed you, like, massively. Come on." Lena takes my arm. "We have catching up to do."

Inside, we line up behind Keith at the order counter.

"I have *so* much to tell you." Lena clings to my arm as if she doesn't want to lose me. "The spring dance, Eric Peterson—"

"You're going to the dance with Eric? What happened to Gene Connell?"

"That didn't work out, but—"

"Come on. Out with it." It feels so good to be here with Lena, to be excited about things that my best friend is excited about. This is my *real* life. This is where I belong.

Keith picks up his burger and sits at a table by the windows. It's my turn to order. I'm at the counter, still listening to Lena, still looking at her and nodding about all her good news. "One Sam's Super-Lean Burger, no fries and a Diet Coke."

"You're the second girl on a diet today."

I whip my head around. Juan Pacheco's dark eyes are on me, his lips in a dazzling sideways smile.

He punches in my order. "Will that be all?" His name tag with JUAN in capitals is pinned to his spotless white Sam's Shack shirt. The way his cap sets at an angle over one eye is really annoying.

When did Juan Pacheco get a job at Sam's? He doesn't belong here. He doesn't belong in any part of my life, and I'm telling him so the first chance I get without an audience, the next time he pulls that . . . that smile business or calls me Princess. Gah!

"The same order for me, except I want fries." Lena's voice sounds low and sexy. "And put them together." She wraps her arm around my shoulder. "My treat. I just got my allowance."

"Thank you." I barely move my lips and keep my eyes down. We wait for our order, then pick up the red plastic baskets with our hamburgers and sit next to Keith's table. He's already devoured half his burger.

While I peel back the paper wrapper, Lena gushes with news. She's not just going to the spring dance with Eric; they're a couple. "Mom bought me a super outrageous dress when we were in the city last weekend."

"Kind of early, isn't it?"

"I couldn't pass it up. You'll understand when you see it." She nibbles a French fry. "So you're coming over, right? I mean, you have to. It's been eons."

I remove the top bun and take a bite of my Super Lean Burger. "Uh huh. Hmmm." My full-mouth sounds are neutral. They could mean, "Sure," or "Maybe," but it seems to satisfy Lena.

"So talk to me." Lena takes the first bite from her burger.

At the next table, Keith pushes up from his chair. "I'm going back to ask some neighbors about Quicken. Pick me up at Mitch's, okay?"

With Keith gone, I have no way to avoid answering Lena. "I'm not sure what to say."

"Well, it kind of hurts, you know?" Lena says.

"What?"

"You're treating me like I'm not good enough anymore." Her voice has an edge again, like it did when we first met outside.

Boy does she have that backwards. "I'm sorry. It's me, not you. I don't like where I'm living. I hate the school." I swallow and choke, covering my mouth with my napkin and giving myself a moment to get it together. The beginning of my confession hasn't gone well and I'm feeling pathetic.

"And that would be where?" Lena asks. "You, like, vanished, and I don't even know your phone number. Someone else answers your cell."

I'm trapped. My web of half-truths and evasions is coming undone. I can't escape answering Lena's direct question this time—I have to tell her. This is going to ruin my life.

I look Lena in the eye. "I don't have a cell right now."
I hand her a piece of paper with my home number scribbled on it. "We moved into a place that doesn't have . . .
good reception." I cough behind my hand. "Las Pulgas."

Lena gazes at me without speaking.

19

Lena stops chewing. She swallows, sips soda through a straw, and wipes her hands on her napkin, taking her time as if she's preparing to do surgery.

"Say something." I want to shake her.

"That's . . . interesting."

I should have made something up. Why didn't I have a story ready? "Have you ever seen Las Pulgas?" I ask her.

Lena wads her napkin and drops it into the empty red plastic basket, but she doesn't answer.

"I didn't think so."

She shifts her eyes toward the window. "My mom said something once about great bargains, but—"

"*Bargains* is the operative word."

"Wait. Wait. I *do* know more. My mom has a friend there. She lives in uh, uh," Lena snaps her fingers. "Barranca Canyon?"

"There's a canyon in Las Pulgas?" We are not seeing the same place.

"Mom says the views from her friend's house are great, just not the ocean, of course."

"Your mom's right. The views are not to be believed." I'm seeing Dumpsters, plastic lounge chairs with their webbing dangling from their seats, and a flat-roofed carport.

A tap on my shoulder brings me around in my chair.

"May I clear your table, Princess?" Juan waits, holding out his hand in the direction of my almost empty basket and Coke can.

What is the matter with him? "Yes, you can take them." I sit back out of his way while he stacks our baskets and wipes off the table. His lips part into that annoying sideways smile, then he moves to the empty table next to us and arranges the napkin holder and catsup, as if he's doing important executive work.

Lena stares after him and then back at me. "Princess?"

"It's a joke. At least *he* thinks it's funny."

"So are you sharing, or what?"

"He's in my class at Las Pulgas High. That's all." No, that really isn't all, but I can't explain what I feel. *But one thing I know, I've had it with Sam's.* "Come on, Keith's waiting for me," I say, ready to escape.

Out front, we hug each other again. "Call me, okay? I'm sorry I've been such a dope. I've really missed you, Lena."

"That makes me feel sooooo good. I thought you wanted to dump me."

"Never!"

"You know, Nicolas still talks about asking you to the spring dance."

I'd almost given up on the dance, but now visions of that red strapless dress float in my head.

"Maybe we could double. That would be so awesome."
With another hug, Lena walks away, then looks over her
shoulder. "Bye, girlfriend."

As I return to our old neighborhood, I feel better than
I have any time since the move. Lena and I are still friends,
and even if Sean won't be in town for the dance, I may have
a date anyway. That means I might at least appear to be the
Carlie Edmund I used to be. *But if Nicolas asks me, how
am I going to buy that dress? I'll call the Franklins. Give
them my new number. Maybe they'll let me babysit some
more.*

When I pull up at Mitch's house, Keith's on the sidewalk, talking to four guys I know from Channing's track
team. He motions for me to wait, then turns his back.

"I just love being your chauffeur!" I shout out the window.

He ignores me, but Brent, the kid with a baby-face who
tries to leer and always fails, leaves the huddle. When he
reaches the Tercel, he leans down to look inside.

"So how's it going in Las Pulgas?" He was always trying to get me to notice him—a sophomore.

"It's good."

"Yeah. So, you're okay hanging with the fleas?"

Step on it, Keith, and let me get out of here. I look past
Brent, then tell him, "Go back with your play group."

"Sure." He slaps the side of the car. "New?"

"Keith! I've got to go!" I've had it with baby brother's
little friend.

Brent returns to the huddle and gets between Mitch
and Keith. "So does the Las Pulgas track team, like, hop
over the finish line?"

102

All the guys laugh except Keith, who snatches a tan gym bag from Mitch's hand and hurries to the car with it slung over his shoulder. His jaw is clenched and his face flushed. Mom used to call him her time bomb when he stomped through the house looking like that.

While Brent hops in place, the others egg him on. Finally, Mitch shoves him and he falls onto the grass, still doing his flea imitation.

"He's quite the comedian," I say, as Keith settles into the passenger seat and slams the door. I put the car in gear and make a U-turn, keeping my eyes ahead and not looking at Keith's friends. "Any Quicken sightings?"

"Nobody's seen her around here."

"What's in the bag?"

"Stuff I left at Mitch's house last month." Keith rolls the top of the bag shut and tucks it between his feet. He leans back and closes his eyes, his signal that he doesn't want to talk. He's done that for as long as I can remember; sort of shuts everyone out when he's down.

When Keith used to turn sulky, Dad would knock on his door and they'd stay in his bedroom for a while. Sometimes they'd occupy the garage and ban Mom and me while they huddled over the workbench. Solder sputtered under a hot iron, the polishing wheel hummed and at the end of a session with Dad, Keith would come back to the house making eye contact again. Neither Keith nor Dad ever answered questions about what the "men" had been up to.

My eyes blur, and that spark of happiness I'd felt after seeing Lena sputters, then dies. Anytime I think about how it used to be, something very complicated happens to me

103

and I can't separate the feelings of guilt and anger and grief. They all mush together, like a soup made with spoiled ingredients that I can't digest. I step on the gas and hurry back across town and to Las Pulgas.

When I open the door to the apartment, the sound of voices comes from inside—Mom's and a man's. I look at Keith, but he just shrugs and starts into the kitchen, then stops so suddenly that I slam into him.

"Jeez, Keith, what—" I don't finish because there at the table with Mom is the man from the apple orchard. He's in our dinky apartment without his gun, and somehow his hawk-like features aren't menacing. His eyes aren't at all the way I'd imagined them in the shadow of his hat brim, either; instead of a black look, I'm getting a steady gray gaze. And there on his lap is a contented, purring Quicken.

"Look at who Mr. Christopher brought home," Mom says.

"She showed up a few days ago. She's a little lean, but healthy enough." The man rubs behind Quicken's ears. "It's lucky you're the only new tenants around here. Made you easy to find."

I stroke Quicken's back. "Oh, fur person, have I missed you."

Mr. Christopher hands her to me. "Keep her inside for a while. My grandmother always put butter on cats' feet when she moved them. She said that by the time they'd licked their paws clean, they'd stay in the new place."

"Thank you again, Mr. Chris—" Mom begins.

"It's Jeb."

"Then please call me Sarah."

I look at her, then back to the man who doesn't look like a Jeb. A Jeb should be chewing on a straw and scratching himself. By all criteria, this guy's hot, old, but definitely hottie material.

Mom walks Jeb Christopher outside; then, after he's gone, she leans against the door and says, "What a nice man."

20

It's almost 2:30 when I arrive at school for my first Saturday play rehearsal. I grasp the handle of the door to Room 9, then consider running back to the car and escaping. *I should never have let Mr. Smith talk me into this part. I'm not an actress. How can I learn all those lines?*

∽

"Once you give your word, Carlie love, you have to keep your promise."
Yes, but . . . well, you promised to be here forever.
I tighten my grip on the door handle and yank.
Didn't you, Dad?

∽

When I open the door to Mr. Smith's classroom, he looks pleased that I've showed up. He was probably worried that I'd change my mind. Well, I have, but—
"Welcome, Miss Edmund. We're just starting." He brings another desk into the circle of students and motions

for me to sit. Hearing Mr. Smith's honey-warm voice calms me, but I can't forget it's the same voice that coaxed me into this mess. Directly across sits K.T., her eyes fixed on me like gun sights. *I thought she was out of the play.*

Next to her on one side is Chico; on her other side, Juan. Anthony sits by Chico, studying his script. I shudder to think of what's ahead of me, working closely with the most disturbing Las Pulgas dwellers.

I still can't remember why Anthony is so familiar; he catches me looking at him and I quickly thumb my script, scouring for the first mention of my character.

Mr. Smith takes the seat next to mine. "This afternoon we're reading and discussing Act I. K.T. please note any props for this act, and use the copy I gave you to begin making your Prompt Script. You have a challenging first act, Chico. Even with this abridged version, Iago has a lot of lines."

"Got it covered, Mr. Smith."

"So let's begin. Jamal, Roderigo has the opening lines."

I follow the dialog, avoiding anymore eye contact. When Chico gets to 'damn'd [by having] a fair wife,' I feel his stare but refuse to look up. *How am I going to get out of this part? How am I going to get out of this school?*

I'm buried in my own plots of escape when Mr. Smith taps my arm. "Desdemona? That was your cue."

"Sorry." I flip the pages, searching for my place.

"Give Brabantio's line again, Pavan." Mr. Smith signals Pavan Gupta, who plays my father.

Pavan reads my cue. "'Where most [do] you owe obedience?'"

" 'My noble father . . .' " My voice cracks. I can't read this, not facing K.T. and Chico, not facing anyone. I don't want to hear those words out loud. Desdemona is telling her father goodbye in this scene. I've already said goodbye to my dad—I can't do it again, not here.

Pressing my fingers against my eyes, I wish I could escape from this rehearsal. It's the same wish I made over and over in that hospital room last October when all I could think about was getting away from my father's dying. That wish to escape still thunders in my head and makes guilt rain down inside me. *I'm a terrible daughter.*

"Is there a problem, Miss Edmund?"

I shake my head, keeping my eyes on my script and willing the tears not to trickle down my cheeks. "I need some water."

"This is a good time to take a break anyway," Mr. Smith says.

"Yes!" Jamal is the first one up. Dolores follows him out the door and I hurry after them.

I wait in line at the water fountain, then drink long and deep.

"You got the jitters?" It's Dolores.

"No. Just thirsty."

Dolores steps up and takes one more sip of water. "It's K.T. Don't look at her, and you'll be okay." She never raises her voice. It's as if she has one low volume setting for everything she says. She's already down the hall and entering the classroom by the time I realize how relieved I am that at least one person besides Mr. Smith hasn't leered, glared or growled at me.

At the door, Jamal holds it open so I can follow him inside. "Thank you," I stammer. I'm beginning to appreciate even the smallest act of kindness.

When we start again, Brabantio stabs Desdemona with words as deadly as any dagger. "I'd rather to adopt a child . . ." Then he says he doesn't want her in his home ever again. I stumble through the scene, focusing on Pavan Gupta, trying not to hear my real dad, who I imagine might say these things to me, now that he can see into my heart, now that he knows the secrets I'm ashamed to admit.

I take Dolores's advice and don't look at K.T. I also don't look at either of her bookends, Chico or Juan. Anthony had to leave early, so I have one less pair of eyes to avoid. It helps to make fists and hide them under the desk.

Every time Juan speaks, I force myself to concentrate on the page. "Honest Iago, My Desdemona must I leave to [you]."

How can he sound so, so Othello-ish? I don't have any lines here, and I wonder what I'm supposed to do while he talks to me.

"Come, Desdemona. I have but an hour

Of love, . . . To spend with [you] . . ."

When Juan says this last line before our exit, the temperature in the room shoots to boiling. My face is on fire; then I glance at Chico and gasp. His sneaky evil look is perfect for Iago and it's leveled at me. I *hate* this play. I hate that creep Chico. Juan Pacheco I despise.

I'm exhausted and grateful when rehearsal is over.

K.T. stops me at the door. "So next time you think you can drag yourself through that part, you know, say all the

Des-da-mo-na words you're supposed to?" She does a shifty-head move in time to each syllable.

"Sure. Next rehearsal, no problem."

She snorts and, taking that as "dismissed," I start toward the car.

"Wait up, Princess." When I look back, Juan is jogging to catch up. I take out my keys and hurry to the car.

"Late for something?" He's right behind me.

"I've got homework." I've already opened the door and scooted behind the wheel.

"Sure. Just thought I'd tell you about Keith. See you tomorrow, Princess."

"I'm not a—what about Keith?"

"It'd be good if he'd stop dissin' the track team. He's talking to someone at Channing and some bad stuff is getting back here. The runners are steamed. You better tell him." Then he goes to join Chico and K.T.

As I back out and roll past the three of them, Chico and K.T. give me identical Las Pulgas scowls. Juan tosses off a quick wave. He's driving me crazy. I can't think when he's taunting me with that—that smile of his. I hate him for being so sure of himself. No, for calling me an uptight princess. He doesn't know anything about me. He's nothing but a judgmental jerk.

Mom's at the kitchen table studying when I come back from rehearsal. "I've got to finish one more section, then I'll make dinner. Want to make a salad?" She doesn't wait for my answer before diving back into her books.

While I wash and shred lettuce, I prop the script over the sink. We'll be going through some of Act II on Sunday, so I need to know what I have to do. The first part is a lot of Iago implying all kinds of rotten stuff. Great. Better yet I have a—"Oh no."

"What's wrong, honey?" Mom asks in that tense, protective tone I hear whenever she senses the tiniest danger for Keith or me.

"Uh, nothing." *Othello kisses Desdemona?* I'd forgotten there was kissing involved in this part, but it's right there in the stage directions. I will not kiss that—jerk. *That* has to be changed.

At dinner Mom talks about the real estate course, and then she circles around into Quicken, which leads to Jeb Christopher and what a really *great guy* he was, to come here and bring back our cat.

I wonder what she means by a *great guy*, but I don't ask. I stuff more salad into my mouth and wash it down with milk.

"So give us a report on your day," she says.

"I saw Lena at the Shack." I tell about lunch with Lena, leaving out the part about that Juan person. It annoys me to even think about him, let alone talk about him.

"How did the rehearsal go?" she asks.

"Good." I choke and gulp more milk.

She turns to Keith. "Did you see Mitch today?" Mom keeps trying to kick-start a family conversation and nobody's playing along.

Keith grunts.

"Do you feel okay, honey?"

111

"I'm good."

He's always in some kind of funk, but he hasn't been this down since right after the memorial service. I know tonight's gloom is all about our visit to Channing and Brent's stupid hip-hoppity flea impersonation. And probably seeing our house painted green, too—that ugly color. What's become my Las Pulgas growl rumbles at the back of my throat.

"I have some things to do before I fall into bed. The kitchen's all yours." Mom yawns her way up from her chair, gathers her real estate books, and disappears down the hall. Her shoulders are more rounded than I remember. It's probably the books, and that disgusting cashier's job.

Keith shares kitchen duty with me, and, since the dishwasher went belly-up last week, tonight it's my turn to wash and his to dry. Quicken curls up next to her cat bowls. Her ribs show and she eats and drinks every few minutes, as if she's making up for a long hunger strike.

"Aren't you glad Quicken's back?" I hand Keith a clean plate.

"Sure. Why wouldn't I be?"

"You're so grumpy."

"And you're Miss Sunshine, all of a sudden?"

"Sheesh. Sorry I'm bothering to talk to you." I shake cleanser in the sink and scrub hard. Keith tosses the dishtowel on the counter and leaves.

I dry my hands and kneel to pet Quicken. "Please tell me you don't like Jeb Christopher and that you'll never go back there again, okay?" I carry her to my room and she purrs when I hold her close. I love her warm, familiar sound. "I've missed you so much."

112

I close my bedroom door and put Quicken down. She hops onto the foot of my bed and snuggles into her cushion.

Tonight the neighbors aren't thrashing each other in the next apartment. I think I've figured out that on Saturday nights, they either go out or watch a TV program they agree on. At least I get a break one night a week.

There's not much homework and I'm tired of studying Desdemona's lines. I peel back the pages of my journal to the last entry I wrote and crossed out so long ago, that night at the Franklin house. I add another line through the sentence.

"Sometimes bad things happen . . . even in Channing."

"Don't give up writing from your heart, Carlie love."

My heart has nothing to say.

21

This is the beginning of the third week of my sentence at Las Pulgas High. Lena's emails and phone conversations with news about Channing keep me both sane and insanely jealous. She's on the Spring Fling dance committee; the table centerpieces are going to be violets and the cloths blue. If I were at Channing, I'd be on that committee. I'd be choosing the centerpiece colors—and not blue, either.

I'm running these thoughts through my head while Mr. Smith returns our essays from last week.

Last night when we talked, Lena said so many girls had signed up for Sean's tutoring that he had to add two more hours a week and one on Saturday. Her words, "God, is he hot!"

I know. I know. That's when I pounded my pillow with my fist and Quicken leapt off her cushion.

"And Carlie, Nicolas is calling you. He told Eric."

I'm glad someone is. I haven't heard from Sean in over a week. Can he be so busy with French lessons that he can't at least pick up the phone and talk to me?

Mr. Smith's voice brings me back to Room 9. "As

usual, I'm reading two of the best papers. With your permission, Miss Edmund, I'd like to read yours."

"Uh, sure."

It's hard to sit still, listening to my own words being read aloud. I try to keep a blank look, but I can't stop fiddling with my pencil, then rubbing the edge of my desk with both thumbs. When I glance across the room at the clock, Juan's eyes are on me and I tangle my fingers in my hair. Why did I write such a friggin' long essay? K.T. fixes me with her usual look of contempt, and I don't have to turn around to know I'm the main attraction for Anthony and Chico. I'd so like to become invisible.

When he's finished, Mr. Smith hands me my paper. "Well done, Miss Edmund. An excellent piece of nonfiction."

It might have won first prize for the nonfiction category of the Scribe's contest this year at Channing. *Who will win it now? Not me.* I crumple my A paper and stuff it into my backpack.

Mr. Smith holds up a second essay. "The next is by Mr. Chico Ramirez."

I expect some kind of gang war essay, with gnarly descriptions of muscled combat, but Chico's essay ties in long-distance running with setting goals and reaching them. The biggest surprise is that it's well written.

At the bell, I stuff my notebook into my backpack and head toward the exit. While Mr. Icky's backpack searches make mornings hell, I hate the five minutes between classes almost as much. Elbows out and push—that's the only way to make the trip. By chemistry, I'm as tired as if I'd run laps with Keith, but at least it's my final class and I'm close to being sprung for the day.

I'm working the combination on my locker when K.T. and her "girls" swing their way down the hall, spreading attitude ahead of them like confetti. They sweep around me, slam open the swinging door to the girls' restroom and file inside. I had considered a quick bathroom break before my next class but I change my mind.

Tossing my geometry book into the locker, I lean in to retrieve chemistry and while I have my head stuck inside, I hear K.T.'s voice. She's coming toward me, so I stay put.

"I'm creaming her next time I catch her anywheres alone."

"You got a plan?" That sounds like her main sidekick, the tall girl with big teeth. I worry about bites when she's near me.

"Do I got a plan?" Today K.T. sounds like she's chewing on gristle. I hope *I* have nothing to do with her mood. "Whaddya think?" She's one of the most physical people I've ever met, so even though I'm not looking at her, I know she *whomps* Big Teeth in the arm.

"Hey! Des, you sniffin' somethin' in that locker of yours?"

I step back and close the door. "Very funny," I say.

"I'm going to do you a number-one favor."

Please don't. I hold my chemistry book to my chest like a shield.

"Do not pee in any of these bathrooms starting today. Go to the annex instead." K.T. smiles, but humor's not involved.

"Excuse me?"

"Something's goin' down around here soon." She leads her gang away, but calls over her shoulder. "Don't want our star to get messed up."

When her back's to me, I make a face. *Some favor.* Now I have to plan an extra walk around the back of the school to the so-called annex if I need a bathroom. *And for what? Is she pulling some kind of newbie joke on me?*

At least in chemistry, I have a nonviolent lab partner—nonviolent but very unfriendly. He'd been working alone until I arrived, then Mr. Mendoza stuck him with me—the future English major.

"Hi, Doc." I keep trying to soften him up. I nicknamed him Doc because he's already decided to be an orthopedist and plans to apply to Columbia University. He didn't tell me; I overheard him telling someone else. He talks to other kids, just not me.

While he sets out the experiment, he grunts commands at me. I'm not allowed to touch the set-up. He may let me hand him stuff if I'm careful.

"So what's the—"

"A combustion experiment." He sets a Bunsen burner on the counter, along with small, square pieces of screen.

"Can I—"

"Light the burner when I tell you."

Mr. Mendoza strolls past as I hold the matches at the ready, trying to look productive. "Remember to use all the fire-safety precautions during this experiment," the teacher says.

"Okay, light it now." Without looking at me, Doc adjusts the flame, something else he won't let me do. Then, using tongs, he slowly lowers one of the screen pieces onto the flame. "Make notes," he commands.

"Like what?" I grab my notebook and a pencil. He snorts, but I ignore him and say, "Just tell me so I don't screw up your lab report, okay?"

"Flame doesn't penetrate the screen when lowered from above."

I write, then wait for the next step.

By the end of the experiment, I have one page of dictation. "So why did we do this?" I know my question annoys him, but how else am I to learn anything in this lab?

"We're observing heat dispersion."

"Hmm." I'll have to read the chapter to find out what I need to know. But Doc's already packing away the Bunsen burner and preparing for the next experiment. We're always ahead in lab. *He's* always ahead in lab. I begin plotting how I can screw up his A in this class.

After chemistry, I have one more stop at my locker before I can quit the stuffy halls of Las Pulgas High until tomorrow. I stack the books I'll need for homework into the crook of my arm, close my locker door and chart my passage to freedom. When I'm near the girls' bathroom, the door swings open and hits the wall with the force of an explosion. I jump back; the loud scream is mine.

A blonde wearing nothing but a bra and panties falls into the hallway. K.T. swings after her on crutches, then tosses them aside and pounces on top of her. Locked together, they roll across the floor, K.T's cast thumping with each rotation. The gang of six jams together in the doorway, yelling and waving what the girl had been wearing.

The girl screams as K.T. rips off her bra and the hoots from males in the area are deafening. Mr. Icky pushes the growing crowd aside and plucks up the nearly naked blonde by the arm. With his foot he pins K.T. to the ground, and Principal Bins is suddenly there, his jacket off and wrapped around the victim, whose face is streaming with tears.

Mr. Icky hands K.T. her crutches and marshals her down the hall toward the office. The principal follows, keeping the girl close to his side. "Show's over," he calls to the gawking bystanders.

The gang of six trails after the rest of the students jostling toward the exit. "K.T. got her good," Big Teeth says. "That'll shut her down."

One of the gang who has beads knitted into her hair sends them chattering against each other as she swings her head. "That skinny witch shoulda knowed better."

Another, the shortest one, scurries to keep up with the rest. "What'll happen to K.T. this time?"

"She'll get some time off from school, that's for sure, but maybe not so long. Bins is gonna see what's on that wall in there." At the exit, Big Teeth separates from the others. "Catch ya tomorrow."

When the door closes on the last student, I exhale. I'd been holding my breath and I'm still pressed against the wall biting my lips, staring at the open door to the girls' restroom and letting the sudden eerie silence crowd around me. The surveillance cameras hover like vultures overhead, scanning, patient. I don't want to alert them to my being here, so on cat feet I step inside to see what provoked K.T. into ripping off someone's clothes. The peeling gray paint is covered with the same initials, phone numbers and gross poems about body parts that I've seen here since day one. The first stall door droops from a single good hinge, and one mirror has a crack from corner to corner. I don't get what that fight was about.

But as I turn to leave, there, next to the light switch by the exit, is a crude drawing that sends my stomach into spasms. A chair is tipped on its side. Dangling over it is the lifeless form of a woman hanging by her neck from a thick rope.

I escape into the hall. *What did that drawing mean? Was it some kind of gang code?* Doesn't matter. It's a terrible thing that'll make going to the annex bathrooms much more appealing. I hurry outside.

Keith's at the curb, but he's not alone. Chico, standing a couple of inches shorter than my brother, has his hands in Keith's face, flipping him off. Keith shoves him and Chico's hands ball into fists. He's about to take a swing when a police car, lights flashing, drives up to the front of the school and two officers get out. Chico turns the swing into a wave and jogs off.

22

Our dented Tercel sweeps up to the front of the school and parks behind the police car. Mom's out almost before the car stops rolling.

"Are you all right?"

"It has nothing to do with us, Mom," I say holding both hands up as if that will calm her down. "Some kids got in a fight."

Still she's shaking as she puts her arm around my shoulder and says, "Let's go." Mom's Las Pulgas Market uniform has perspiration stains under both arms, and if she combed her hair today, it was early this morning.

My brother doesn't say anything when we climb into the car. He avoids eye contact with me, leans back against the seat and does his ostrich impression. Nothing's wrong so long as he closes his eyes.

The last thing I want to talk about is K.T.'s fight, so none of us has anything to say.

When we reach the apartment, Mom starts for her room. "I need a quick shower and—" She opens the door and closes it behind her, still talking, and forgetting that

121

we're not with her. "—put my feet up for half an hour." The last part is muffled.

I follow Keith down the hall. "What was that about today?" I ask him.

He looks at me like I'm talking in a foreign language.

"I saw Chico take a swing—" I get out these few words before he snaps at me.

"It's none of your business." Keith steps into the bathroom, then closes and locks the door.

I'm not letting him get away with that answer. "Whatever you're saying to Mitch about Las Pulgas is getting back here, so you'd better stop."

"Mind your own business," he growls through the door.

"Keith—" I pound on the door, but he cranks the water on in the shower so he won't hear anything else I try to tell him.

That night, my brother eats in his room. Mom never let us do that in Channing, but this is one more thing that's different here. When I ask why Keith gets special treatment, she says, "He needs some time without women."

Mom holds her real estate book in both hands, but she doesn't turn the pages, so I'm sure she's reading the white spaces instead of the words. I flip through the script without paying attention to which act I have in front of me. We don't talk, and I know this silence is about the two missing males in our lives. I keep seeing Chico at the curb, ready to pound on Keith, and I wonder what else is going to happen to my brother at school.

What would you do about this kind of thing, Dad? Go to the principal? Buy Keith some boxing gloves? I know

Dad would handle this mess so differently than Mom, who seems willing to let our mole burrow deeper and deeper into his hole.

I glance over the top of my script; even after a shower, Mom looks wilted, but she's so into her thoughts that I know she's not really here in this box of a kitchen. I wish that were true for me, too.

Later, when I check my email, it's as pathetic as the rest of my life. Sean writes that he's bought his ticket, so he's set to visit New York before the break and he'll talk to me soon.

"Right!" I hit Delete. Then I change my mind and retrieve the message from Trash. "U R so lucky! Out of school early AND going to NY. Carlie." My finger hovers over Send. Then I backspace over Carlie and write, "Love, Carlie." I backspace again over "Love," and type "X."

Quicken is tucked into a tight ball on my desk, and when I stroke her, she stretches out. "You are my best fur person, aren't you?" I tell her. She rolls over and lets me stroke her belly and under her chin.

I'm too tired to shower. I'll just—

The crash that makes my wall shudder sends Quicken under the bed. I'm up from my desk chair instantly and on the opposite side of the room to listen.

"No more money on the horses! You hear me?" The woman's voice on the other side of my bulletin board is shrill. I remember her face from that day I knocked at her door and asked about Quicken.

Her husband's loud gravelly voice shouts back. "I make the money. I'll spend it on what I want."

What she says next changes my mind about not taking a shower. I need to wash away her voice and block out the ugly sounds coming through my wall. Rummaging through my desk and shuffling my journal aside, I dig out the earplugs I used for swimming class last year. Quicken's low growls come from under the bed.

I push the foam plugs into each ear and relax to the soft pulse of my blood. Before closing the drawer, I touch the embossed letters on my journal, but I don't open the leather cover to look inside.

⌒⌒

Tuesday's here again, and another rehearsal night has arrived before I've read over my part. I stake out a quiet corner behind the gym bleachers during lunch and cram "My lords" and "Alacks" and "Alases" into my head. After Scene ii in Act V, I have no more lines. Othello murders Desdemona, and even though I hate the plot, I'm grateful not to have more to learn.

I take a moment to close my eyes and get ready for social studies. I've done the homework; I've studied for the quiz. I deserve a break from it.

The door to the boys' locker room opens, but I don't pay any attention to the footsteps and voices that echo in the empty room. But when I'm about to get up from my seat, I hear, "That effin' Edmund."

Is that Anthony's voice?

"He's a dip shit." I'd know Chico's snarly voice anywhere. That evil jerk is stirring up trouble for my brother.

I peer through the gym's bleacher seats at the three of them huddled together. I can't leave now, so I stay crouched without moving. They're at the opposite end of the gym, so I can't hear everything they say.

"Channing . . . that ass—." That's Anthony again.

"Grits says the guy's good and we need—" I don't recognize this third guy's voice.

Chico interrupts. "Ain't happening, man, Grits or no Grits."

"I say we nail him now and shut his mouth."

I'd like to strangle Anthony Mancuso.

"We'll get him, but not until the motherf—" The bell signaling the end of lunch drowns out the rest of what Chico says.

The gym door opens and closes, and now I'm alone. I have to warn Keith. They're going to jump him, but I don't know when.

The second bell rings before I reach my seat in social studies. I sit right in front of Chico Ramirez, of all people, who's already there, his eyes tracking me as I head down the aisle.

I suddenly want to be a female version of Rambo. I want to take all of these creeps down and reduce Las Pulgas High School to rubble.

23

Saturday and Sunday always whip by during the school year, but since I started going to Las Pulgas High, it's even worse: I blink and they're gone. The weekdays are different—they drag, and so do the weeks themselves. Week four seems more like week four hundred.

As I cross toward the annex, I hear louder than usual crowd noise coming from behind the main building. I turn the corner and see what looks like most of the student body outside the gym, but I can't see what's caused the excitement, even when I stand on my toes. I make my way to the annex steps and go to the top so I can look over what's sounding more like a mob than a student gathering. There's a police car parked at the curb, but that's so common, I didn't even notice it at first. Since I've been in this crappy school, I've seen the police almost as much as my teachers.

Probably some Las Pulgas creep at work again. Not K.T.—she's just back from three days' suspension. She's behaving like a bored saint now, because even though the naked girl's parents dropped the charges, Bins says he'll file more if K.T. gets into one more mess this semester. Disgust must be etched permanently on my face after these weeks of exposure to the low-lives at this school.

I start to enter the building, but when the crowd begins shouting, I glance over my shoulder. The gym door's opened and two police officers are coming out with a guy between them. He stumbles, head down, his sandy hair falling over his eyes. One officer holds a tan gym bag in his free hand. They've got my brother.

"Keith," I mutter, gripping the door handle until my fingers go numb.

As I watch the drama of the cops with my brother, someone grabs my shoulder and spins me around. It's Chico. He shoves me against the building, smashing my back against the metal siding. "He's dead. Tell him."

"Hey!" Juan Pacheco runs up the steps and grabs Chico's arm. "She's not the one who did it."

Chico jerks his arm free "Shove off, Pacheco. I'm giving her a message for her piece of crap brother."

"Did you hear me?" Juan jabs Chico in the chest. "She didn't do it."

Chico backs up and spits over the handrail, then says, "Just remember what I said." He aims his finger at me like a gun. "Your brother better watch his back."

"Come on, Princess. Chico likes to come off like a serious bad ass." Juan presses his hand to my back and guides me to the main building, then down the hall to the office. "You don't want to be out there when the crowd breaks up."

"Wha—what did Keith do?"

"Mega graffiti all over the gym."

"Oh, no." The words come out as if someone hit me in the stomach. "You've seen it?"

He nods. " 'Fleas suck' is the nicest message he spray-painted.' "

"What will . . . happen to him?"

"He'll go to Juvie Court. Get probation, probably. Is this his first run-in with the cops?"

"Of course." I draw myself up, crossing my arms. How could he even think Keith had ever been in trouble like this before?

Juan sighs.

"And you're sighing at what, exactly?"

"The Princess act."

I double my fists and hold them up in his face.

"You don't want to pound on me. I'm on your side." Opening the door to the principal's office, he gently guides me inside. "Call home, Princess." He leaves, closing the door behind him.

The secretary already has a pass ready for me. "We haven't notified your mother yet, Carlie. We're waiting until Mr. Bins returns from a district meeting. You can use his office to call your family."

I close the principal's door and press the numbers with the same care I'd use to set an explosive device. How am I going to tell Mom about Keith? What if the police have already called her?

"Hello?"

"Mom, uh . . . what are you doing?" That was a stupid question. She's not at work this afternoon, so she's studying.

"Like you always say," Mom laughs, "talking to you. Duh!"

She obviously doesn't know. "Can you pick me up at school?"

"Honey, I was planning to."

"No, Mom. I mean right now."

"Are you sick?" Mom's instant fear comes through the phone.

"Not exactly, but . . . Something's happened with Keith."

"Is he hurt?" I can see her clutching the receiver.

"No—but he's been . . . arrested."

There's a second's pause, as if her throat has closed. "I'll be right there," she says and hangs up.

The secretary is busy with a student as I leave. Once I'm in the hall, I keep my head down and push my way through the stragglers on their way to class.

I take the front steps two at a time and smack directly into K.T.'s sizable chest.

"It's Desdemona, the star!" K.T. hops sideways on her good foot and adjusts both crutches under her arms. "You packin' any of those spray cans, Des?"

Behind K.T. are her six friends—a kaleidoscope of colorful hair, but all with their faces set in a single, dark threat.

K.T. balances between her crutches; her friends say nothing, but they all shoot angry messages from their eyes. I'd like to remind K.T. that she could get kicked out of school again if she picks another fight.

I'm keeping my lips sealed; I'm all about wanting to keep my clothes on.

Backing up, I fold my arms across my chest. "Look, I didn't spray graffiti in the gym."

She doesn't say anything; I'm the mouse, and she's the cat who can pounce whenever she wants.

"What do you want, K.T.?" I manage to keep my voice from cracking, but sweat collects at the back of my neck and I want to pick up my hair to cool off. I should've paid more attention to the Aikido class Dad forced me to take when I was twelve. I might've had a better chance to escape, if not take on seven bad junior girls.

"I just want to *ast* you one little question." K.T. swings between her crutches, closing the small distance between us and stopping squarely in front of me. We're eye to eye, which surprises me. I thought K.T. was a lot taller than I was.

"So ask." I don't step back. Even if I wanted to, I couldn't. Big Teeth has edged her way in to stand directly behind me.

"Since we aren't good enough for the Edmunds, why don't you all go back to Preppy Land?" She shoves my shoulder and I mash up against Big Teeth.

"Don't look away, Carlie love. Stare straight at her. Try to look bigger."

I hear my dad's voice, from that day on the trail, when we saw a mountain lion. He'd drawn me close to his side, then flapped his jacket and yelled until the big cat slunk off into the trees.

"If it's the part, you can have it back. I didn't ask to play Desdemona." I shout and lean toward her, in spite of shaking.

"You keep it. I don't pick up leftovers from nobody." K.T. punctuates each point she makes with a right or left head-shift. Even her conversations sound like rap.

"What are you talking about? The part was yours before you broke your leg. I'm the one who got the leftovers, if you want to call a major lead in a major play leftovers." Big Teeth snarls at my back, and immediately, I regret trying to clear up that bit of fuzzy thinking.

K.T. pushes her face so close, I feel her breath on my cheek. "Hey, preppy, where do you get off, telling me I make no sense? You telling me I'm stupid?"

"Look, if you want to hit me, then hit me. I have to go meet my mom and pick up my spray-painting creep of a brother." Any second, I'm getting socked and socked hard.

Big Teeth shoves me from behind and I lurch forward, smack into K.T. We'd both be on the ground if it weren't for her crutches, and for a second I'm holding onto her. When I regain my balance, I let go and step away.

"I'll get back to you later—after you spring your little brother from the clutches of the po-leece!" She swings between her crutches more like they're gym equipment than prosthetic devices. The other girls follow, laughing, punching, and throwing their arms around each other, playing like a litter of pups.

I watch them enter the main building, relieved that they're gone; I'm worried about what K.T. will do when she "gets back to me later."

24

While I wait in front of the school for Mom, I practice what to say. "My idiot brother . . . Keith was arrested because . . ."

When the Tercel screeches to a stop in front of me, I quickly get in, relieved to escape school.

"What happened?" Mom hasn't put on any makeup and her hair hangs limp around her face. Her mouth is tight with tiny lines radiating out from her lips.

"He sprayed graffiti in the gym. The police took him away about half an hour ago."

"I'm going to talk to Mr. Bins," Mom says as she opens her door.

"He's not here!"

"What?"

"He's at a meeting somewhere."

I want to say I'm scared. I need to get away from Chico, and even more from K.T., before she decides to use her crutches on my shins. But when I see how worried Mom looks already, I can't add to her problems. Then I remember how my brother turns off the world when he doesn't want to talk, and I slouch into the seat, closing my eyes, just like Keith does.

Mom slams the car door. "Let's get home and make some calls," she says. "I've got to find out where they've taken him." Mom drives without asking me any other questions. She presses her lips together and clenches her teeth so the blue vein at her temple stands out. Her expression is hard to read. She's not angry. She's not scared. It's more like she's ready to go back into battle after losing the first skirmish.

At the apartment, Mom grabs the phone book and runs her finger down the city government page until she finds the number for the police. She hesitates with her hand over the phone, but before she can pick it up, it rings. The sound is so sharp and she's already so tense that she jerks her hand away, knocking over the mug on the table. Hot coffee sloshes over the side and onto her lap. "Oh, rats!" She jumps to her feet and pulls her pant leg away from her skin. With her other hand, she grabs the phone. "Hello? Yes, this is she." There's a long pause, then she says, "Where is he?"

I lay a paper towel over Mom's spilled coffee, then put both elbows on the table and cradle my forehead in my hands.

"Can I bring him home, then?" She rubs her eyes. "Okay. Thank you." Dropping the phone onto the table, Mom crosses to the sink, dumping out the remaining coffee. "I'm going to change my slacks, and then we can go get him."

When she returns from her room, she takes the keys from her bag and slams her books one on top of the other.

"Come on. You came along to help, so now's a good time to start."

She's using a Wonder Woman voice. I've never heard my mom sound this way. She's always been soft-spoken. Even when she'd get mad at us, her voice never sounded hard like this. I was right; she's ready to do battle. I just wonder who she plans to take on—Keith or the cops.

In the car, Mom grips the wheel and sits with her eyes closed before starting the engine. "What am I going to do?"

I don't have an answer, but when I glance at Mom, I can see that the question's really for Dad, not me.

She starts the car and backs out of the carport.

I trace all the other questions for Dad that must be streaming through her head. *What did you say to Keith whenever there was a problem? What did you tell him in his room or the garage that always got through to him? What would you say now?*

We stop at a red light. Mom closes her eyes again.

A horn honks behind us.

"Mom, the light's green," I tell her.

We park at the city hall complex. "Let's get this over with," Mom says and shoves the driver's door open. She steps out and asks, "Are you coming?" Then slams her door.

As we climb the steps leading to the entrance to the police station, I start to twist my charm bracelet. But then I make fists on the way into the building. At least this is happening in Las Pulgas, where nobody I care about will recognize me.

Inside, the walls are the same stone color as they are

outside, with only a single picture of the governor for decoration. The California flag hangs in one corner and the U.S. flag in another. Otherwise, the walls are bare. A counter with a single uniformed officer is before us at the back of the lobby. Fake leather chairs line the edges of the room, and two women and a man occupy three of these chairs. All their faces are closed, as if they've pulled the blinds over them.

We walk up to the counter. "I'm Mrs. Edmund. I got a call about my son, Keith."

Just like the other people, we have to wait. We watch as each of the waiting women is called to the counter, and each one leaves with a teenage boy. When the man's turn comes, I watch him leave with the girl who, from the strong resemblance between them, must be his daughter. How did this girl look before the tattoos? Not beautiful, but kind of pretty. Her dark hair hangs to her waist. Without the purple and orange spirals, her skin probably would be perfect.

In my mind, I trace the purple line that snakes down her neck, across her collarbone, and disappears under her T-shirt, then trails from under the sleeve and down her arm. *What route does the orange one on her leg take? That has to drive guys nuts.*

"How is she ever going to get a job?" Mom's voice startles me, as if I've been caught snooping somewhere I shouldn't.

"Mrs. Edmund." The uniformed policeman behind the counter calls out and motions us over. When we get to the counter, he hands Mom some papers to sign.

"Will he have to go to court?" Mom asks.

"Yes, and a parent will have to be there."

"Do you know how much the damages will be?" Mom asks.

"That's up to the school and the judge."

Keith doesn't look up when he comes out. With his head down and his hands stuffed in the pockets of his sweatshirt, he shuffles toward us. I wait as Mom goes to him and reaches up to brush his hair back from his forehead. He jerks his head away.

Is she just noticing that he's stopped getting buzz cuts?

"Let's go. . ." Mom leaves the sentence unfinished.

Even she can't say the word *home* when she's referring to our apartment.

Without making eye contact, Keith walks ahead of her and brushes past me like I'm a piece of the furniture.

When we return to the apartment, Keith goes directly to his room and closes the door. Mom doesn't even try to stop him. It's as if she's watching a ghost, something she has no control over.

"I haven't done anything right." Her voice is a whisper. "I signed loan papers I didn't understand and I lost our home. I'm the reason we had to move to this—," she looks around her, "—this awful place we don't fit into."

"I told you Las Pulgas was a rotten idea."

"Not now, Carlie."

"Then when? After a gang member beats me up because my brother's a jerk?"

"That's not going to happen."

"Oh, yeah. Right!" I hurl myself onto the couch and burrow into the cushions.

Mom leans against the living room wall, her hands covering her face. She's not crying. It's more like she needs to shut me out.

I stomp into the kitchen, shake two Tylenos into my palm, and fill a glass with water. With a single swallow, I wash the pills down.

"Give me two of those." Mom slumps into her chair at the kitchen table and unfolds copies of the papers she signed at Juvenile Hall. "How am I supposed to pay for this?"

That's another question for Dad.

Her face takes on that look of a storm in summer. "It's time I stopped asking someone who's dead for help."

That catches me in my chest. Mom never sounds like that when she talks about Dad. She never uses the word *dead* when he's the topic.

I refill my glass, then go to my room and close the door. Quicken stretches up into her Halloween-cat impression to greet me. I take my journal from my desk and hold it against my chest, then lie down next to her cat warmth, stroking her fur and listening to her gentle purr.

"Now what, Dad? What do we do now?"

When he doesn't answer, I get up and go to the closet, where I put the journal on the top shelf.

Mom and I *both* need to stop asking him for help.

25

When that woman in 147 isn't smoking, she's screaming at her husband, so I keep those earplugs in anytime I'm in my room. Between secondhand smoke and the reality show rehearsals, trying to study anywhere in the apartment ranges from challenging to impossible.

I figure I have about five minutes before the fireworks start next door, because Quicken has already scooted out between my legs and into the kitchen. She seems to know when it's time to escape.

I log on to my computer and open my email. *Why doesn't Sean email me?* I'll shoot him a quick message. *No. I shouldn't look too eager. Maybe he's got a girlfriend in Channing. I mean, I'm not there. And I can't bring him here.* "Merde!"

The only message I have is from Lena, who's written again about her dress for the spring dance. "When RU coming to Channing to see it? Or can I, Lena, the one who's supposed to be your BFF, bring the dress over to show you? Oh, and did Nicolas call yet about the dance?"

I'm about to answer Lena when a door slams and rattles my window. The woman in 147 screeches, "I told you we were out of money, and look what you went and did. I'm sick and tired of having your lazy ass around here!"

I hear glass shattering and clap my hands over my ears as another thud from the apartment next door sends a tiny seismic tremor through my room. I gather my books and flee into the kitchen, where Mom sits with a stack of bills and her checkbook. She's still in her brown and gold uniform. It reminds me of what women wear to clean toilets at ballparks.

I drop my books at the end of the table. "Our neighbors are killing each other in the next apartment."

Mom rubs her eyes and says, "I'll talk to the manager."

"Our 'manager' won't do anything," I tell her. "We've complained about the neighbors at least ten times by now. We've begged for the blasting music to stop by ten, and when the manager puts up signs one day, they're shredded and floating in the pool the next."

Mom's face crumples, and she looks old, like the pictures of my grandmother that I remember from our photo album.

"Carlie . . ." She sips from a bottle of cold water and picks at the label, then goes on, "...this won't be forever."

"It'll just seem like it." I'm sorry I've said this as soon as the words are out of my mouth, but I don't apologize. I have no energy for it after everything that's happened today—the nightmare of seeing my brother dragged off by police, being jumped by Chico and having the confrontation with K.T., and then going to the police station—I can't handle anything else. Even my hopes for any kind of relationship with Sean are fading fast.

Mom rubs her eyes. "I know it feels like it, but nothing's forever. You should know that by now." Her voice is so low I can barely hear what she says. Suddenly she's up from her chair and shoves her books away. She stands with both hands on the edge of the kitchen counter, but not looking at me. In a moment she sits down again, and with a sigh, pulls her books back in front of her. "I think I did okay on that test today. I'll know by the end of the week."

I should say something—congratulations, great job. But I don't.

Keith shuffles past us to the refrigerator. "No milk?"

I want to strangle the graffiti criminal.

"I knew I forgot something," Mom says. She sounds like she's just failed a test. "We need something for dinner, too."

I grab my jacket. "I'll go. What should I get?"

She looks as if she doesn't understand the question.

"Never mind, Mom. I'll figure it out. But I'll need some money."

Mom fumbles inside her wallet and hands me five crumpled dollar bills. We won't be eating steak tonight.

"Go with your sister, Keith. It's getting late," she snaps at my brother.

He doesn't answer or look at her, but the front door opens and closes, so I guess he's doing what she asked. We haven't talked since his arrest this morning, but I plan to say a lot once we're alone.

As I step outside, the sound of someone running comes

from behind me and the balcony bounces under the pounding of feet. I turn to face a lean male figure bearing down on us. He whips past, shoving Keith so hard that he falls against the wobbly railing. For a second I'm sure it will give away under his weight and I grab Keith's arm.

Without stopping, the runner flips us the bird, scrambles down the steps to the pool area and disappears out the gate, letting it clang shut behind him.

Keith yanks away from my grasp. "Let go!"

"He almost pushed you off the balcony!"

"I'm okay," he says sharply. "Mancuso's an Olympic sprinter wannabe—and Mancuso hates my guts." Keith juts his chin toward the apartment house. "And he just happens to be a neighbor."

"Anthony Mancuso?" I ask him, but now it all makes sense. *Cassio—that's where I've seen him. He was in the apartment with the guy in the orange jumpsuit the day I was out looking for Quicken.* "He's in the play."

Keith shrugs. "Whatever."

"What? Are you so used to dealing with hoods, now that you've been in lock up?"

He shoves me away and buries his hands in his pockets.

I walk alongside him, matching his steps. "So say something!" I shout.

Keith doesn't break his pace and he doesn't look at me.

"You think you're the only one in this family who's hurting? *I'm* taking the heat for what you did, you know. How'd you like not being able to walk into class without looking over your shoulder?" Stepping in front of him, I put my hands on his chest. "Huh?"

"What do you want me to say?" Anger flares across his face.

"How about why you did it?"

"I—" His anger vanishes, and all I see is the pain that takes its place. "Las Pulgas track sucks."

He's suddenly younger, looking the way he did in grade school. I almost forget what he's done to make my life hell. He doesn't have to say the rest of what he's thinking. He doesn't want to run on a team his Channing friends think is a joke.

"The good news is, Las Pulgas will kick me out. I won't have to be in that rat hole again." He side steps around me and walks down the street.

26

The next morning, I'm burrowed under my sheets, considering how to barricade my room when Mom knocks and comes in. I feel her put Quicken aside and sit on the edge of my bed. She waits until I poke my head out.

"You could stay home today if you want, but you know what I'm thinking," she says.

"I know. I know. Putting it off is only going to make it worse." She's always told me that, as long as I can remember. It's something she's passed down to me from some great-grandmother who crocheted afghans.

"You decide, okay?" She strokes my hair and leaves.

How can I stay home now? I haul myself out of bed, and on my way out, I pause to pick up my Jack-in-the-Box and give the crank a whirl. I wish it had the power to put itself back together. I need one thing in my life that works the way it should. Quicken purrs between my legs. "Thank you, fur person, for being here."

After feeding Quicken, I head to the bathroom. At least this morning, Keith isn't in there before me. He's shut away in his mole hole.

"Carlie love, you're strong enough to take on that whole school."

I turn on the shower, then reduce the flow before stepping under it and letting hot water wash over me. I don't feel strong enough to stand under a pelting stream in the shower, let alone take on Las Pulgas High today.

∽

In Mr. Smith's class, K.T. only glares at me a little more than at everybody else, but once I'm in the halls, she and her gang of six are either in my face. She's also been rapping behind my back:

> She the girl who got a brudder.
> He be paint-man with a paint can.
> Off to Juvie do he go.
> Carlie Edmund's little bro.

∽

In each class I'm on the lookout for Chico. He's a safe two rows away from me in English, but way too close in social studies. I've seen that face leering at me for weeks, but they weren't the angry, spiteful looks he's giving me now. I ease into my desk and feel him glowering behind me, like he's sharpening his switchblade to plunge into my back as soon as Mr. Burk turns the other way. If he makes up his final from today's lesson, I'll be a junior again next year—I won't remember anything that went on today.

I avoid the cafeteria at lunchtime. I need to memorize

more lines, so I decide to go outside. A quiet table or a tree would be good, but good just doesn't seem to happen at Las Pulgas High and I have to settle for the steps to the auditorium. I'm focused on my tuna sandwich and reviewing Act II when Juan sits beside me.

"'How do you, Desdemona?'" His Othello voice fills the air.

"I'd say, 'Well, my good lord,' if I could."

"Rough today?"

"Pick another adjective with more edges." I have to talk through tuna, and I'm sorry I chose fish.

He has a bottle of water and sips from it. "How's the Desdemona part coming?"

"Okay. Lots of lines. Lots of strange language."

"Let's see." He thinks a bit. "'Give me your hand:'" He reaches for my free hand, but I pull away. "You don't know the lines yet, do you?"

"I know them," I tell him.

"Show me," he says. This time he takes my hand and doesn't let go. "'This hand is moist, my lady.'"

"'It yet [has] felt no age or known no . . . sorrow.'" Only the first half of that is true in my case.

"You do know them." He laughs, but stops when he looks at me. "So what's gone down?"

No way am I sharing my feelings with Juan Pacheco. Eyes track me. I douse conversations in the halls. When I pass, whispers follow me like stinging insects, and now my grumpy lab partner growls at me *before* I screw up in chemistry lab. Who knows what Chico and K.T. are planning to do to me? Whenever I go to the apartment, I have to watch out for snarly Anthony, who just might push me over the balcony railing. I give Juan the condensed version. "Chico's close to stabbing me and K.T.'s getting ready to write a rap eulogy in my honor."

Juan hasn't released my hand. I'm about to yank it free and tell him to get away and stay away, when he moves closer and I smell his spicy aftershave and clean clothes that compete with the tuna I've just swallowed.

"I talked with Chico," he says. "He's a hothead when it comes to his reputation, and that's all about how fast he is on the track. He's mad about what your brother sprayed in the gym, but my dad knows his dad, so he's not going to do anything to you. And K.T.? She's a royal pain, but she's got serious trouble at home. She acts tough to get through a lot of bad stuff."

I'm not sure I believe that, and my expression says so.

"Her mom killed herself last year," he tells me, "so she lives with her grandmother now."

Killed herself? Those are such awful words. "That's horrible."

"Yeah. She hung herself, and K.T. was the one who found her."

The hanging woman! That hideous drawing and the way K.T. lunged at that girl, ripping off her clothes—now it all makes sense. And now I understand why everybody cuts her so much slack—her rappy Desdemona, her brawls—everything. Mr. Smith, the principal, even most of the other kids put up with her in-your-face attitude.

"She's always been bossy, so she's made a few enemies. Some of them are mean enough to use what happened to her mom to get back at her."

"The fight when she broke her leg . . . was that about her mom, too?"

He nods. "Some kids at Las Pulgas are trouble, but most aren't." He turns my hand palm up, as if he plans to read it. "My dad graduated from here. After college, he came back because he thought it was a good place to live."

His dad went to college?

He looks as if I've asked him that question out loud.

"Mexicans go to college."

"I didn't mean—" Yanking my hand away, I slam my script on the steps. "I hate to disagree with your dad, but you're choosing the wrong adjective again. *Good* and *Las Pulgas* do not go together."

He leans toward me until I feel his breath on my cheek. "Maybe it'll grow on you."

"Ah, my two leading actors."

Juan moves back and I turn quickly to meet our English teacher's dark, smiling eyes.

"Rehearsing?" Mr. Smith asks.

"Just helping Desdemona with a few lines." Juan's smug voice almost gags me. How did I let him worm his way into my confidence like that? The only difference between him and Chico is he's a make-love-not-war type, but he's still trouble.

My face has to be red because I feel the heat in my cheeks, but Juan doesn't look one bit concerned about being caught pressed so close to me.

"She's almost got it right," he tells Mr. Smith.

I'd love to punch him out, but he's already gotten up and is halfway down the sidewalk, leaving me to face Mr. Smith alone.

The teacher sits next to me in Juan's place on the auditorium step. "I'm pleased to see you took my advice, Miss Edmund."

"Advice?"

"It was about coming to like your classmates, but you probably didn't need me to say that. I think you're doing just fine."

I remember, and now my face grows even hotter. I want to tell him it isn't that I gave Juan a chance, but that he, well, he—

I'm scrambling to think of something to say that'll shift his attention away from that way too-friendly moment with Juan when he says, "I'm sorry about your brother's trouble."

"That's the first time he's ever done anything wrong. Well, not wrong, but really bad."

"I'm sure of it." He gazes at the chain-link fence that separates school property from the sidewalk. "I know how difficult it is to make the adjustment between Channing and Las Pulgas."

How can he know anything about the "adjustment" Keith and I have to make?

"It's taken me over five years," he says.

"What?" I don't try to hide the shock in my voice.

"I stopped teaching at Channing a few years before you started."

I'm glad he's not looking my direction because I have time to close my mouth.

"I'd spent a great deal of my youthful energy getting into trouble, but I stayed out of jail from the time I was fourteen—"

"Jail . . .?" I bite down on my lower lip to shut myself up.

"Luckily someone saw a flicker of intelligence in me, and even a speck of moral decency buried behind some purely bad behavior."

If Mr. Smith had socked me in the stomach, I wouldn't have been struck this dumb.

"I started studying, made it through college with a good man's help and graduated with honors. I felt fortunate to find a position at Channing." He smiles, but it's at the memory, not at me. "Now I'm here, and it's been an interesting journey."

If my vocal cords weren't paralyzed, I'd ask him why. Why not Channing? Why Las Pulgas?

"I'm glad I could persuade you to take on K.T's role," he says, getting to his feet. "I was concerned that we might have to cancel this year's junior play when she broke her leg."

I don't look at him, for fear he'll read my thoughts about K.T.

"She's assertive, so in the end I believe her accident gave us the strong stage manager we needed."

People around here choose very strange adjectives. Assertive? K.T. is a bitchy tyrant.

149

His eyes are on me and I'm sure he's reading my mind. "It also gave us a very fine Desdemona. I have papers to grade before lunch period ends, so I will see you tonight at rehearsal, Miss Edmund. Remember, we'll begin practicing on the auditorium stage from now on."

He's gone before I think to tell him he has to change that scene in Act II. I am *not* kissing Juan Pacheco.

27

After an early dinner, Mom puts the dishes into the sink and sets the leftover soup in the refrigerator. "Keith, you take care of the cleanup. Carlie has rehearsal." She walks with me to the front door and asks, "What time are you through?"

"Mr. Smith said by nine."

"Maybe I should drive you. I worry about those front tires."

"I'll be fine." The tension between us has eased since Monday. My guess is Mom and Keith have talked, but I don't care why. I just care that Mom has stopped biting down on her words as if she's severing heads. At dinner, even Keith grunted in the right places to show he was listening.

"My next paycheck, I'm getting two new tires and our cell phones back. I need to be in touch with you when you're out at night."

I have my keys in my hand and start across the pool area toward the gate when two guys I recognize from the halls of Las Pulgas come through the gate and cross toward

151

me. I circle around one of the tables in hopes they're on their way somewhere and not interested in me. No such luck. They block my path.

"Where you going in such a hurry?" The one closer to me smells of locker room.

"Play practice." I say, trying to sound calm—but I don't.

"Didn't know you lived in this place," he says again, looking around the complex. I know that tactic. Pretend not to be interested in the prey, then pounce when they're off guard. "We got a friend here. You know Anthony?"

"Not really." I shake my head for emphasis.

"You will," the one standing behind his friend says. His eyes are set close, and when he talks, he squints as if he's bringing me into focus "You and your brother will get to know him real good."

"We don't want any trouble."

"Too late for that." He pushes his friend aside and shoves his face inches from mine. "You already got a *pile* of trouble. Channing people should stay where they belong, and that ain't Las Pulgas. You got that?"

I have nothing to say and if I did, I couldn't get the words out because I've clamped my mouth shut to keep my chin from quivering. I'm also not able to move—the pool is behind me and they're in front, blocking me. Screaming is out of the question because nobody here would pay any attention to it. Even my family's immune to the loud voices we hear that always sound like cries for help but aren't.

The gate into the pool area clangs and the woman from Apartment 147 swaggers toward us. "Any of you got change for a buck? I gotta do some laundry and I need quarters."

They ignore her and head toward the stairs.

"Bullies. Hate bullies." She lights a cigarette. "You okay?"

"Yes."

"Better get yourself some mace, honey. Around here, a girl needs protection." She returns through the gate and goes into the laundry room at the end of the carport.

The loud neighbor with a vocabulary that could fill a dictionary of banned language has just rescued me. I like her suggestion about getting mace, but a bulky bodyguard is an even better idea.

It takes me a minute to make my legs move. Then I run for the Tercel and lock myself inside, where I sit shaking until I can steady my hand enough to start the car.

I back out slowly, as if I can take the Tercel and sneak out from the carport, and get away without being seen or heard.

⌀

I've memorized my Act I lines, but that's only because I don't say very much. While I don't have many lines in Act II either, I do have that sticky scene about Desdemona's dad. I hate that I have to say any of those words, but I *totally* can't stand that I have to say them to Chico and put up with his Iago glares. Every time I rehearse, my throat dries up and I choke, even when I'm practicing alone in front of the mirror.

And in Acts III and IV, Desdemona never shuts up.

It's after six and I run from the student parking lot across from the auditorium. The front door is unlocked and I hurry into the entrance hall. There are only night lights on and they cast eerie shadows. I was jumpy enough already. Now I'm really freaked.

As I rush into the auditorium, Mr. Smith is onstage. Next to him is Anthony, who tracks me as I come towards them. Then, without taking his eyes from me, he says something to Chico, who licks his lips.

"Come up, Miss Edmund. I know some of us still need scripts, but it's time we practice moving and interacting with the other characters. I'm going to be "blocking"—by that I mean telling you where to stand and when to move. This act may be a bit rough, but let's see what we can do with it. Desdemona, I'd like you to use this prop." Mr. Smith hands me a small white handkerchief.

He places a metal chair at the front of the stage. A folding table in the wings has water bottles, candlesticks and fake daggers. Off stage to the left, there's a light panel where Jamal and K.T. huddle around the switches that control the curtain and all the lights.

Once we've started, Chico stumbles on every other line, so it's hard to believe Iago could trick anyone into believing Desdemona and Cassio are an item, but he's definitely been typecast. The vilest Las Pulgas male is playing the worst Shakespearean villain. When we get to the scene between Juan and me, I can't concentrate. I avoid looking directly at him, even though that's exactly what Mr. Smith keeps directing me to do.

"Even I don't believe Desdemona is innocent, Miss

154

Edmund," Mr. Smith calls from his seat down stage. "She has to look Othello in the eye."

Easier said than done. First I keep losing my place in the script. Then I keep remembering the feel of Juan's hand around mine and his closeness on the steps earlier today. I fidget so much with my handkerchief that I drop it twice before the stage directions even call for it.

K.T. shakes her head, and in a stage whisper that everyone can hear, says, "Better get us an understudy ready." When I look at her, she glares back. She may seem not so tough to Juan, but I've seen her fight and I don't like turning my back on her, even with witnesses.

Mr. Smith gets out of his chair and scoops up the handkerchief. "Let's try it this way. Othello says, 'Your [handkerchief] is too little.' He pushes her hand and the handkerchief falls. Now, you can't see it fall, either one of you, and you won't if you're *looking* at each other, correct? Othello says blah blah blah, and Desdemona says, 'I am very sorry that you are not well.'" He says her lines in a falsetto voice and everyone laughs at the tall, elegant black man flicking the lacy handkerchief like a girl.

The tension melts and I get through the small scene. I have a long scene coming up that I don't know at all, so I go backstage and sit down to study. It's hard to concentrate with Juan's voice booming from the other side of the curtain. Phrases like *kisses on her lips* and *her sweet body* keep distracting me as I try to learn my lines.

How can Othello be such a dope? Iago's a sleaze, and if Desdemona weren't so lovesick and blind . . . . Well, then there wouldn't be a play, would there?

I'm so tired. Between play rehearsals, Keith's trouble, the commotion in the apartment, the loud music that blasts me awake at odd hours, and now this latest crap from Chico and Anthony and his friends—I'm just not sleeping very much anymore. I put my head down on the table next to my script and close my eyes.

"All cast and crew on stage, please." Mr. Smith's voice snaps me awake.

Yawning, I gather my script and grope my way around the curtain.

"All right, everyone, based on tonight," he looks at the cast, "we have to add a few hours of rehearsal."

A collective groan interrupts him.

He ignores the students who sink in their seats or hold their heads. "And on Saturday nights, we'll add another hour of practice until we open." He holds up his calendar. "Anyone have conflicts?"

"As long as it's after two on Saturdays, I can make it," Juan says. "I work until one-thirty." He looks at me and I pretend to make notes on my schedule.

"All right, cast and crew. I will see you tomorrow, with eyes bright and homework completed." Mr. Smith shuts down the lights, leaving the floodlight on in back until everyone files out, then he locks the stage door. "Gentlemen, we shall walk the ladies to their cars, if you please."

I wait until Anthony and Chico head out to the parking lot, then I pull out my keys and hurry toward my car. Juan falls in beside me, his arm brushing against mine. "So are you ready for our big scene, Princess?"

"I've already written a letter telling my mother to notify the police if anything happens to me on that stage."

"Princess, I'm hurt."

"And I don't *want* to be," I tell him. We reach my car, and I say, "Thanks for the escort."

"My pleasure." He walks across the now empty parking lot toward the street.

I follow behind, my headlights casting a giant shadow of him on the pavement. When he reaches the sidewalk, he turns right and keeps walking. *Where's he parked?* Then it hits me. He doesn't have a car. I slow and roll down the passenger window. "Want a lift?"

"Are you a safe driver?"

"Get in."

We drive past the school to the main highway. "Which way do I go?"

"South to Escondido, then left. I'll tell you where to stop."

Escondido's the opposite way I take home. I shouldn't have offered him a ride. I'm going to be later than I told Mom I'd be.

Soon he says, "Stop here." He points to a hotel with an iron-barred front door and ground-floor windows. On the second and third floors, light glows from behind drawn curtains.

"Is this home?"

"Home to many."

The front door swings open and the bars clank shut behind a man who's leaving. He's reached where I'm parked when the door opens again and a woman sticks her head out. "¡Bastardo!" she shouts.

"¡Calla la boca!" the man yells over his shoulder, then

gets into a car and guns the engine. His tires squeal as he backs up and makes a quick left onto Escondido.

"Carmen and Miguel are at it again," Juan said.

"Yes, I see."

"That sounds a bit like the 'Super Princess' talking."

"Get off the princess stuff, okay? I'm just not used to people yelling at each other on the street. Is that a crime?"

Juan shrugs. "People get upset. They yell. It's no big deal."

"We don't do that."

"We?" He arches one eyebrow.

"Look, I'm tired. Let's just forget it." I fiddle with my seat belt.

"By we, you mean the upper classes in Channing?"

"Holy crap, Juan. You are such a pain. I didn't mean *we* in any big sense. I meant my family, that's all."

"So you don't yell because you're not Mexican like me or," he nods toward the hotel, "those people."

"What? Look, I don't care if you're Mexican, Martian or . . . Malaysian."

His laugh barely ruffles the air in the car. "Go ahead and lie to me, but remember what our favorite playwright said, 'To thine own self be true.'"

I need to ward him off, along with the headache that's ready to pound behind my eyeballs. "I don't have anything against Mexicans or anyone else from Las Pulgas."

For a moment he looks up and stares at the roof of the Tercel.

"Now what?"

He turns his head so his eyes meet mine. "It's no use."

"I'm tired. I've got tons of homework to do and two scenes of dialog to memorize. If you think I'm some kind of bigot, you're wrong. But I don't have the energy to argue about it tonight."

"Well, you're a very pretty bigot."

"*Merde.*"

"See?"

"What are you talking about?"

"French."

"So because I study French, I'm a bigot?"

He doesn't answer.

"That's so . . . dumb. It's important to know another language, appreciate a different culture. Can't you understand that?"

"Sure I do, but why do you study French? Because you live in the middle of a densely populated French-speaking state?" He leans over and kisses me, stifling my witty response. Then he says, "Adios."

I don't have time to react to his kiss before he's out of the car, loping across the lawn, dodging broken bicycles and shopping carts. He doesn't go in the front door, but heads down the driveway alongside the hotel.

That was so . . . unfair, untrue. I crank the car and make a sharp U-turn. Absolutely baseless! "Grrr."

Why is he making me so crazy? So what if he lives in a hotel with Carmen and Miguel and who knows how many other people? What's that to me?

I live in a dump of my own, so we have a lot in common. The difference is, he doesn't care if I see his dump.

How can he be so sure of himself? He was even sure I'd let him kiss me. As I turn onto the main highway I trace my lips with my fingers. "I'm not letting him do that again."

28

By the time I ease the Tercel into the carport, I have a strategy for getting through this play. I'll be the super-prepared Desdemona, knowing all my lines. Then I'll square off with K.T. and look her in the eye the next time she has some ratty thing to say about my acting. So far, I've survived two run-ins with her and lived. I might as well go for a third time and see how charmed my life is. As for Chico and Anthony and Juan, I'll pretend they don't exist except as Iago and Cassio and Othello.

I park the car, get out cautiously and wait by the door. I listen, looking into the shadows, and have my fist curled around my keys in case I need to use them as a weapon.

A cat yowls and something with a long tail scampers across the driveway to dive under a Dumpster. My throat closes and feels like it did when I came down with the mumps. I flash on a memory of Dad, sitting on the edge of the bed, pushing tiny spoonfuls of ice chips into my mouth, then stroking my hair and telling me I'm beautiful, despite of my bullmastiff jaws.

"Carlie love, this is going to take time. Be patient. Take small pieces of the ice and let them melt. That's my girl."

This is a lot worse than the mumps, Dad.

Locking the car door, I hurry from the carport toward the gate. I wish I had my cell phone. Calling Mom, hearing her voice while I cross from the carport to the apartment would make me feel a lot safer.

Once I reach the pool area, I run toward the apartment building and mount the stairs, holding onto the rickety handrail.

I sprint to #148 and, hand shaking, jab the key at the lock. On the second try the key slips in, but won't turn. The carport gate opens and clangs shut. Someone's entered the pool area. Still twisting the key, I pound on the door until it opens, pulling me forward.

"Carlie? What on earth?"

"My key—got stuck." I focus on removing the key so I don't have to look at Mom. I feel like the blood has drained into my feet, and my face must be the color of paste.

"You're later than you said you'd be. I was getting worried."

"Sorry." I suck in oxygen before facing Mom. "I gave someone a ride home."

"A ride? Carlie—" She's on alert, code red. I've broken a major rule.

"It was a friend from the cast, Othello . . . I mean Juan Pacheco, who plays Othello."

"Oh." She takes a deep breath and her exhale is a loud

sigh. "I don't—never mind. I'm glad you're home safe." She locks the deadbolt on the door. "Nicolas Benz called twice. He said he'd call again at about ten." Mom tilts her head and looks at me questioningly. "Date?"

"Maybe." I can't think about a date while every nerve in my body is still short-circuiting. I need to be alone in a quiet place, somewhere I can concentrate on something besides the scary track team guys who're out to get any Edmund they catch alone. Unfortunately, that quiet place is the room next to the loud smoker and Gerald. "I have to get some homework done," I tell my mom.

"Me, too," she says. As I start for my room, Mom reaches out and takes my hand. "I feel better when you're not out alone after dark."

"It's only a few more weeks, Mom. Then the play is over." I don't tell her there's *no* time I feel better anymore.

She takes my hand, then lets go and drops into her usual chair at the kitchen table. Rubbing her temples, she opens a book. "See you in the morning."

Quicken pads down the hall in front of me and goes into my room. Then she jumps onto her cushion and carefully runs her tongue down her side and along her tail. Her ritual has a calming effect as I lean against the closed door. *Wake up your computer, check your email, then do your chemistry assignment. Focus, Carlie. Calm down and stop being so wired.*

I follow my advice and open my inbox. The first message is from Sean. *About time.*

"Had some problems with Mom these past few weeks. When can I see you?"

I type: "How about I come over on Saturday?" Send.

Lena has left three messages: #1: He's calling tonight. #2: Did he call? #3: Well?

The sharp rap on my door jolts me back to reality. So much for calming myself, and when I look at Quicken's cushion, it's empty. She's probably under the bed and who can blame her? We're both on edge.

"Call for you." Mom pushes open the door and hands me the phone, mouthing, Nic-o-las. She blows me a kiss and leaves, closing the door behind her.

"Hi," I say.

A voice says, "This is Nicolas."

I hear the way his mouth forms the O in his name. Sometimes I feel like calling him "Nic" to see how he'd react to the missing two syllables. Then I picture his blue eyes set deep under dark honey eyebrows, his hair like the sun, the way his appearance in any class changes the climate in the room. That's one kind of chemistry I do understand. Any girl in Channing would be willing to pay him to take her out.

"Sorry you're not still at Channing." The rich sound of his voice reminds me of what I don't have anymore.

Nobody's sorrier than I am, Nicolas.

"I made debate captain this year. We'll be going to Washington, D.C., if we win at the state level. Are you on the team at Las Pulgas?"

"Uh, no." *Las Pulgas doesn't debate. They use their fists to settle disputes.* "No time." I don't want to hear about Nicolas Benz and his fabulous year at Channing. *Is he*

164

going to get to the point? "I'm glad you called," I tell him. "What else is new?"

"I talked to Lena, and I was thinking that maybe if you didn't already have a date for the spring dance, we could double with her and Eric."

"Double. That's sweet. I'd like to go."

"Great! I'll call you and get directions to your new—"

"You don't have to do that. I'm, um, going to stay at Lena's, so you and Eric can pick us up there." I hate the chirpy sound in my voice.

"Right. Okay. I'll still call you. I guess I'll need to find out what color dress you're wearing. You know, for the corsage."

"Sure. Thanks, Nicolas. It'll be fun." I click the phone off and drop onto my bed. I've got a date for the spring dance. And not with just anyone—with NicOlas Benz— next to Sean, he's the hottest guy at Channing. I can put up with a bit of ego if I get to go to the dance.

Do I finally have something I can write about in my journal? Maybe. I open my desk drawer, but the space where I usually keep it is empty. That's when I remember putting it on the closet shelf.

Next door in #147, a door opens and closes and heavy footsteps enter the bedroom. The woman yells one of her favorite cuss words. He yells back. From a few doors down, music blasts familiar hip hop.

I cradle my head between my hands. I'll think about my journal some other time.

Keith's familiar footsteps come down the hallway, then I hear the scrape of the deadbolt and our front door opens.

"Shut that damned thing off!" He shouts and his voice echoes around the apartment complex. The music goes quiet.

I see Juan's shrug and I hear him say, "People get upset. They yell. It's no big deal."

Then I hear my voice. "*We* don't do that."

We do now.

"Carlie," Mom calls from the kitchen.

"Yes?"

"Check your room and see if Quicken's there. I thought I saw her run through the living room."

I kneel to look under the bed. The space is empty. She's not behind the desk and the closet door's been closed since I got dressed this morning. I can't believe she's run out again. And it's way too late to go look for her tonight.

29

"You have half an hour of free writing today." Mr. Smith leans against his desk. "This is your midweek treat. No grammar exercises, no tests. Just the opportunity to *express* yourselves on paper. Make it a short story, or nonfiction—about something real. Maybe some of you would like to try poetry." He looks over at Jamal. "I'll be available to help with any questions."

The rustle of notebooks and pencils coming out of backpacks subsides as students settle over blank papers. Across the aisle K.T. writes, erases, then writes some more, while I twirl my pencil, waiting to come up with an idea.

I lean my head on my hand, doodling absent-mindedly. All I manage to get down in words is the familiar date: October 22.

"Carlie love, you have to start sometime."

You've told me that before, Dad.

"Did you listen?"

I sigh and mumble, "No."

Jamal leans towards me from behind and says, "What?"

I shake my head. "Nothing."

K.T. shushes me.

"Grr!" I bend over the paper so my nose is only inches away from it, my pencil pressed at the start of a blank line. *Make it fiction. Change how the father dies. Avoid writing two words: guilt and anger.*

The story falls out of my head onto the paper. I've filled almost two pages without stopping when Mr. Smith says, "That's time."

At the sudden sound of his voice, I press too hard on my pencil and snap off the point.

"I'm hoping some of you will share your writing aloud. The rest of you can do *my* job and be the editors. There are no grades, only comments. Who will begin?"

"I wrote a poem about homework," I hear from behind me, as Jamal clicks open his notebook and shuffles papers as if he's preparing for a congressional filibuster. "Ahem.

'English Homework.

I read my English homework steadily,

Reviewed it with my eyes,

To see that I made no mistake,

In any clause or part—'"

"Wait. Wait. Wait." Mr. Smith tugs the paper from Jamal's hand. He reads and then looks up. "Very nice, Jamal. However, Emily Dickinson is not totally unknown to me. Now if you want to play with her poetry and work it into something humorous, I have no problem with that. That's called parody. You'll simply have to say that's what you're doing." He returns Jamal's paper.

K.T. shoots her hand in the air. Sometimes I think she
wandered into high school by mistake and should really be
in a fifth-grade classroom.

"All right, K.T. What do you have for us?" Mr. Smith
asks.

"Got a short story idea." K.T. clears her throat and her
eyes cut to me before she holds up her paper and reads.
"This is gonna be about a girl named Gloria and she can
draw pictures that's so real, people who see them think they
are real."

I cup both hands over my eyes to keep from staring at
her. When I peek between my fingers, Mr. Smith is giving
K.T. his full attention. I drop my hands and fold them on top
of my desk. *How can he listen to this and not laugh?*

"I'm gonna make her draw a big dog, and that dog is
gonna get up off the page and run away. Then I'm thinking about her drawing a lion, and the police will come to the
house and shoot it. Gloria's mom knows her daughter has
to stop drawing animals because it's too dangerous. That's
what I got so far."

She drops her paper on the desk and crosses her arms
as if to say, "Tell me what's wrong with that."

I'm beginning to wonder how much K.T. plays with
our heads. Hard rapper who can read Desdemona when she
thinks about what she's doing. Kick-ass fighter when she's
wronged. Penitent and saintly girl when she's close to being
expelled. But her story idea definitely puts her in grade
school.

Why is she staring at me? Why is Dolores staring at
me, smiling like she's waiting to see me trip over an invis-

ible wire? Jamal whispers, "Better tell her something. She's got that look on and this time it's aimed at Y. O. U."

Mr. Smith removes his glasses and rubs his eyes. "Comments? Remember there's always something good to find in someone's writing. Then there's always a way to improve it. Who will start?"

I pull out binder paper from my notebook and pretend to take notes. No way am I saying one word about K.T.'s story. I look back at Jamal, who noisily flips pages in the book of poetry I now realize he always carries under his arm. A few rows away, Pavan Gupta is bent over his own paper, erasing. Dolores leans back in her seat, looking at K.T. with a bored expression.

K.T. breaks the silence. "I see you writing lots of stuff on that paper you got. What does it say?" K.T.'s staring at me.

"Some, uh, ideas?"

"Let's hear 'em."

"Umm. Uh. Well, . . . I like the theme of your story." I take a quick look at the doodles on my paper. A dog with a wide grin. A lion on its back, its eyes crossed, and a smoking gun lying next to it. "It's . . . magical."

"And?"

K.T. isn't letting me off, so I might as well tell her what I think of that piece of junk. "Yes, magical. So when you write it you'll need to develop the magic more. Maybe another animal that befriends the artist?" *Making the story longer wasn't going to improve it.* "One more thing—you need to show us the girl more. How she looks, how old she is, why she likes to draw. That would help your story come alive." *Or not.* "The mom isn't really . . . what I mean is we need to know a little more about her, but the girl should make her own decision about drawing."

When I look across at K.T., she's still got me in the crosshairs of her dark eyes. "I always make my own decisions."

So she's Gloria. I got it. "Well, then," I fiddle with my pencil. ". . .you know exactly what Gloria would do."

K.T. uncrosses her arms and writes on her paper.

"Well done, Miss Edmund." Mr. Smith points to Pavan. "Next."

Pavan has written a new version of Cassio's part. In his revised story, Cassio speaks up and ruins old Iago's plot to make Othello jealous.

"How come we can't use that guy in the play?" I flinch at the sound of Chico's voice.

"Then your part would be quite short," Mr. Smith says.

"Sweet," Chico says.

"What about your free writing? Do you care to read it?" Mr. Smith asks him.

Like K.T.'s story, Chico's is short; but unlike hers, it's good. In a single page, he tells about a kid who runs the 10k and pushes himself to win. His reputation is more important to him than anything else. When he loses, he's bitter and takes out his anger on a close friend with unexpected results.

Chico is definitely a low-life who writes. Maybe he'll stab me with a pen when he decides to do me in.

"That's one good story, man," Jamal says.

Pavan Gupta twists in his seat and says, "Hey, Chico.

I like the part about revenge. It makes the guy kind of sad, even if we don't like him."

"Excellent work, class. I'd like to see your writing, make some comments and give you a chance to rewrite for extra credit. Still no grade, and a rewrite is not required. Homework is on the board. Cast, don't be late for rehearsal tonight."

K.T. stops me at the door. "How come we didn't get to chew on something you wrote?" She shows her teeth, but it's not because she's smiling at me.

"I didn't write much."

"There you go again, thinking I'm stupid. I heard all that scratchin' you were doing with that pencil and I seen those pages full of writing."

"It's a rough draft."

She snorts and shakes her head. "Right. And the other ones the class heard were perfectly polished."

I inhale and I'm sure my eyes go round. *Perfectly polished?*

She shifts her head and looks as if she's very satisfied with how she's shocked me.

"So long, great writer." She's off her crutches these days and hobbles on a rubber-heeled walking cast that's already covered with more graffiti than the gym after Keith redecorated it.

30

Keith's court hearing is set for 9 a.m. on Thursday. I shower early so I can have hot water to wash my hair, and so I won't have to hurry because the delinquent wants to look good for the judge. Mom has to drop me at school, then speed back across town to the civic center for the hearing, so it's going to be a rushed morning.

"Carlie, can you bring me some coffee, please?" I can tell from Mom's voice that she's stressing.

I dress, then take coffee to her in her room.

"Oh, thanks, honey." She takes a quick sip. On the bed she's laid out the dark suit she used to wear for fund-raising auctions. "What do you think?" She holds the jacket up. "Subdued was a good look for extracting money from reluctant bidders. Maybe it'll work to extract a light sentence from the judge."

I can tell she'd like me to say the suit will work the miracle she wants, but I guess my expression tells her what I'm really thinking.

She sighs. "Sorry I asked."

I've done it again. Even when I don't say things to

173

upset Mom I upset her anyway, but the suit won't make things easier for Keith. I'm sure he'll get the standard punishment for graffiti, along with his two-week suspension from school. Mom's already talked to the principal and promised to pay for the damages. But like everything else for us these days, the big question is how much?

She puts on her skirt and the long-sleeved blouse with the tailored collar. Turning sideways, she studies her image in the dresser mirror. "Next to the kitchen, the one thing I really miss is my full-length mirror."

Finally something I can agree with. "Totally," I tell her.

"It's going to be okay," she says.

I pray she's right. There's nothing left to crash down on our heads, except maybe the sky.

As if she reads my thoughts, she says, "Your brother's a good kid who's done a stupid, rotten thing—the first bad thing he's ever done. That has to count." She picks up a framed picture from her dresser. In it, Keith's about five, holding Dad's hand. Mom is at Dad's side, and I'm seated in front of them. "An easy-payment plan would help with the damages." She thumps it back down.

I know Mom's expressions well—there's one about grief, one for worrying over money and us—and now this new one that's more like anger. It doesn't come often, but when it does, it flickers across her face as quickly as a summer storm and with the same kind of threat. I've only seen it a few times before today—the day the movers arrived, the first time we entered this apartment, and just after Keith's arrest.

I place my hands together like I'm really praying this time. *Don't let the sky fall.*

∞

After Mr. Smith returns our free writing with his comments, he spends the rest of the period on grammar "issues" that he picked out from our papers. Since grammar is not a favorite of mine, I shield my closed eyes, trying to look as if I'm following the exercises; instead, I'm reading what he's written on my assignment and suggested I do to revise my story.

"This is a very touching story that reveals so much about loss. I think you can heighten the empathy for your main character by showing more details about how she's managing the tragic changes in her life."

The truth is . . . she's not.

I picture Keith in a striped prison uniform with chains at his ankles, Mom in her Las Pulgas Market uniform, me inside my catacomb of a room with a weak, flickering candle stub.

In French, I doodle stars dropping from the sky, their tiny, sharp points jabbing into the head and shoulders of a cowering figure.

By chemistry, I've switched to doodling fangs and claws.

I should have stayed home sick.

Before my next class, I'm at my locker when I spot K.T. hip-hopping toward me on her gaudy walking cast. I work my combination, watching her from the corner of my eye.

"Yo, Des."

I'm weary of this combat, but I force what I hope is a neutral expression onto my face. "Yo, yourself, K.T."

175

K.T. moves her head side-to-side, keeping time to that beat only she hears. "Got somethin' for you to read." She reaches inside her abused notebook and rips out a piece of lined paper from the rings. "You got opinions on everything, so give me some of those super-thoughts on this."

I take the papers and read the first line. "'The Artist.' Your story?"

"No. My Gettysburg Ad-dress."

I stop a long blink in time to avoid a confrontation. "You already wrote it?"

"I'm quick."

"So what do you want me to do?"

"You're, like, the genius writer. Fix it. I'm turnin' this in for extra credit." K.T. holds out her hand, waiting. "Well?"

"Well what?"

"Gimme yours. You know—a trade."

Dawning horror must register on my face.

"What, I'm not good enough to read what you wrote?"

"No. I mean I haven't made the changes Mr. Smith suggested. I'm—

I can almost see the storm clouds gathering over her head. She can slam people to the floor and rip off their clothes even on crutches. What can she do now that she's got both hands free? She cocks her head and I jump back; then I reach into my locker and fish out my English paper. "It's not, I mean, I haven't—"

She plucks it out of my hand and examines it. "So it'll be rough. I'll see what I can do." She swivels on her rubber heel, and over her shoulder says, "I need all the extra credit I can get to bail outta eleventh grade, so make it good."

K.T. stumps down the hall, my paper fluttering like a captive in her hand, my heart pumping like it's working out all by itself. I can't stand that *she's* going to read what I had trouble letting Mr. Smith read. *She's my editor?* I stare at K.T.'s smudged writing. *And I'm hers.* I can just imagine what she's going to come up with: "Do this, Carlie. Do that, Carlie." I take a breath, then mutter to myself, "She's going to love telling me what to do with my story, as if she'll have a clue."

Jamal passes by and twirls his finger next to his head and looks at me like I'm nuts.

Buzz off, Jamal. I pull my French book from the locker and slam the door. I've got a whole scene to learn by Friday, Keith's assignments to collect from his classes, my own homework, and now I have to edit K.T.'s story. *What else?* Oh, right. "I have to make two hundred dollars like that," I say to myself and snap my fingers. Jamal just shakes his head at me.

"Talkin' to yourself is bad, Des. Like, whacked, you know?"

∽⷏

That afternoon, when Mom picks me up at school, she tells me that Keith was sentenced to two weeks of county service in a new juvenile correctional program for boys under sixteen. Now I realize just how much special treatment K.T. gets at school. My brother gets two whole weeks for a little paint, while she gets one weekend of detention and only three days' suspension for attacking a girl and ripping off her clothes.

The good news for Keith is that, while he has to pick up roadside debris, he doesn't have to spend any time in detention.

"He has two Saturdays to report to the Cal Works office for roadside clean-up duty," Mom says. "He's to be there by eight in the morning, work until two, and have his report form signed."

She parks the Tercel and takes the small bag of groceries from the back seat. "The school sent the judge an estimate for seven hundred fifty dollars in damages."

"Seven hundred and fifty dollars?" What I really mean is, "That's more than three red strapless dresses." I trudge through the gate and up the steps behind Mom. No way can I ask for help with my Spring Fling dress now.

"I can pay it off at fifty dollars a month." She sighs. "It means no cell phones yet, but I found a sale on tires, so I'm getting two new ones. That'll make me less nervous when you're out at night."

I follow her inside to the kitchen, plop in a chair at the table and push aside a real estate book to make room for my backpack.

"It could've been a lot worse," Mom says. "The damages aren't so high as I expected." She sets the grocery bag on the counter. "We'll—" The phone rings and she picks up the handset. "Edmunds' residence."

Mom leans against the counter and cups her hand around the receiver. "Oh, hello, Jeb." The pinched look around her eyes and mouth relaxes.

What does he want now? We're fresh out of cats.

I signal to her, then mouth, "Ask if he's seen Quicken."

When Mom clicks the phone off, she hums as she puts canned beans into the cupboard. "Quicken's safe. She's staked out Jeb's barn that's filled with fat, juicy mice."

"So is he bringing her back, or do I have to go get her?"

"He didn't say."

"Just freakin' wonderful."

"Thank you, sweet daughter of mine. You sound just like your brother on a bad day." Mom takes a plastic bag of lettuce from the refrigerator. "Now please wash some lettuce for a salad and stop being such a pain." She holds the lettuce out to me, then goes on. "I was very happy when I came into this room. Do you know why?"

"No, Mom. I'm not a mind reader."

"Because I passed the real estate principles section of the practice test."

I sigh. "That's good. How many more do you have left?"

"Too many, but thanks for at least asking." As she clears the table she says, "Jeb invited us to dinner Friday night."

"What?"

"I'd love a nice dinner for a change, wouldn't you?"

"Sure, if you made it."

"Let's drop it, okay? I'm too tired to argue." Mom takes the plates from the cupboard and sets the table. "All I ask is that you be pleasant at dinner."

"I'm not going."

"You don't have rehearsals on Friday nights, so you'll be coming. End of discussion."

"Then I get my cat back, right?"

"Oh, Carlie." She tries to pull me close but I push her away and she drops her arms at her sides. "Of course we'll bring her back."

31

I expect to walk into a musty farm house when Jeb opens the door for us, but the air smells clean and the walls are creamy under soft lights. In the living room, a fire brightens the warm room. He already has the dining room table set, and the wine and water are poured. Three candles flicker in the center of the table and reflect in the polished wood.

As we follow him into the kitchen, the smell of roasting meat reminds me of our house in Channing. I hate Jeb for having what I used to have—a place that feels safe and that smells like home instead of a secondhand store.

"Hope you're hungry," he says. "Everything's ready." Jeb hands each of us a dish to put on the table, then he picks up a platter of carved roast. "Sit where you like."

Mom pulls out a chair across from me and Keith goes to the opposite end of the table from Jeb.

Jeb serves each of us a slice of roast. "There're potatoes and peas in those covered dishes. Salad anyone?"

I'd like to push my plate away and hate his cooking, but my stomach and mouth have other ideas. I chew the roast and potatoes slowly, watching the candlelight dance, thinking that Dad should be sitting on my right, and thinking that we should be playing the "take turns to talk about our day" game. And I'm thinking that I should've never let K.T. have my paper.

Mom brings up the topic of Quicken. "She's never wandered off like this before. We've had her since she was a kitten."

"Three gophers have met their maker since her arrival. So the long and short of it is, you can't have your cat back." Jeb holds his glass up and drains his wine, as if to seal a bargain. His features are softened by the candle glow, and it's hard to remember how it felt to be afraid of him that first time in the orchard. Tonight he doesn't remind me of a hawk in the least; just an annoying, bossy cowboy.

"But, she's my cat," I say, "not yours."

Mom holds up her hand in a signal to stop. "Maybe we should give Quicken a little time here, honey. She doesn't like the apartment, and if she keeps running away, I'm worried she'll get hit by a car."

"Did you use butter on her paws like I told you?"

Why can't Jeb butt out? "I used margarine," I say.

"Like I said, you should've used butter."

I cut the meat on my plate so the knife scrapes the china. *We can't afford butter for bread, let alone for Quicken's paws.*

"She never did anything but sleep and wait by her food bowl when she was with us," Keith says.

Did my brother just say something at the dinner table?

"Your fault, not the cat's. Those little round cans are

182

the curse of the feline family. Takes all their instincts away and they forget how to be self-sufficient. Just like people. Without a can opener or a frozen food section, most of them would starve."

He's got an opinion on just about everything.

"Jeb, your dinner is fabulous. I . . . we really appreciate having good food like this. I've been so consumed by this move and the real estate classes that I've let all my culinary skills go into retirement."

"Understandable." He pushes away from the table, his hand resting by his plate. "It took me three years after my wife died to take up cooking, and that was mostly because Chinese take-out was beginning to wreck my stomach."

"Well, you've certainly mastered the art." Mom waits, and I know she wants one of her well-brought-up children to add a compliment.

But Jeb doesn't seem to notice the family dynamics. "Paula studied at Le Cordon Bleu, so I'd been very spoiled. There are still some things I can't or won't even try."

"Like?" Mom asks.

"Crepes," he says. "I love apple crepes."

"Mom makes some wicked apple crepes," my brother says. Keith should really stop talking.

"Well, then, I'll have something to look forward to the next time we dine together." Jeb looks at Mom. "Deal?"

"Absolutely."

Jeb gets to his feet. "Keith, you can give me a hand clearing the dishes. Carlie, I'm assigning you pie-cutting duty. Sarah, you get to be waited on for tonight."

Who is this guy, telling us what to do? Keith's already

jumped up and started taking away the plates. *And how can Mom look like that? She's nodding, doing whatever Jeb says.*

Jeb's pie is apple. No surprise in that, but I'm surprised at how it tastes. The fresh apples and his homemade crust explode with flavor in my mouth. When Jeb offers seconds, even I accept. Tomorrow I'll just skip lunch. This guy is scoring points and I'll eat his pie, but no way am I falling for his line like the rest of my family.

At the end of the table, Mom eats Jeb's pie, yumming and smiling with each bite. Mona Lisa has returned to planet Earth, smack in the middle of Jeb Christopher's house.

When we've finished our dessert, I volunteer Keith and myself to do the dishes. Hauling him into the kitchen and keeping my voice low, I tell him, "We need to talk."

"Huh?"

"Are *you* dense?" I jab my finger toward the living room.

"Mom and Jeb?"

"You *are* dense." I toss the dishtowel at him. "Dense people dry."

I slam the dishes into the sink full of soapy water.

"Are you bent on trashing his china?" he asks me.

"Who cares about his china?" I hiss. "What are we going to do? I mean, this is screwed up, isn't it?"

Keith picks up a plate, dries and stacks it in the cupboard. "What are you on about now?"

"We don't know *anything* about him. Neither does *she*. What's she *thinking*?"

"She likes apples?"

"You are so dim."

"It's genetic; something we share." Keith tosses the towel across my shoulder. "You finish. I'm joining the happy people."

"Right, jerk." I snatch the towel off and dry the last of the silverware, leaving the sink filled with dessert dishes in sudsy water and the cupboard doors open. Jeb can do the rest himself.

In the living room, Mom and Jeb sit on the sofa in front of the fireplace, and Quicken lies curled up next to Jeb. Keith's in one of the leather chairs on either side of the sofa, his long legs stretched out toward the fire. I lift Quicken and take the chair opposite Keith, putting the cat in my lap. She rubs against my arm and butts her head against me, like she always does when she needs petting. I stroke her fur and expect she'll make a circle on my lap and purr. But no, she jumps down and returns to her spot next to Jeb.

I know hearts can't break, but I think they shrivel from too much pain. Right now, mine's down to the size of a raisin. It's all I can do to sit across from that man, Mom on his one side and Quicken on the other. I shove my back against the warm leather of the chair and wish Jeb would go up in a poof of smoke.

"Carlie, Jeb has offered to give Keith a job helping around the orchard while he's suspended." Mom smiles at me as if she's modeling the expression she'd like to see on my face.

"And when he returns to school, I could use some help on the weekends," Jeb says. "There's even a job in summer."

185

"What do you say?" Mom asks Keith.

I'm screaming inside my head. *I think the idea sucks!* I don't want more of Jeb Christopher in my life, and if Keith works for him, that's exactly what I'll get. I stare at Keith the same way that used to send him scurrying behind Mom when he was a toddler. *Say no, Keith!*

Keith shrugs and says, "Sure."

Aaarg! I need to work on a new stare.

⌒∞

Jeb insists on following us in his truck as we drive back to the apartment, and he waits by the pool until Mom waves from the stairs before he drives off. He knows this place isn't safe; no wonder he keeps his gun with him when he's in the orchard.

I ignore Mom and Keith's conversation about the job and keep my eyes on the dark windows to Anthony Mancuso's apartment, wondering if he's safely asleep or out there somewhere in the shadows, watching.

"Carlie," Mom calls, "come inside and close the door. I can't afford to heat the entire city of Las Pulgas."

Mom and Keith are in the hall.

"Consider this a mini-family meeting." Mom beckons, then reaches her arm around me. "I wasn't too happy with some of the attitude at Jeb's tonight. He's been generous with his offer to Keith, and I expect you both to be polite in his company. Am I clear?"

"Keith sprays graffiti in the gym and gets a job. How

fair is that? I do nothing and have one month to scrape up two hundred dollars."

Mom takes me by both shoulders and spins me around so we're face to face. "Why do you need two hundred dollars?"

This is a family meeting—the first one in a long time—Mom is almost through with the real estate class, and whether I like it or not, Jeb's making Mom's life more . . . interesting. My dress problem shouldn't sink the boat. "I want a dress for the Spring Fling."

"That is so lame—" my brother says.

"Stop right there, Keith. There's nothing lame about Carlie wanting a new dress for a special night," Mom says. "Why didn't you say something?"

I shrug. "What good would it do?"

"At least I'd know what's making you such a grouch." Mom shakes her head. "I picked up another shift at the market, so by the end of this month I'll have a little extra to help you get your dress. You have no idea how good it feels, being able to say that. Now come here. I need a group hug."

I let Mom draw me close and Keith stays in the circle a second before pulling away and slouching off to his room.

Mom holds me close a moment longer. "Dump the grumpy-girl attitude, okay? It doesn't suit you." She waits, but when I don't say anything, she sighs and lets go. "I'm turning in early for a change. Goodnight."

When I go into the kitchen for a glass of water, I check the phone for messages and it's Sean's voice that I hear.

"Hey. Give me a call at my aunt's. Dad and I are here for dinner."

I play the message again to hear his voice and give my heart time to rein itself in. Still, my hand shakes as I dial the familiar babysitting number. I didn't know how much I missed him until right now.

Mrs. Franklin answers. "I'm so glad you called. I desperately need a sitter for next Sunday afternoon. Any chance you're available?"

You'll never guess how available I am, Aunt Corky. "Sure."

"Excellent. I'll let you know the time when our plans firm up with the other couples. Here's Sean."

"So how's my favorite ex-Channing girl? Are you still coming over tomorrow? Or I can head your way—"

"No, I'm coming, but I, uh, can't until after five-thirty. Is that okay?"

"Absolutely. I'll be at Aunt Corky's. Dad's going out of town on business. Oh, and I'll wait dinner until you come."

The words are ordinary, but how he says them makes me feel very special, even on the phone. And he's . . . fun. Why is that the first word that comes to mind whenever I think about him? But he *is* fun. Kind of like when Lena and I used to hang out.

Lena must pick up my vibes because I'm on my way out of the kitchen when she calls. It's so good to talk about things that have nothing to do with my troubles in Las Pulgas. There are no burning issues with Lena. Actually, there're no issues at all. All we talk about is Channing's Spring Fling, where Eric and Nicolas are taking us to dinner, her dress again, and when am I coming to see it?

I can't put this off any longer. "The only time I have is Saturday morning. I've got lots to do later, and Sunday I'm babysitting." Seeing Lena that day means I have to make two trips to Channing, with play rehearsal in between. But that's just the way it'll have to be.

"At last!" she screeches. "This is so going to be fun, like old times." I imagine her jumping up and down, just like she did in third grade.

"I'm excited, too."

"So what are you wearing for the dance? Have you bought it yet?"

"No. I'm still busy unpacking and stuff. Maybe next week."

"Are you going with your mom?" The way she says it, I know she wants me to ask her to come along, but I can't. I might be shopping at the Happy Hollow Discount Shoppe.

I sprawl across my bed. "I'm not sure when I can go." Again I've dodged asking her, but I haven't really lied. "I'll call you, okay? Oh, I almost forgot. Can you ask your mom if I can sleep over the night of the dance?"

She does a loud squeal and we end our conversation with Lena really happy. Me, too.

After I hang up I go to my desk and check my savings account online. Fifty-five dollars and ten cents. In just five weeks, I have to come up with at least two hundred dollars or it's definitely the discount shop.

Talking to Sean, and then Lena, reminds me that I'm running out of excuses to keep Channing away from Las Pulgas. I pick up Quicken's empty cushion and crush it to my chest, missing how she purred comfort into my room.

"I hate you, Jeb Christopher!"

189

32

Saturday morning, I drop Mom at work, then drive Keith to the Cal Works office. The car's mine for the day.

"What time do I have to pick you up?" I say to my brother, trying not to sound put out. But today my schedule is tight, and picking up Keith makes my time crunch worse.

"They said after two." He makes a sour face.

"Be thankful it's only a couple of Saturdays, bro."

"'Bro.' Very funny." He slams the door and joins a group of people standing around a man who's handing out high-visibility yellow vests.

I don't envy him a day picking up garbage along roadsides, just like I don't relish having to spend the day of *oohing* and *ahhhing* over Lena's new dress. At least now I have a hope of buying something decent since I'll earn some babysitting cash on Sunday. For the first time, I pray that the Franklins will stay out late for once. Mom might be able to help me with some of the dress money, and if I'm lucky, there'll be a sale somewhere on an awesome red strapless dress.

I park a few blocks away and walk toward Lena's. No

sooner do I step onto her porch than she's out the door to meet me. "You're here! Finally!" She looks past me. "Where's your car?"

"It's—"

She drags me inside, as if I might change my mind and leave. "Do you have any idea how long it's been since you've come over?" I don't get a chance to answer this question, either. "Since Christmas! Over four months," she tells me.

In Lena's room, I sit on the small blue-and-white checkered couch nested in the bay window. Sheer curtains hang over them and the midmorning light filters through, creating a soft, hazy glow. A crisp duvet and matching shams give off a scent of laundry softener. The room hasn't changed, but it feels twice the size that I remember.

How can I go back to my black-sheeted window?

"Here it is!" Lena twirls out of the closet pressing a shimmery blue dress against her body. "Is this the most beautiful dress you have ever laid eyes on, or what?"

Two waves surge inside me. The first is relief. The second is regret for feeling that way. The dress is not beautiful. It isn't even close, but I try to look as if I love it. Lena peels off her sweater and slips the dress over her head. She lets it slide down over her hips and twirls with arms outstretched.

Say something, Carlie. "You're right. I've never seen a dress quite like that. It's—"

"Mom and I found it in L.A. It's a designer original— one of a kind."

Thank heavens. One's plenty. "Are those tassels at the hem?" I ask, trying to hide my disbelief.

"Different, right?" Lena holds up the skirt in front of my nose, as if I couldn't spot a tassel from a foot away.

"Very."

"And it's my favorite color."

I've often wondered if pale blue is really Lena's favorite color, or if her mom's told her it is so often that Lena actually believes it now. Blonde, blue-eyed, Mrs. Knudson looks great in blue. On Lena, it's only so-so.

After Lena changes back into her regular clothes, we go to the kitchen and she pours two glasses of orange juice, then dumps taco chips into a bowl. The Knudsons' housekeeper sweeps around our high stools at the marble island.

"Eric says he's buying me the biggest orchid at the florist's. Isn't that cool?"

"Sweet." I sip my orange juice.

"So, tell me about your dress. You didn't buy it yet, right? Do you know what you're looking for?"

The door leading from the garage opens and Mrs. Knudson comes into the kitchen with bags dangling from both arms. "Lupe! Come take these bags."

The housekeeper puts her broom in the utility closet and hurries to help Mrs. Knudson.

"Carlie!" Mrs. Knudson wraps her arms around me. "It's been too long. How's your mother?"

"Good."

"And you're going to the dance with Nicolas. How wonderful!"

"Carlie doesn't have her dress yet, Mom. We're talking about what she's going to buy."

Mrs. Knudson pours herself a tall orange juice and sits on the stool across from us. "Lovely. I'm just in time."

"I was thinking strapless, maybe red."

"You can't do red." Mrs. Knudson's voice is suddenly sharp.

I sip more juice and swish it around in my mouth, tapping the glass with one finger.

"Mom's, right. We'll clash."

"Red goes with blue," I say.

"Oh no, dear. Besides, you need a pastel. It's a spring dance. And definitely not strapless." Mrs. Knudson shakes her head.

"I don't look good in spring colors. I'm a winter."

"How about brown? That's a winter color," Lena says, as if she's solved the problem.

"Since when did brown become a pastel?"

"I'm just making suggestions," Lena says.

Mrs. Knudson pats my hand. "Believe me, red isn't right for this dance. We should go shopping together, like we used to. It'll be fun."

I crunch down on a taco chip and fill my mouth with more juice.

"What about tomorrow? I'm doing lunch with some friends. You girls can shop and meet me when we're finished."

"We can hang at the mall all day." Lena brushes her crumbs onto the floor.

Suddenly the Knudsons' spacious house is closing in. I drain my glass and set it on the counter. "Listen, I have to go."

"You just got here." Lena's expression turns pouty.

"Sorry, but I've got to, um, pick up Keith. He needs a, a ride. Thanks for the offer, Mrs. Knudson." I stammer my way out of the kitchen and into the wide entry hall.

"Are you coming tomorrow?" Lena stands at the open door, looking confused.

"I'll call you later." I start to take my keys from my pocket, then tuck them back inside. "I have to ask my mom. Um, she might need me to do something."

"Where's your car? How are you getting home?"

"I'm meeting Keith at Mitch's. The car's there."

As I walk away, Lena calls from her doorway. "Remember, just no red."

Nodding like a Bobble-head doll, I start down the sidewalk.

That didn't go well. Something's different between us, and I'm ashamed to admit it's called jealousy—not only on my part, but on Lena's, too. Has it always been like this and I never saw it?

By the time I reach the Tercel, I'm starved. A Sam's Shack special half-priced burger is exactly what I crave, even if Juan's there. This was my hangout long before he showed up.

When I enter the Shack and walk up to the counter, he smiles at me and for a moment I forget what I planned to order. "A . . . Super Lean Special."

"Something to drink?"

"Just water."

"I'm off in a few minutes. How about eating lunch with me?"

I can say no way, or I can say yes and act as if eating lunch with Juan Pacheco is as humdrum as conjugating French verbs. "Sure. I, uh, guess."

"Great. Take a booth."

As I scoot across the vinyl-padded seat, I wonder if this is a mistake. What if someone sees us? He's just a kid from Las Pulgas who happens to be in my English class and who happens to be in a play with me and—

Juan comes from behind the counter with two burgers, one water, and a large Coke. Tossing his white cap and apron onto the seat, he sits down across from me. "So, Princess, what brings you to the old Shack?"

I give him my best-annoyed look. "My name is Carlie."

"What brings you to the old Shack, Car . . . lie. How come you're in Channing?" He bites into his burger.

"I still have friends here, you know. And I used to come to Sam's all the time. I don't have to change my entire life around just because you work here."

"Want to go over a few lines? We've got a hot date this afternoon."

"What?"

"Our big scene, Des."

"No. I do not want to rehearse." Before I know it, I'm twisting my bracelet. Sweet Sixteen is spinning around my wrist. I tell him, "I want to forget all about that play for a while. I'm sick of going to practice and studying that part. K.T. needs to get that cast off and be Desdemona again."

"So what's got your 'spleen' hot?"

My face must go blank.

195

"Haven't you been listening to Mr. Smith's Elizabethan lectures?"

"You're taking Shakespeare way too seriously. Nothing's got my *spleen* hot. I'm just fed up with all of it."

"Hmmm. Got it. Something bad went down between you and your friend, so you came here to take it out on the Mexican kid." He holds his hands up in surrender. "Go ahead. Shoot me."

Now I laugh. In spite of how I feel about Lena and her stupid dress and her stupid mom and her stupid beautiful, light, spacious, airy bedroom that doesn't smell like secondhand smoke, or have a battling couple on the other side of her bulletin board. "You're absolutely right, but I forgot my gun, Pancho."

"Name's Juan." He reaches for my hand and I don't move it away. "'Have you pray'd tonight, Desdemona?'"

"'Ay, my lord.'" The words are out of my mouth before I can stop them.

The ride back to Cal Works to pick up Keith is a blur. I only remember Othello and two half-eaten Sam's hamburgers, one that the Moor of Venice didn't finish and one that Des didn't finish either. I remember that I didn't pay for lunch—Othello did. I realize I've spent over an hour with a Mexican playing a Moor. That my spleen isn't hot anymore. That it floats inside me on clouds. And that I'm more confused than ever before about my life.

33

A little after two, I park in front of Cal Works behind other waiting cars. As a county bus pulls to a stop by the main office, people emerge from the cars and head toward the bus. Like me, they're here to pick up an underage criminal, and I join the moms and big brothers on the sidewalk.

The door to the bus wheezes open and a man steps down. He stands next to the bus with a clipboard. "Come along, ladies. Give me your name and form a line."

A procession of yellow-vested teenage boys files out from the bus and the man makes a tick mark as each one says his name. Keith steps off last and lines up with the others.

As soon as I catch his eye, he turns on that disconnected look he's perfected over the years.

Now the man faces the lineup. "Listen up, ladies."

The tallest boy in the lineup yells, "Rodney, you are one sweet comedian, man."

Rodney jabs a finger at him. "Stay in line, Grits, and keep quiet for a change."

"Grits." I repeat the name. Where have I heard that weird name before?

Rodney opens a door on the side of the bus, saying, "Put your vests in this storage bin. Be sure they're stowed correctly, snaps secured, vests flat and facing one direction, front sides up."

The boys remove their vests, fasten the snaps, and one by one follow Rodney's orders. "I look forward to seeing many of you next Saturday." He climbs back on the bus, swooshes the automatic door closed, and drives away.

As Grits walks over to Keith, I hold out my arm and tap my watch, but Keith ignores my "Let's go" signal.

"So, old Grits got you through the day, right?"

"I guess," Keith answers.

"I know you been aching to ask all day, so go ahead."

"What?"

"Why *Grits*? Let me tell you about it." Grits points to his throat. "They call it chronic laryngitis. It's 'cause I talk too much and I get real excited about stuff. Shouting's what I'm all about—at least I was. So how come you're here? Me, I got a few too many tickets and the cops got pissed."

"Stifle it, Grits. Give us a break for a change," one of the boys says and shoves past.

Grits ignores him. "So, why *are* you here, anyways?" he asks Keith.

"Graffiti."

"Artsy or fartsy?"

I'm surprised when Keith laughs and says, "Fartsy, I guess."

I haven't heard Keith laugh in like, how long? Almost a year.

"They gave you two weeks, right?"

Keith nods.

Grits cracks his knuckles. "You must be the guy that *redecorated* the gym."

Uh, oh. I don't like where this is heading.

"Yeah." Keith looks down.

Damn it, Keith. I step closer and reach for his arm, but he turns his back to me.

"Who's this?" Grits juts his chin in my direction. I'm holding my breath, wishing Rodney would come back so we could get away with all limbs unbroken.

"My sister. She's giving me a ride."

"Hey, Sis. Grits here." He salutes, then turns his attention back to Keith again. "So what's your beef with my team?" He squints at Keith.

Now I remember. Grits is the name I overheard that day in the gym when Chico and his friends vowed to get Keith. Grits is on the track team.

"No beef, at all, really," Keith says, staring into the dark eyes sizing him up. "I just got mad and made a mistake."

The boy punches Keith on the shoulder, but it's playful. "Mistake is my middle name, dude. I knew you and me'd hit it off, even with your fartsy paint job. I seen you run at Channing. You're good."

"Do you run?" Keith asks.

"You betcha. Best freshman 10k time ever at Las Pulgas." Grits points at his feet. "See how far those things are from my hips? That's the reason. I can outrun cops—and used to, before I seen the light. I can also leave most of the long-distance boys in the dust."

199

Grits's gravelly voice becomes white noise. From the look on Keith's face, he's deep into his own thoughts. Probably about running.

Keith shakes his hair back from his forehead and looks up at Grits.

"So what's your best time?"

"In 10k, 31.35. That was last year. Coach says I'll do better now that I got more stamina. We'll take the inter-district championships this year for sure. Channing's going to pick our dirt outta their teeth."

∽

It's after two-thirty when Keith and I get to the apartment. The first dress rehearsal starts at three. If I shower and change, I'll be late.

Too bad. I'll just have to be late.

I move fast and get into the shower. When I pull a strand of hair under my nose, it smells like hamburgers and fries.

I'll just be later.

A quick shampoo, rinse and towel dry, then into clean clothes.

I plug in the hair dryer and set it at hot, but then turn it off again when I see the tube of White Orchid Glaze in the drawer. I've been doling out my favorite scented hair product for weeks, trying to make it last for special occasions.

Special times coming up: The dance. My mall date.

Do I care about my hair smelling like White Orchid for Nicolas? "Not really." *Sean? Absolutely, but we'll be playing at the toy store.*

I drop the tube back into the drawer and turn on the dryer again.

Click. Off.

I don't care that Juan Pacheco will be all over me today while he smothers Desdemona. "I don't."

But I snatch up the glaze anyway. Flattening the tube to extract the last dab, I rub the fragrant cream into my damp hair and comb it through. "At twenty-five dollars a pop, I won't be scoring anymore of you for a while," I say as I drop the empty container into the wastebasket. "*Au revoir.*"

As I finish, my watch clicks around to two fifty-five. I grab the keys and run out of my bedroom and right into Keith.

"You got a fire in there?" he shouts, falling against the wall.

"Rehearsal—late!" I'm out the front door, then poke my head back inside. "Mom's got a ride home from work, but she won't get here 'til after six, so you have to make dinner, okay?"

I don't wait for his answer.

34

On my way across town, most of the traffic lights cooperate and I push the last two yellows. Now's not the time to get a ticket, but I don't want the rehearsal to last beyond five-thirty because of me. Seeing Sean tonight is important. I miss him. And now that I'm thinking about it, I realize I miss him a lot more than I miss Lena.

I park close to the auditorium and race to the building. Inside the auditorium, I push the door closed and lean against it. I'm tired and I'm stressed. *Please let me get through this play. Please let me get through this year.*

"Our star has arrived." Mr. Smith's voice booms across the auditorium.

"Sorry I'm late." I hurry down the aisle and onto the stage.

"We're just getting underway. Now, my dear Desdemona, put on this long skirt so you can practice moving around in it, and let us continue."

I love how he talks to me. With only these few words, my heart beat slows to its normal pace and my thoughts dim about everything that's bad in Las Pulgas.

Up on the stage, Jamal and K.T. are stacking a third mattress on top of two others in the center of the set.

"Almost ready?" Mr. Smith asks, then sits in his chair downstage.

"Here," K.T. tosses a roll of furry material to Jamal. "This goes on the bed, loose and sexy, okay?"

Jamal smoothes the material over the mattress.

K.T. puts her hands on her hips and scolds him. "Hey! This is no army bed! I said, 'loose and sexy.'"

"Then *you* do it. I got no idea what you mean by 'loose and sexy.'" Jamal jumps off the mattresses as K.T. hobbles over.

She huffs and shakes her head, then climbs onto the bed and musses the material.

Jamal throws up his hands and goes to sulk in the wings.

"There. Now we got us a good place for a romantic murder." K.T. slides down the mattress pile and examines her handiwork. Over her shoulder, she yells at Jamal. "So what about hanging that red corduroy stuff on those flats you built? I'm not the only one on the set crew, you know."

"Who made you the boss, K.T.?"

"Jamal, you sound just like you did in fifth grade. Get your sorry self over here and do your job."

I laugh, but behind my hand. I don't need K.T. coming down on me today. Besides, I'm impressed by the way she pictures the bedchamber—another interesting surprise from old K.T. I'd like to see inside that head of hers. I'm beginning to think it's more complicated than I expected. I just wish she didn't have my English paper; I'd feel better if she lost it before she has a chance to read it.

Jamal picks up a roll of corduroy and a staple gun. He climbs a stepladder and staples one end of the fabric to the top of a flat, then he looks at K.T. "Suppose you want this 'loose and sexy' too?"

"You got it."

When Jamal folds the footstool and takes it off stage, Mr. Smith tells him, "Bring up the lights, Jamal." A white circle of light shines on the fake fur. "Now take them down a touch. A bit more. There. That's perfect." He clasps his hand to his chest. "We have ourselves a Rococo bed chamber."

At center stage, the mounds and creases of K.T.'s fake fur catch the light, disguising the stacked mattresses. The flats that form the corduroy walls create a dark crimson bedchamber, intimate and somehow ominous, now that it's the color of blood. Her room looks exactly as it should if Desdemona slept there and Othello came to her, jealous and ready to take her life.

"Wow!" Escapes my lips. I'm not the only one who reacts to K.T.'s set, but I'm the loudest.

K.T. stands next to Jamal at the control panel, shifting her head in time to that mystery tune. "All it takes is talent," she says and bows to everyone on stage, her magenta-tipped hair catching the lights.

"Places," Mr. Smith calls.

With the long skirt, I'm clumsy climbing onto the fake fur. Once I'm on the bed, I lie down and close my eyes. I know all the lines, all my cues and how to look afraid. I've practiced in front of the mirror until I've convinced myself I'm about to be killed. To get that look exactly right, I've thought first about K.T., and then Chico or Anthony. Over the weeks, I've become very convincing—more so every day that I have to deal with that bunch.

"'Yet I'll not shed her blood.'" Juan's voice becomes deeper when he gets into his part. As he approaches, I listen to the way he forms words like "monumental" and "alabaster," words that enter the room like broad-shouldered men. Shakespeare wrote them, but Juan Pacheco gives them life.

I feel his lips brush mine.

"'She wakes.'"

That's my cue. What am I supposed say? I knew it when I climbed onto the mattresses, but somehow I don't know now. Opening my eyes, I stare into Juan's face, and the only parts of me that I can feel are my lips.

"'Who's there?'" He feeds me the line. "You know, kind of like the second part of a knock-knock joke."

I'd like to strangle him but I can't. Instead, he does me in and the big scene ends as it always does, with poor Desdemona begging for her life. One day I'm going to rewrite that scene. It's time to turn tables on that big jealous bully.

35

As I ring the Franklins' doorbell, my stomach ripples like it does when I drive too fast over highway dips. Sean's at the door before the chime fades.

"Yahoo!" He shouts and scoops me into his arms and twirls me around. "You're just the girl I want to see." He presses his cheek against mine and leads me into the kitchen, his arm around my waist.

Feeling him close, my stomach settles and I'm thrilled to be here.

"Aunt Corky left us some of her healthy snacks, but I wrangled a couple of cheeseburgers from Sam's Shack, just in case yogurt and carrot sticks aren't enough."

"She's not here?"

"No, but you have a job all Sunday afternoon. Here's her note."

"Carlie, please be here by 2. We'll be out until at least 8." At the bottom she'd written: "No more of those candy sprinkles for the children, okay? I have my rules."

Mrs. Franklin is all about rules. No snacks at bedtime

for the kids; only free-range chicken. Nothing except organic, triple-washed, quadruple-checked anything in her fridge. How did anyone think to name her *Corky*? That name has such sparkle and fizz.

Sean takes the wrappers off the cheeseburgers and puts each one on a plate. I'll have to do without food all day tomorrow if I eat this, but he's set the kitchen table with place mats, flatware, and water with lemon slices. I can't exactly say, "No thanks."

"Milady." He pulls out my chair and snaps my napkin across my lap.

I can never quite figure this guy out. It's like he majored in nineteenth-century etiquette.

"So, why the great need for cash?" he asks, sitting across from me.

"College, mostly."

"Okaaaay. Now tell me what you're *really* saving for." He bites into the cheeseburger.

I'm such a bad liar. As I look across at Sean, I remember Dad—how he held my face between his hands and said, "Carlie love, you are the worst liar in the world. Your face is a map to your heart, so give it up, Sweetheart, and just tell me the truth." So I did and he forgave me, and now I can't even remember what it was about; only the lesson stayed with me.

"Okay, I lied, a little. I am saving for college, but right now I need a new dress."

"A-ha! The Spring Fling."

"How do you know?"

207

"Sam's Shack. Lots of gossip flying around that place—like, you're double dating with Lena and Eric Peterson."

I peel off the top of the bun and bite into the open-faced cheeseburger. I want my mouth full because I'm close to saying, *Why didn't you ask me first?*

"Let's go shopping. The stores are open until ten."

"You are the most confusing boy I've ever met." Being with Sean is kind of like being with Lena, but without everything centered on him, and without the kind of moody seismic tremors that cut trenches between us. With Sean, everything is about having fun together. Still, I wish he'd be a tiny bit jealous about my date with Nicolas. "I'd love to go shopping with you," I tell him and stack my plate in the dishwasher—an old habit from so many babysitting stints here.

I put my arms around his neck. "You're my favorite burglar, Sean."

"And you're my favorite girl." He kisses my forehead and briefly presses his cheek to mine. I close my eyes and lift my face, waiting for his lips, but he steps away. "We'd better go," he says.

I try to cover my embarrassment by grabbing my glass and chugging water while Sean clears the rest of the table.

⸰⸱

Once we're at the mall, Sean takes my arm as if I'm his steady girlfriend and I let him because it's nice to pretend that I am.

"Where to shop for the perfect dress is the question." He stops in front of the store guide display and runs his finger down the list of Women's Apparel.

"There's a Dress Mart at the end of the mall, but I don't think they do formals," I say.

Sean wrinkles his nose, as if the words Dress Mart smell bad. "This is the Spring Fling, Carlie, not a Sadie Hawkins dance. Come on. I have a friend whose mother just happens to work in the best couturier department in Channing."

"Think budget," I say, but Sean's already taking off down the center of the mall, dodging the oncoming pedestrians. I run to catch him, saying, "Seriously, Sean. I'm broke. Really."

"Budgets are out the window when it's a special occasion like this one." Sean turns sharply and strides through the elegant entrance of Très Elégant, the most exclusive shop in town.

The jazzy mall music fades inside the store, where a live piano concerto floats across the displays. I grab his arm. "I cannot afford this store. I can't even afford to breathe the air in here." I'm tugging on him now because something has to make an impression. My words sure aren't. "Let's go," I beg.

"Not to worry," Sean says as he steps onto the escalator. "Come along. We're going to the second floor—Designer Evening Wear."

"Oh, man," I say, watching him ascend. He might as well be heading to the moon for all the good going up there will do him. I *so* can't afford this place!

"Well?" he says, looking down at me from the escalator, then disappears.

This is nuts. I can't afford something from the recycling bin outside and he's talking about designer formals. My favorite French swear word is on my lips, but I keep quiet. I hop on the escalator and I'm on my way to the moon.

When I catch up to Sean, he's already talking to a woman seated behind a desk.

"This is she?" The woman speaks as if she towers over both of us.

Sean nods. "Carlie, meet Miss Lily."

I attempt a pale smile. It's the best I can do to look happy about what Sean's up to.

"*Enchanté*," Miss Lily says as she extends her hand.

What am I doing here? How much is this going to cost? Well, it doesn't matter, because if it costs more than fifty-five dollars, I can't buy it. The sample spray at the cosmetic counter costs more than that in this store. What part of broke *doesn't Sean understand?*

"So we're looking for something sleek and elegant, but youthful," Miss Lily says, looking up from under dark eyelashes. "Turn, *s'il vous plaît*." She twirls her hand at me.

I do a slow one-eighty.

"*Huit.*"

The way Miss Lily says the size, it's like it's engraved on a stone tablet. Miss Lily has declared me a size *huit*, so eight it is. No diet is ever getting me into a six before the dance.

"Come," Miss Lily says, then parts the dressing room double doors and ushers us in.

I've never seen a dressing room like this one. It's bigger than my Channing bedroom. The floors are dark polished wood. A rich, ivory-colored leather couch is against one wall. A tall palm sits behind the seat at one end, and an oval coffee table holds a single orchid—white, with a tiny crimson center. The walls are glass panels, and at the back is a thick, leopard-patterned curtain.

"What did you have in mind?" Miss Lily asks.

"Red. Strapless?"

She frowns.

"Red?"

Again she frowns.

"Strapless?"

"No. But slender straps, of course,."

"Of course." I shoot a look at Sean, but he's studying the orchid blossom.

"And because this is a spring event, a pink. Not pale, but hot—with pizazz," she says.

"Pizazz," I repeat.

Miss Lily separates the leopard curtain and leaves us seated on the couch.

"What are you thinking?" I hiss.

Sean pats my hand like I'm a pet poodle. "Trust me."

When the curtain parts again, a girl only a few years older than I am glides into the room. She wears a deep pink dress that shimmers under the lights. It curves around her breasts, nips in at the waist and drapes effortlessly over her hips. It's gorgeous and I can't breathe.

Sean tilts his head from one side to the other, considering.

As the first model struts back through the curtain, a second enters. This time the hot pink dress flows against the model's thighs, like water washing against her skin. Small rosettes form narrow straps, and each rose glitters with a tiny crystal at its center.

"Now *that's* pizazz," Sean says. "What do you think?"

"I can't!"

"Good."

Miss Lily returns.

"We'll take that one," Sean says.

I collapse against the back of the couch.

36

Huit fits almost perfectly. With a small adjustment to the straps, the gown looks as if it's been tailor made for me.

"Return on Monday, Carlie. It'll be ready then." Miss Lily embraces Sean. "I'm so pleased you're to live here after graduation. Michael speaks of your plans to share a dorm room at Elmhurst. He's very excited."

When is Miss Lily going to ask me to pay? She hasn't even mentioned money. There was no price tag, and I don't have the nerve to ask. Well, it doesn't matter, does it? I can't afford it, no matter what. Wait until I get Sean Wright alone. I'm going to wring his fabulous neck.

Once we are in the main mall again, I get in his face with both hands braced against his shoulders. "And just how do you think I'm going to pay for that dress? I told you—"

"You get so worked up over everything, Carlie. I made a deal. It's good for Miss Lily, and even better for you."

"What deal, and when did you make it?"

"When you were getting dressed, that's when. And anyway, the deal is that you tell all your friends where you

213

bought that drop-dead gorgeous pizzazzy dress, and she lends it to you for the night."

"She can do that?"

"She sure can. Some of her clients wear a dress once and return it. The store policy is 'Never Question the Customer.'" He turns and leads me down the crowded walkway. "All you have to do is look stunningly beautiful, which you will, and return the dress in good condition, which you will. Okay? Now come on."

By the time we walk out of the mall, it's nine-thirty. Sean says, "Thanks for the great time, Carlie."

The feel of his hand at my back is wonderful and suddenly I can't say a word. I haven't got a single clear thought to express.

At my car, he says, "High school's been a major drag. I'm ready to join the real world." He opens my car door. "You're a great friend, you know that?"

"Me? You're the one giving all the special help to the down-and-outer. All I do is just hang with you."

"That's what I mean—you hang with me. That's very—I appreciate it."

My skin simmers under the spot where his fingers brush against my arm. I wish he'd say something, like, "I hate that you're going to that dance with another guy." Maybe I have to say, "Take me to the dance."

"I want pictures, okay? I have to see you in that dress, your hair very—" He scoops my hair between his hands and piles it on top of my head. "Yes, up like this, and with pink orchids in it—make them small. You'll wow 'em, and

Lily will love you for it." He kisses me as he always does: lightly on the cheek.

I can't get anymore confused about the guys in my life than I am right now. Sean excites me, but treats me like a pal. Juan infuriates me, but his face keeps appearing like some dark, haunting vision that supercharges my heart. Nicolas is awesome, but he's totally into himself.

When I pull into the Franklins' driveway, I get out of the car and walk around to stand next to him. "Sean . . ." *Now what, Carlie? Are you going to say, I want you to take me to the dance, not Nicolas? Are you going to beg and say, "Please really kiss me?"* I gaze down the street without saying anything.

"This sounds serious," Sean says.

In my head, I hear Dad's voice: *"Carlie love, you can't expect people to read your mind. When you don't understand what someone means, ask them to explain it, and then really listen to what they say."*

I look Sean in the eye. "Is something wrong with me?"

He tips his head on an angle and seems puzzled. "Wrong?"

"You . . . treat me like a, a sister. I don't want to be your sister. I want—"

For a moment, he seems unsure, as if he hasn't heard me. Then he pulls me to him and wraps his arms around me. I'm melting and our hearts are beating against each other's chests.

He's telling me there's nothing wrong with me and I'm listening, Dad.

"You aren't like a sister to me. You're a special girl in my life."

I can't breathe. I'm waiting for the shooting star to cross the heavens and hear his next words: *I love you.*

"If I could love a girl, Carlie, I'd love you." He steps back, puts one hand on my shoulder, and lifts my chin with the other. "But I'm in love with Michael, Miss Lily's son. I thought you knew . . ." He looks away as if he's thinking of what he can say next.

My shooting star fizzles as the light comes on inside my brain. All this time, I thought I had to keep him away from Las Pulgas or he wouldn't love me. He wouldn't love me if I lived in a mansion. He wouldn't love me—ever. "Oh. Uh—I didn't understand."

"And now that you do?" His face reflects the anxiety in his voice.

I open my mouth, but nothing comes out. Suddenly I have no words.

"Carlie?"

"I—need to get home. Uh, I'll call you. And you call me. Uh—I'm sorry." I start to get into the car. "Sean, thank you for . . . tonight. I—"

But he just waves over his shoulder without turning around to look at me, then walks silently into the Franklins' house.

37

I wonder if you can be arrested for driving while sobbing? During the trip from Channing to Las Pulgas, I follow the familiar route, but trusting more to memory than eyesight. I should have told him it didn't matter he was gay, but it isn't true. "It friggin' matters a lot!" I say out loud.

At the stop sign, I pound the steering wheel with both hands and my horn blasts. A motorist passing me jams on the brakes and the car behind him screeches to a stop. I speed away—I have to get home before I cause an accident.

When I reach the carport, I sit for a while and press my fingers against my swollen eyelids. I don't want to go into the apartment all red-eyed and with a runny nose. Then Mom will freak and Keith will have some clever comment that'll make killing him my only option. When I open the driver's door, the overhead light flickers on and I check my face in the rearview mirror. Then I double-time it through the pool area. This has become a dangerous route and I want to make it to the apartment fast. I take the stairs two at a time and look down towards Apartment 152. The win-

217

dows are dark, and so are the ones at #148. *Nobody's here?* I jam the key into the lock, but it won't turn.

At the sound of someone climbing the steps, I look around. It's Anthony. My skin erupts in a million icy pin pricks as I twist the key hard, but still it doesn't turn. Jiggling it and using both hands doesn't open the door, either. When I try to yank the key free, it won't budge.

"Locked out?" Two words in Anthony's voice and I'm freezing into a panic.

"No—it's the key. It's stuck. I can get it."

But he's already next to me, smelling of sweat, with his Las Pulgas track shirt sticking to his chest. He brushes against me as he reaches for the key. I fall back, but he closes the distance and braces his hands on the wall, locking me between them.

"So, are you and Pacheco doin' it?"

I almost ask, "Doing what?" before my brain thaws. "No!"

"Hmm. That's not what I hear."

"I hate Juan Pacheco. I hate—" I start to say, *I hate everybody in that school*, but I swallow the words. This isn't the time to tell Anthony anything that might set him off. He's scaring me, but so far, at least he's not hurting me.

"Whaddya hate? Las Pulgas? Maybe I could change your mind." He bends his arms and brings his face close.

"No!"

He pushes away as if I've slapped him, and fixes me with dark eyes that reflect me cringing. This is like the moment just before a rainstorm, when the air is charged and still.

He snatches the key from my hand and I yank my head back so sharply that I bang it against the wall. Pain radiates from the back of my skull as I suck in air and choke.

"Chill, will ya? I'm not into punching out girls, even the sisters of creeps." For a moment I think he might pin me against the wall again. But then he forces my key into the lock and works it back and forth until it turns. The door swings open and he says, "It's your brother I'm taking out. Remind him."

He jogs to his apartment. When he's at the door, he faces me and for a second he looks like a little kid who's just been told nobody likes him. Then he's Anthony again—hard eyes and a jaw that works back and forth like a crushing machine. Once he's out of sight, the rest of my body thaws out so I can move, but my legs feel rubbery and barely carry me inside. My hand is shaking and my lungs scream for air as if I'm surfacing from a deep pool.

I lean against the closed door and reach for the light switch; when I'm sure my legs work again, I go into the kitchen for water. On the counter I find a note propped against the toaster oven. It says:

"Keith and I have gone to a movie with Jeb. We should be back by the time you're home, but if we're late, lock the door. Love, Mom."

First Quicken, now Keith and Mom—all gone. Jeb's emptied the apartment of every living thing except me. "*Merde.*" This has been one terrible night so far. I remember the worried look on Sean's face while he waited to hear what I was going to tell him—if I'd say I never wanted to see him again. I didn't say it, but I might as well have. *What*

219

will I do if I don't have Sean to call me "Milady"? What if I don't have him to tell me I'm special and beautiful, and that I'm his . . . friend?

I punch the air with my fist. I should be punching myself for being so stupid.

I head into my catacomb. My homework isn't doing itself, and I'm sure K.T.'s hastily scribbled story needs work. I have to keep my mind off being alone, and I have to wonder if K.T., the last person in the world I want to know anything about me, is reading my story right now? Did she just turn to page two and find out how I really feel? Why did I put all of that on paper, something I couldn't even write in my journal?

I take out the paper K.T. shoved at me.

"Gloria got her name because her mom sang in the church choir before she was born and she liked the 'Gloria Hallelujah' parts. Gloria could of been famous. That's cuz when she drew something it came to life like magic. One day she drew a big dog cuz she wanted one really really bad, but that dog got up off the page and ran away. She felt terrible, so the next day she drew a cat to, but it crossed the street and got run over by a car. Now she felt super terrible. If Gloria had a mom that mom would tell her to stop drawing pets for herself cuz she used to tell her what to do and not to do. Like she told her not to put up with junk from nobody. Her mom was like that too. She didn't put up with people who treated her bad. Gloria got that trait from her mom, so she was tough and the jerks let her alone. When Gloria's mom skipped town unexpected, and left her on her own is when she started trying to draw stuff. She wanted some animal friends. She didn't try to draw a mom to cuz who knew what might happen if she did? The End."

That stupid story isn't so stupid, now that I know about her mom. K.T. misses her, and she's somehow figured out a way to get through day after day, grieving and surviving.

I sit back in my chair with my brain doing crazy eights. I wrote the same thing in my free-writing exercise, except it's my dad who "skipped town." I can't believe I have anything in common with K.T., yet here it is, right on this piece of paper.

I hold my pencil over the first sentence. Not a bad start, really, and the next four are kind of catchy in a rappy sort of way. What if K.T. turns this into a rap? Maybe that's the best suggestion. It's got a story, sort of. The cat shouldn't get creamed. Maybe it just leaves her. I can relate to that one, too.

I like the idea that she wishes she could draw her mom but can't. It's bad enough bringing a dog and a cat to life and then having them leave, but if that happened to her mother, it'd be like going through her death all over again.

"All over again." I drop my pencil and look up from K.T's paper. That's how I feel in that scene, when Desdemona says goodbye to her father. I press my fingers against my eyelids until splotches of light and dark are all I see.

Get this done. You've got your own homework, Carlie.

I sit straight in my chair, pick up my pencil and line out the parts K.T. should delete, then I write my rap idea on the bottom of the paper. I add one more comment: "This story has a sad message about a girl who's lost a mom." I fold the paper, but then unfold it and write something else,

"Acting tough might be part of the answer, but I don't think it's enough to get rid of what's hurting inside. Thanks for trusting me with your writing."

Maybe she'll lighten up on me if I try some honey. I sigh. *Or not.*

Tucking the paper back into my notebook, I wonder if she's at her desk, writing notes on my story. And what kind of notes? *Huge mistake, Carlie. Huge.*

"Carlie love, stop worrying about what you wrote."

I wanted you to—

"You wanted me to die, so both of us could stop hurting."

Yes, but—

"Do you think you're the only person who has feelings they're ashamed of?"

I shake my head.

"You can't help being human."

I lay my head on my desk. *But there's more, Dad. You know that.*

"I know, but you're entitled to be angry about what's happened."

I'm not entitled to hate you.

"Who says?"

Dad's voice is so clear; I sit up to look around the room. My desk light shines on my papers and because I haven't turned on the overhead light, the corners are shadowy and the wall behind me is dark. The still air stirs only slightly when I stand up with my hands outstretched. I want him to be here. I want one more moment with him.

But I'm alone. I blow my nose, then swipe my eyes.

Suddenly our front door opens and closes. I'm up and

tense. Rapid footsteps come toward my room. *How did any-one slide the safety off? Did they cut it?*

I'm clutching the black sheet at my window. When my bedroom door pops open and Mom pokes her head inside, her face pale.

"Carlie! Are you all right?" she shouts.

She crosses the room in two quick steps and holds me. "Honey, you left the safety chain off and the door was ajar. I was so scared. You have to remember to use it all the time."

I have to remember so much that I can't remember any of it. I fall against her, crying.

"It's time we talked," she says. "It's long overdue." She pulls me to sit next to her on my bed and holds me until I stop sobbing.

"Now tell me what's happening." She pushes my hair out of my eyes and rocks me from side to side the way she did when I was little.

"I've got a serious case of nerves. The play is really hard, and I'm behind in a couple of classes."

"I used to know all about your classes. Now I don't even think about anything else, except real estate laws and the Wednesday specials on canned goods."

"It's . . . just nerves." I'm still not going to tell her about the threats to Keith, or to me.

"And the dance? What about the dress? Did you look yet?"

"I've got it covered. Well, Sean helped. It's a long story."

She hugs me closer. "I'm missing some of the best parts of your life, aren't I?"

I don't answer because I want this moment to last. I don't want to ruin it with tales of the "best parts" of life at Las Pulgas.

"So when can I see this creation?"

"I can pick it up next week." I sit up and blow my nose. "Maybe I'll call Lena tomorrow while I'm babysitting and have her meet me at the mall after school on Monday. She's super ticked off about my not shopping with her, so I've got some making up to do. But that means I'll need the car."

"I can ask Jeb for a ride to work. He told me he'd help anytime. It's because of Quicken, you know. He tells me our cat is the best thing that's happened to him in a long time."

A scowl draws my face tight. I look up through my lashes at her.

"Carlie, stop with that look. You have no idea—" Mom rubs both temples with her fingers. "Jeb and I . . . Well, it helps to have someone to talk to, someone my own age who understands about being forty plus and not living the life they'd expected, not knowing about the direction to take the way they always did in the past. When I was twenty-five, everything was in place—your father, you, Keith, my friends." She smiles, but it makes her face regretful, not happy. "That's all there is between Jeb and me, so I don't need those looks of yours, okay?" She points at me and waits until my expression shifts back to normal.

"Who is this Juan Pacheco, anyway?"

Mom's been busy, but her radar hasn't been totally

down. I explain about the poor Mexican kid who works at Sam's Shack and does a great Othello impression. Then I veer quickly to Mr. Smith, the most awesome teacher ever. I save Sean for last, because I don't know how to explain what's happened between us.

"He's . . . he's my best friend. No—he used to be."

Her eyes are studying me, seeing what I wish wasn't there. "Did you have a fight?"

"Not exactly, but he'll never speak to me again because I let him down."

"Maybe I can help. I . . . I know something about letting people down." The way she says this makes me ache to tell her everything.

"He's gay, Mom, and I love him, but I hate him for . . . not being able to love me back—at least not the way I want him to."

I tell her the rest of what happened and how I regret letting him think I didn't want anything else to do with him when I left.

She traces her finger along my cheek. "You were upset. He has to understand that. And, Carlie, you still have time to tell him how you really feel."

After she leaves I curl up, missing Quicken at the foot of my bed, and aching because I may have lost Sean, the one person left in this world who made me feel special.

38

Sunday, while Kip and Jessie watch afternoon car-
toons, I close myself in Mr. Franklin's office and pick up his
phone. I punch in Sean's cell number and wait, hoping he'll
answer because I don't want to leave him a message. But I
also have no idea what I'm going to say or how I'm going
to say it—if he picks up. It rings a few times, and then his
voicemail answers. I hit End.

When I call Lena, I have to listen to twenty minutes of
her "news" before she stops to inhale. Then I grab my
chance to jump in.

"I found my dress for the dance."

The silence has a chill, and I can picture her drawing
her mouth tight. I know what comes next—she perfected
her snotty act around the time we entered second grade. She
discovered that saucy tilt of her head when we started junior high, and by the time we were freshmen in high school,
she knew the effect of parting her glossy, peach-scented lips
and sighing. And now I hear that sigh.

"Lena?"

"I thought we were shopping *together*."

"We talked about it, but . . . it just kind of happened. I didn't go *looking* for it, you know?" I wait a few beats for her to say something, but when she doesn't, I plow ahead, hoping to get her back to being happy. "How about you go with me to pick it up after school tomorrow? About three?"

She's slow to warm up, but after I say, "like old times" she comes back with "I do still need a small evening bag to go with my dress."

"Super. Let's meet in front of Très Elégant."

"Perfect. I'd love to paw through their shelves," she says.

Paw through their shelves? "Lena—"

"Mom's calling. See you tomorrow."

The dial tone is all that's left of our conversation. *You don't paw through shelves in Très Elégant.*

I'm ready to press redial and cancel when I hear Jessie screaming in the TV room. I've got some kind of cartoon crisis and I'll have to worry about Lena later.

⁂

On Monday morning I lie in bed, waiting for the shower to stop, then drag myself into the steamy bathroom and draw a sad face on the mirror. *How much longer will I have to share this bathroom with Keith?*

By the time I've showered and grabbed toast, Keith's eaten the whole box of cereal and used up what was left of the milk. Mom comes back into the kitchen, fastening the last snap on her Las Pulgas Supermarket uniform. "I'm set with a ride from work, and Jeb says he'll swing by to get me, so take the car and pick up your dress this afternoon. I can't wait to see it." She hugs me. "This is so exciting. And someday I want to meet your friend Sean. He sounds like one interesting boy."

Keith—The Diabolical—leers at me. "Oh, he's *interesting* all right."

"What's *that* supposed to mean?" I say.

He takes an empty mug from the drainer and fills it with hot cocoa. Then he picks up the mug, extending his pinky finger with a flourish. "Just what I said—*interesting*."

My insides constrict. Why is it I find out about Sean being gay *after* my brother does, and only by asking? My face goes hot. "You're a twisted piece of snot, Keith!"

"Carlie! That's disgusting." Mom shakes her head and scoops up a stack of papers on the end of the table.

"Big sister scare little brother," Keith says with an evil grin.

"Keith, that's enough from you, too. Sean is Carlie's friend, and besides you know better than to spread rumors that can hurt people. Get yourself ready to go to Jeb's. He's expecting you, and I'd better get good reports from him about you."

Keith gulps his cocoa.

"I liked you both better when you were three," Mom says. "Okay, let's get on our way. Anything you need from the lovely Las Pulgas Market?"

Keith shakes his head.

I give him another look that I hope screams *you are a jerk head*.

"You have a test in algebra next week. Do you want me to pick up anything from your locker?" I ask him.

"No."

"Good. I didn't want to get it anyway."

"Look, you two. That's enough. I'm already tired and I haven't even started my shift yet." Mom kisses Keith's cheek and musses his hair before he can duck away. "Quite a mop you've got going there. Do you need some money for a haircut?"

"No," he says.

"He's not going to run anymore," I tell her.

"That's none of your business," Keith growls.

I go for sarcasm. "Gee, thanks Carlie, for bringing all my assignments home every night. And I really appreciate your dropping me off at Cal Works and picking me up every Saturday."

Keith holds up two fingers. "Twice."

I yank the front door open, then look both ways before stepping outside. Every time I come or go from this place I know what it's like to live in a war zone. I poke my head back inside. "Mom, I'm going to be late for first period if we don't go right now."

"See you after six," Mom says to Keith. She takes her coat from the back of the couch and closes the door behind her.

The traffic is fairly light, so I make the trip to the Las Pulgas Market in less than ten minutes. Neither of us talks, but as Mom gets out, she says. "I want you to stop talking like that to Keith."

"He's—"

"Your brother." Mom gets out of the car. "And he's hurting as much as we are."

When I finally look up, she's already inside the store.

When I get to school, I'm later than usual, and there's only a single parking space at the very end of the lot.

Our decrepit car clock reads two forty-five just like always, but my watch says I'm going to be late. Grabbing my backpack, I race toward the main entrance and line up behind three others kids in the security line. Only five minutes till the final bell.

Every time I pass through security my skin crawls. I pray Mr. Icky won't search my bag again. He's done it three out of five days, every week. Am I particularly suspicious-looking?

Today the wand guy lets me through instead.

I'm making good time until four guys break away from a group and come at me, forming a wall I can't get around. I find myself staring into Chico's scowly face, and recognize two other guys beside him from that incident at the apartments. The fourth one is the sulky-faced Anthony.

"So, when's your creep of a brother coming back to school to get creamed?" Chico asks.

He already knows when Keith's due back so I don't answer him.

"You tell him we're waiting," Chico says, shoving me aside. Each of them makes a point of shouldering me as he passes and Anthony squeezes my upper arm hard.

The final bell rings as I slam my way into Mr. Smith's classroom, still shaking. Keith doesn't stand a chance against these guys when he gets back.

As I head for my seat, I slide K.T.'s story with my suggestions onto her desk.

"What's this?" she asks.

"It's your story about the artist."

K.T. looks at the paper. "Got lots of marks on it."

"It's a critique, K.T." I wait, but she takes her time reading my comments and doesn't pay any attention to me. Then I remind her that I'm waiting by asking, "And my . . . paper?"

"Oh, yeah. Here." She pulls out a folded sheet of notebook paper from her pocket. It's been creased so many times, it looks more like scrap.

I growl on my way to my seat, but low enough so she doesn't hear me. Once I sit down, I unfold the paper and smooth it out. She's scribbled red pen in the margins and even between my lines. She's written more than Mr. Smith did. I shove it into my notebook without reading her notes. I just can't right now.

39

That afternoon, I pull into the mall's underground parking, turn off the ignition, and sit in the quiet car. Lena's "paw through the shelves" remark and the way she said it still runs through my head. Mrs. Knudson uses that small undercurrent of spite in her voice sometimes. The first time I noticed it was when I'd won the eighth-grade poetry contest and Lena came in third. When I showed her the ribbon, Mrs. Knudson parted her lips enough for her even little teeth to show. "How sweet, Carlie. It's a nice little keepsake." The word *jealousy* flits through my mind as I recall the incident.

At the time, when I'd asked Mom why Mrs. Knudson didn't like me, her exact words were, "Remember, you have a terrific imagination. Keep the real world separate from the imagined one, Carlie." I wonder what Mom would say now, if I told her what Lena's mom had said last Saturday about my dress for the dance. I didn't imagine one bit of *that* conversation. But they used to be friends, so maybe Mom didn't see what I did.

When I reach the main gallery, Lena's ahead of me,

texting. She ends her message and holds out her arms when she sees me. Her expression's like the old Lena, and I feel ashamed for thinking my friend would turn spiteful on me.

"We haven't done the mall in a hundred years. I'm so into shopping today, and it's double fun now that you're here. I'm, like, totally in need of a break from my schedule, which you have to know is intense. I'm doing Spring Fling decorations, arranging the DJ, and trying to sleep occasionally. I have news and more news, too!" Lena links her arm through mine without stopping for a breath, and as we enter Très Elégant, her cell chimes the French national anthem and she answers it.

"Hi. What's up? That is so awesome! Right. Bye." Lena texts, then closes the cell again.

"That was Paula. You remember her—the exchange student from Paris? She, like, sent to Paris for her Spring Fling dress. I am totally green. Imagine a new dress all the way from France?" She scans the marquee. "Accessories, second floor. There's a really awesome purse waiting just over our heads and it's all mine."

I step onto the escalator behind Lena. "Oh, before I forget—" she chatters on, "—you have to text or call me on my cell. My computer crashed. We think it's the hard drive. Can you believe it? I'm getting a new one when my dad comes back from South America, but that's two weeks. He says I can . . ."

Lena goes on and on, but by now I've tuned in to another station.

I seem to have a BFF who babbles, who never asks about how I feel, or cares about what's happening in my life.

233

What should I do, just listen and listen and listen to talk, talk, talk?

Lena steps off the escalator and looks over her shoulder at me. "So where do you pick up your dress?"

I point to the couturier section of the store.

"Oh, *couturier*. Do you want to do that first?" The mean undercurrent that's so like Mrs. Knudson's is back in Lena's voice.

"How about if I pick up my dress while you 'paw through the shelves.'" *Talk about undercurrent.* "I'll probably finish first; then I'll come find you."

"No way, Carlie. We are together on this mission. Come on, couturier first." Lena leads the way to the desk. Without being asked, she speaks for me. "We're here to pick up a dress for—"

"Carlie. I'm so happy to see you again." Miss Lily comes from behind her desk, and I'm the recipient of the two-cheek European-style kiss. "Your dress is ready, but I want you to model it for us first. I've told all of my ladies how amazingly beautiful you are in it." She takes my hand saying, "Come."

The dressing room is still as glamorous as I remember. I flash back to Sean sitting with me, watching the models, helping me choose the perfect dress. A small tornado whips around in my belly. I wish—I don't know what I wish. Yes, I do. I wish Sean wasn't gay. Mostly I wish he could be here with me instead of Lena.

My dress hangs by its tiny rosette straps from a golden hanger and it's more beautiful than ever before.

From behind me Lena gasps.

"Your friend also appreciates how lovely this is for you." Miss Lily hands the gown to me. "Here is a pair of heels to use. It will look so much better with the right shoes. Now try it on and I will gather my ladies."

I strip to my underwear and carefully step into the dress. "Can you zip this for me?"

Lena yanks the zipper to the top.

"Whoa. That's a tad rough, *mon amie*."

"It stuck."

I step into the pink heels and face the mirrored walls. "Well," I say, "what do you think?"

"It's fine. Of course, I asked you not to get something pink."

"No. You said not to buy a red dress. This isn't red." But I'm *seeing* red. Flames lap around Lena, who is now tied to a stake in my mind. And I want to scream, "Witch!"

I'm relieved when Miss Lily returns with two other Très Elégant saleswomen. Their chatter covers the tension between Lena and my pizazzy pink self.

I change quickly, and Miss Lily boxes the dress, carefully tucking it between folds of tissue paper, then tying it with Très Elégant ribbon. She kisses me again on both cheeks, pressing the box into my hands. "Have a wonderful time at the dance."

Lena has her back to us, fingering a chiffon skirt on a mannequin. It was a mistake to do this with her.

"So what kind of purse are you looking for?" Maybe I can salvage the rest of the afternoon if I sincerely try to help Lena buy the right accessory.

"It's getting late. Maybe I'll wait to get it another day."

Lena is already on the escalator, her head slowly disappearing from my sight, so I can't argue.

"How about a Coke?" I say, not giving up.

"Sure. The Food Court's close."

Maybe humbling myself will ease Lena back into a good mood. "I can't shop today. I'm pretty broke."

Lena doesn't answer, but when we've bought our drinks and found seats, she says, "Are you broke because of that?" She points at the Très Elégant box.

"Not really." I don't want to get into how much the dress cost. "It wasn't that expensive. You might say I got a—"

"Hey! It's the Des."

K.T. and her gang of six encircle us. I almost snatch the box from the seat and hold on to protect it.

"Being a mall rat's not what I expected of the star."

"I do more than act in Mr. Smith's play, K.T."

"When do you do all that fancy writing?"

It's in her eyes. All that I wrote about my dad, all that I wrote about how I feel. Why does she have to be here now? Today?

"Who's this?" K.T. points at Lena, who sits without moving anything but her eyes. They dart nervously between K.T. and the six girls at her back.

"Lena Knudson. She's my friend, so be nice."

"I'm always nice. You know that." K.T. grins at the six girls, who laugh. "So what you got in the fancy box?"

"A dress."

"Lemme see."

I think Lena's shrinking inside her clothes.

"It's nothing special."

K.T. fingers the ribbon. "The outside sure looks kinda special."

I'm not getting rid of her until she gets her way, so I untie the bow, lift off the top and peel aside the tissue.

"Holy—" K.T. exclaims. "Get your eyeballs ready to pop. Lookit at what Des has bought herself!"

The gang of six clusters around the table, closing in around Lena and me.

The girl with tightly beaded hair extends a finger but K.T. slaps her hand away.

"It's okay," I tell her. "Touching won't hurt it." Picking up my dress has just become an event, instead of a chore to finish so I can escape Lena's sour looks and ping-ponging moods.

K.T. sets one hand on her hip and does an exaggerated head shift right and left, so that her dangly earrings dance above each shoulder. "So *where* you gonna wear this?"

"She's going to Channing's Spring Fling." I turn around to see if Mrs. Knudson has suddenly appeared, but it's just Lena, doing her best imitation of her sarcastic mom.

"Whoa. Excuse my asking," K.T. says and hops back, pretending to be threatened. Her gang moves behind her like a chorus line. "We'll be travelin,'" she says and leads them away.

"Thanks," I call after them.

K.T. looks back, suspicion in her eyes.

"Glad you liked my dress." *Glad you interrupted a perfectly horrible conversation is more like it.*

She sticks one hand on her hip and says, "It'd be better in red. And I'd dump those strappy flower things."

She can't let up for a minute, can she?

Like always, her gang plays its way across the Food Court. Big Teeth shoulders K.T., then K.T. slings her arm around the girl's back and does a hip-hop move on her rubber heel. I watch until they merge with the mall crowd. And I'm the girl left behind with the elegant dress and the sour-faced friend. Staring after them, I feel lonelier the farther away they get.

Lena slurps the last of her Coke through a straw and crumples the plastic cup. "So what's all this, 'Des' stuff?"

"I'm in the junior play. That's my nickname."

"For?"

"Desdemona."

Lena tosses her crumpled cup into the trash. "How many nicknames do you have at Las Pulgas?"

"Two. And one isn't meant to be flattering." I don't want to explain Juan's to her.

"How come you didn't tell me about the play?"

"It just never came up. I'm sorry, Lena, but you don't know what kind of mess I've been in since my dad died."

Now that I've played the "Dad Card," Lena switches from bitchy to sweet. "Can we come? I mean Eric and me?"

"You want to?"

"Sure. I saw posters at Sam's, but I didn't know my best friend was the star."

She's chatty. She's happy. As long as the pizazzy pink dress doesn't enter the conversation, and as long as I'm the one with major problems, Lena's just fine.

"Sure, if you'd like to—that would be, uh, great." I can almost hear the "uh" escape. It's like a huge, carbonated burp. Finally, unexpectedly, I've invited Channing to Las Pulgas.

Relieved?

Yes.

Scared?

Absolutely.

And here I thought K.T. and the track team were the scariest part of my life.

40

After Lena drives out of the parking garage, I sit in my car without putting the key into the ignition. The Très Elégant box fills the passenger seat and anxiety fills the rest of the space, as I picture Lena and Eric sitting in the Las Pulgas auditorium, staring at me while I pretend to be lovely, innocent Desdemona. On the way out of the Food Court, Lena even suggested asking Nicolas to join them at the play—sort of like a rehearsal for our big double date.

I'll break my leg like K.T. did. Mr. Smith will have to cast somebody else, maybe Dolores. She knows a lot of my lines.

By the time I reach the apartment, it's almost dark. But tonight the lights are on in our apartment windows. Clutching the box I hurry up the stairs, grateful that I've made it past the pool without having to fear for my life. As I hurry past Apartment 147, the door snaps open and Gerald and his wife come out. He doesn't seem to notice me, but she does.

"Hi, honey. You've got the joint all to yourself tonight. Me and Gerald got a date." She flicks her cigarette ashes over the balcony, then follows her husband down the stairs, calling, "Wait up!"

Inside the apartment I say, "Mom, I've got the dress."

She comes down the hall barefoot, still in her gold and brown uniform. "Let's see it. I've been waiting for this all day."

I undo the ribbon and hold up the dress.

"Oh! It's absolutely beautiful." Mom's eyes glisten as she wraps me in her arms.

"Are you crying?"

"Yes. And don't try to stop me. I need this cry."

Keith pokes his head out of his bedroom, sees us and ducks back inside.

Mom steps away and holds the dress against me. "Try it on. I have to see you in it right now!"

I change, dig quickly through my closet for heels, and check my jewelry box for the small sparkly earrings. When I pull the dress over my head, I'm careful not to snag it on my bracelet. I twist my hair into a knot and pin it in place.

Mom's waiting in the living room, her hands folded in her lap.

"Carlie—" She presses her fingers to her lips. "I just wasn't prepared for you to look so— so grown up."

Mom's loneliness is real and as depressing as the room itself. I can almost see a form in the space next to her, where Dad would be sitting, looking at me, his daughter, in a pizazzy pink dress.

"Now tell me again about the orchids. What kind should you wear?" Mom blots her eyes with her Las Pulgas Market apron.

Keith goes into the kitchen without looking at us. He bangs a cupboard door shut, rummages noisily in the refrigerator and clanks a pot onto the stove.

"Sean said he thought I should have small pink ones. What do you—"

There's a knock at our door. "I'll get it," Mom says. She looks through the security peephole, then unlocks the door for Jeb.

"Come in. Sorry I haven't changed for dinner yet."

"Who's this?" Jeb stops in front of me. "Must be a movie star."

"Isn't she beautiful?"

"Mom!"

"No—your mom's right. You *are* beautiful and she has every right to say so," Jeb says, then he calls toward the kitchen, "Hey, Keith! Come in here and tell your sister she's a knock out."

"You're a knock out, Carlie," Keith says in a monotone.

"Thank you, Keith," I reply, mimicking his insincerity.

After Jeb and Mom leave, I change into my jeans and join Keith in the kitchen.

"What's left to eat?" I ask. I'm starved after the tense day with Lena.

"Chicken."

I carve some slices from the last of the whole bird Mom roasted Saturday. "So how is it to work for him?"

"Jeb?"

"No, King Ludwig of Bavaria."

Keith laughs. This is the second time I've heard that sound this year, but once Chico and his friends have at Keith, he won't be laughing.

"Ludwig's okay. He doesn't bug me. Gives me a list of stuff to do, then leaves me alone to do it."

"What kind of stuff?" Maybe I could work at Jeb's too. Then when Mom visits, I can make sure it's really a friendship and nothing else between them. Besides, working in an orchard might be more fun than babysitting for Aunt Corky.

"I put crates together. Fix stuff that's broken. That kind of thing."

It doesn't sound very interesting, but I could probably do the crates. "Um, do you think you could fix something for me?"

"Like?"

"My Jack-in-the-Box."

He shrugs, then says, "Give it to me. I'll try."

I eat the last of my chicken. "Do you ever see Quicken when you're at Jeb's?"

"Yeah. She's fat and full of all kinds of rodents—including one pesky squirrel." Keith bites into a chicken leg and chews.

"Pesky?"

"Jeb's word. I think he's in love with that cat."

"I don't care. She's *my* cat." I remember how she wouldn't sit on my lap at Jeb's, how she went to him instead. She *was* my cat. I go to the sink, wash my plate and stack it in the drainer. My English homework isn't doing itself, and I've got a whole scene to memorize by next rehearsal.

On my way from the kitchen I stop next to Keith. "What are you going to do? I mean about the track team."

He shakes his head. "Nothing. Anthony tells me to wait until next week. I keep thinking he's going to jump me, but all I get are some names insulting our ancestors."

"I don't get it. If they start something on campus, Bins will suspend them all. But here, they could probably get away with pounding on you."

"My guess?"

I shrug. "Yeah."

"It's about showing off. They want everybody to see me get hurt."

"Guys are so weird."

"Right. I guess you forgot about the naked girl fight in the girls' room. I sure haven't."

"No boy on campus will ever forget that. See you in the morning."

"Carlie." Keith's at the sink washing his own plate. "Jeb's right. You do look awesome in that dress."

He can't see my expression because he's facing away. My mouth is set to reply with a smart comeback to top his usual sarcasm, but there's no sarcasm in his voice. I head to my room without saying anything. It's because I don't know what to say.

After changing into pjs, I pull the covers around me, then think about how Keith and I sat together and . . . talked—that he said something nice to me. If I weren't so tired, I'd take my journal down from the closet shelf and put something in it about a pizazzy pink dress and my real brother—the one I glimpsed tonight. The one who'll try to fix my favorite toy.

Sleep pulls me and I feel something I haven't felt in a very long time: a speck of stillness in the center of all those funnel clouds that make up my life.

41

The next day after school, I take a quick peek inside the Très Elégant box and finger the tiny rosettes along the straps. I'll wait to try the dress on after I finish my homework—kind of like a reward. The dance is still two weeks away, and if I keep putting Miss Lily's dress on and taking it off, I'll wear it out before the big night. But it feels so good.

I finish the chemistry chapter notes that I'm sure Doc did days ago, and then I open my notebook and take out my story. I've put off reading K.T.'s comments as long as I can, but now I have to do it.

At the top she writes, "Mr. Smith nailed it. You got to describe the person's feelings more and let me understand how she gets through the days since her dad died. I liked the story alot. I didn't find no grammer problems either."

K.T. didn't write any ugly things. She didn't draw ghoulish pictures like I'd imagined. The rest of the comments are smiley faces or "Here's where you can put in more about how the girl feels."

I pull out a clean sheet of lined paper. I know how I'll

write my story this time. *"And the next time I open my journal, Dad, I'll write how my heart is trying to listen."*

"My dad died of cancer in the month when spirits walk among the living. He's still here because I know he doesn't want to leave. He's still here because I'm having a hard time letting him go. I need him to help me sort out the feelings inside me, like the funnel clouds that drop from the sky when you least expect them. You may think I'm mad, but when you read my story, you'll see that it's not about madness. It's about hating the person you love most. It's about the guilt that keeps October's dark chill in my heart and won't allow the spring come in."

I'm almost finished with my rewrite when Mom comes in and hands me the phone. "It's Lena."

Maybe she's changed her mind about coming to the play. "Hi," I say into the phone.

"You are not going to believe this," Lena says.

"Okaaay?" I know there's gossip at Channing just by the way she sounds.

"Sean Wright."

I don't have to hear the rest to know what she's about to say, but I have to stop her or be dragged into a story I don't want to hear, especially not coming from her.

"We've been spending a lot of time together," I say. "Is that what you've heard?"

"What?" Lena shrieks.

I yank the phone away from my ear, then as smoothly as I can manage, I say, "We just started seeing each other last month. Nothing steady. He knows I'm going to the dance with Nicolas."

"Well, uh, uh—why didn't you tell me?"

Good question, Lena. Maybe it has to do with the fact that you never really gave me a chance. "I tried, but you always had so much going on—"

"You need to know something." Lena's gossip is festering and she's not about to keep it to herself.

"Oh, I know about Sean. He's seeing someone in New York. But that's okay."

I think I hear her teeth clamp together.

"I'm glad you called, Lena. But I'll have to get back to you later. I'm already late for rehearsal."

I press End before she says anything more about Sean. Then, before I lose my nerve, I punch in his phone number and wait. *Please pick up this time. Please.*

When I hear his voice I stammer, "Uhh. I—I—"

"Carlie? What's wrong?"

"I don't . . . I don't care. I mean I *do* care, but I don't want to lose you. I *can't* lose you." I know I'm not making sense and I sound desperate.

"I thought you knew I was gay. I'm open about it, and I think most people know."

For a moment, his breath is the only sound coming through the phone. Then he says, "I wanted to ask you to the dance and I *would* have, but I thought maybe you didn't want anyone to see us together."

I can't make my mouth open.

"You always came here and wouldn't let me go to your place."

"No! That's wrong. I couldn't let you come to *this* apartment." I wave my arm around my room, as if he can see what I mean. "It's beyond bad, Sean. I—I" *What am I?* "I'm a total idiot."

"Not a total one, just one who's having a hard time with change. Right?"

"Yes, very." When I say this, in my mind I hear Juan calling me Princess.

"Hey, I understand, Carlie. Really." The warmth of his word, *understand*, spreads through me like a soothing mist.

"Please come over, Sean. I really need to see you."

"Me, too. You won't forget pictures, right? I mean of you in the dress?"

"You'll be getting dozens."

"That's great. I can't wait."

Before I hang up, I give Sean my Las Pulgas address.

"Bye, beautiful," he says.

After he's gone I say, "Bye, beautiful," back to him, holding the handset to my chest. He wanted to ask me to the dance. He would have asked me if I hadn't made him feel like I was ashamed of him. "I *am* a total idiot."

I double-time past the kitchen. "I'm late to rehearsal. See you later, Mom." I'm out the door before she looks up from her books.

∽

The next day, when I'm supposed to hand in my story for extra-credit during English, I don't. It takes me most of the day to work up the courage to give Mr. Smith the rewrite, but after chemistry, I go back to his classroom.

"Am I too late to give you this?" I ask.

"Ah, the very touching story. No, you're not too late. This'll be interesting to read. I'm glad you're resubmitting it."

As I hand him the paper I tighten my grip on the edge. This is the most I've revealed about Dad's death. I still don't know if I'm doing the right thing by putting all of that in words, but it's too late now. Mr. Smith stacks my paper on top of others.

"You seem distracted. Is it because of what you wrote?"

I nod. "Partly."

"A parent's death is the hardest loss to accept, and it's never easy to put how you feel about it on paper." He points to my story. "You did an excellent job here."

Obviously, my attempts at making the story a piece of fiction didn't work.

"Are you worried about the play?" Mr. Smith asks.

"A little. Nervous, I guess." Our dress rehearsal had more glitches than any of the earlier ones. We're getting worse, not better. Dolores tripped on the hem of her dress, Jamal missed his first entrance, and I blew the same lines in my opening scene with Brabantio. Everybody, including Juan this time, glared at me, not just Iago. "I'll go over those scenes I had trouble with."

"You'll be fine."

I hope he's right. My stomach knots every time I think about Lena and Eric in the audience, watching me.

After picking up Keith's algebra assignment, I start down the hall. I pass through security at the main door and hurry down the steps.

The track team has gathered out front, like they do every afternoon for practice, and Grits, who's back from his suspension, waves to me. Anthony's eyes track me and the others give me their death-ray looks, especially Chico. Why can't I have just one day when I don't feel like I'm prey?

42

The word *jitters* takes on real meaning starting at seven Saturday morning, when my eyes snap open. Only twelve hours before the curtain goes up, and I, Carlie Edmund, have to morph into Desdemona of Venice in front of a live audience.

Between now and then, I have the usual boring routine of homework, dropping and picking up Keith at Cal Works and . . . I run my tongue over my teeth . . . some basic grooming.

In the bathroom, I stare into the mirror over the sink. "I've forgotten all of my lines!"

"There's a line out here you've forgotten, too," Keith yells.

Sharing a bathroom with my brother is more painful than having a wisdom tooth extracted and it's been going on a lot longer. "Just give me a minute," I tell him through the door.

"You've got thirty seconds. I have to pee."

"Grrr." I yank the door open. "I need to get back in there as soon as you're done, okay?"

Keith mimics me like he used to when he was little, repeating "I need to get back in there." He closes the door and snaps the lock. "Later!"

"You're a creep, you know that?"

"A creep who now controls the bathroom!"

I drag myself into the kitchen and pour cereal into a bowl. Mom's books and papers still litter the table, so I decide to eat at the counter.

"Good morning, honey. I'll take Keith to Cal Works this morning," she says. "That'll give you a break."

This is good news. Now I have an extra hour to go through my scenes again. "Another test?" I point at the books and papers.

Mom sighs. "Of course, but I'm on my last lap now." She picks up her book and almost immediately I can see her mind leave the kitchen and she forgets I'm here.

I'd love to be able to focus like she does. But I just don't have that kind of mind. I'm a "here, there, and everywhere" kind of thinker. Thoughts of Sean thread in and out with others about Keith's return to school next week, then they merge with Othello's dark face and Juan's side-ways smile. With all of that turmoil in my head, it's no wonder I can't remember Desdemona's lines or Doc's chemistry lessons.

I get some milk from the fridge, then open the script to that first scene, when Desdemona leaves her father. Since I've blown this scene every time in rehearsal, all the actors on stage have memorized my lines and whisper them to me. But I *know* them. I just can't *say* them.

It's all about the guilt that I can't shake—all those

253

times when I wished the dying would end because I couldn't stand to watch it anymore. It's about how I feel sometimes when I look around this dump, knowing we wouldn't be here if Dad were alive.

I set the glass down with a *thunk* and say, "I'm going to go study, Mom."

"Don't worry about it, honey," she says without looking up.

Keith stumbles past my room, smelling of fresh soap and shampoo. "Shower's all yours."

I drop my script and catch him in the hall. "How can you be so . . . so . . . calm all the time?"

He shrugs.

"Chico's still out to get even when you go back to school, and I'm getting more than my share of the heat," I tell him.

"Just stay clear of him," he says.

"Ha! I'd laugh if you'd start being really funny. So, have you thought what you're going to do to keep them from creaming you?"

Mom comes out of the kitchen. "What's this, about someone creaming you?"

"Nothing," Keith says and starts to leave.

Mom grabs the back of his T-shirt and says, "Hold it. I want to know what Carlie's talking about."

"The track team is on about beating me up when I get back to school Monday."

"Beating?"

"Forget it, Mom." Keith pulls his shirt from her grasp. "I gotta get dressed for my date with a garbage bag."

"I'm calling the principal. This is going to stop right now."

"Calling Bins won't make any difference," Keith says as he darts back into his room.

"What do you know about this?" she asks.

"Just what he said, Mom." I can't tell her Chico wants blood, and that he wants it where everyone in school can see it. I can't tell her about the creepy run-ins I've had with the track team, or the times the hair on my arms stands on end in social studies because Chico sits behind me. Then I realize I don't have to. She knows things are bad at school. It's all over her face. She just doesn't know what to do about it.

Once Keith and Mom leave for Cal Works, the apartment settles into a quiet hole again—depressing, but a good place to go over lines. When the phone rings I ignore it at first and sit on my bed, eyes closed, repeating lines and cues. But the constant shrill sound is annoying, so I hurry to the kitchen and answer the call.

"Carlie, it's me," Sean says.

"It's about time you called. Where *are* you?"

"New York."

"Oh." I can't keep the sound of disappointment out of that monosyllable.

"I saw my Mom and now Michael's here. We've been going around to the sights. You know—all the places New Yorkers never go near until someone from California visits."

"Michael."

"Miss Lily's son. We're rooming together at Elmhust, remember?"

I *know* who Michael is. His name slipped out more from feeling the sting of rejection than from trying to identify him. A trickle of jealousy hits my stomach as I picture Sean and Michael enjoying the Statue of Liberty or Central Park, while here I am, crouched inside a crappy apartment in Las Pulgas.

"I just remembered that you open tonight and I wanted to tell you to break a leg."

"I've got a serious case of stage fright." It feels good to confide in him. "I wish you were here." *I wish I were in New York.*

"Michael sends his best, too. His mom told him about how knockout beautiful you are in that dress."

"You're good for my ego, Sean. Thanks."

"Guess you're excited. Play's almost over. The dance is next weekend."

"Come home soon, okay? I miss you." I think I like having Sean as my friend. *Keep telling yourself that, Carlie, and stop feeling sorry for yourself.*

After the call, I can't settle back into studying my part and I punch up Lena's number.

"Hi, Lena. It's me, Carlie."

"I know. Caller ID."

"Tonight's the big deal. Are you and Eric still coming?" *Say, no—please.*

"Of course. And Nicolas is, too."

I scream inside my head. Part of me wants my friends there and part of me doesn't. It's very complicated.

"I bought a ticket for Nicolas today—from Juan at the

Shack." Lena says Juan's name with a hint of familiarity, as if she'd done more than buy a ticket from him.

"Oh. Well, good. That's great." I hope I deliver more convincing lines on stage tonight.

"So did you need something else?" Lena's question surprises me. It implies that I've interrupted something important, or taken her away from a more interesting conversation.

"Uh, no. Just checking in."

"Okay, then. We'll see you tonight," Lena says.

Click.

"Bye . . . Lena," I say to dead air. I set the phone on the charger, thinking that my best friend didn't tell me to break a leg.

43

Mom drops me at the auditorium a little after six and leaves to pick up Keith and Jeb at the orchard. She helped me with make-up and braided my hair, so all I have to do is twist the braid into a knot at the back of my head. But the extra preparation's made me a little late.

When I check in, the rest of the cast already has tic marks by their names—I'm the last to show up. Dolores and the girl playing Bianca, the only other female character, are putting on make-up when I walk into the girls' dressing room.

"K.T. was getting ready to take back her Desdemona part if you didn't show up soon," Dolores says in her soft voice.

"I'm not that late." I hurry to undress, slipping into a creamy-colored underdress, then getting into the dark red costume and hooking it together at the side. The bodice lacing is the slowest part of getting into Desdemona's costume. When I finish, I turn around to see myself in the only full-length mirror I get to look in these days. The square neckline of the costume is trimmed with lace, and the long sleeves are soft and flowing. I add a silver chain-belt at my waist and adjust the skirt so it doesn't trip me.

A loud *bam, bam, bam* on the dressing room door freezes the three of us, then K.T's stage manager voice comes from the other side. "Cast backstage in five."

Dolores shakes her head. "Nobody should ever give her any power. It just makes life miserable for everybody."

I appreciate Dolores's quiet humor more every day. "What would I do if you weren't in this play with me?" I say to her.

She smiles. "You'd have to get cozier with K.T., I guess."

"Come on." I sling my arm around her shoulder. "I don't want to cross her and her Prompt Script tonight."

K.T. has carried that script around, with all the scene changes, all the props and lighting cues since we began re-hearsing and now it looks like a permanent piece of her. When someone blows a line, or Jamal doesn't have the lights exactly where her book says it should be, she yells out the line or thumps her way to the light panel and takes control. I think about Mr. Smith's word, "assertive," and grudgingly admit he was right. She does her job as if the pay is good, even if she makes the cast and crew miserable a lot of the time.

The three of us line up in front of K.T. for a costume check, something she instigated after reading an Internet article about putting on a school play. At dress rehearsal, K.T. gave me two minuses for hair braiding and bodice lac-ing. Tonight I've done both right. She's about to move on to inspect Dolores when she spies my Sweet Sixteen bracelet.

"I thought I told you that ain't period."

"It brings me luck, K.T."

"Not tonight. Take it off."

I'm ready to scream something when Dolores reaches out and grabs one end of K.T's script. "It brings her luck." Dolores says this in the same quiet, even tone she says everything else, but this time, underneath that soft tone, there's a touch of steel.

For a minute, I'm sure K.T. is going to turn physical. She fixes Dolores with those hard eyes; then as quick as a barracuda, she snatches her script back and marches away.

I do not believe she buckled under to Dolores. "That was interesting."

Dolores shrugs. "Sometimes she just can't have her way."

"Not with you in charge." I hold up my wrist. "Thanks. I . . . I really needed this tonight."

She and Bianca go inside the dressing room and the murmur of the gathering audience becomes gradually louder from the other side of the curtain. I picture Lena, her arm linked with Eric Peterson's. Next to Eric, Nicolas Benz will be examining the dented metal seat back in front of him or glancing overhead at the peeling paint, a repair that's supposed to be possible with the proceeds from tonight's performance.

Why did I invite my friends from Channing? I'm twisting my bracelet around my wrist, then pacing and wiping the trickles of sweat from my neck.

Mr. Smith steps from the wings and blocks my path. "A bit of stage fright? Good. That makes for a splendid performance." In a dark suit with a white shirt and silver-and-blue-striped tie, he looks more like a successful banker than a Las Pulgas English teacher. "It is almost time for me to speak to our esteemed audience." He takes both my hands in his. "You will be wonderful, as will all the rest of your castmates." As he leaves, I consider ducking out the back door and running away.

I'm panicked. I make a sound like someone gargling, then collapse in the nearest chair. If I get through this, I will never act in a play again. I lean forward and bury my face in my arms.

"Yo, Des. You're not getting ready to hurl are you?"

"Go away, K.T." If Dolores can tell her what to do, so can I.

"Be kind to the crew. They can do mean things to you when you're up on that stage. Know what I mean?"

I'm having thoughts about strangling her when her hand on my shoulder stops me short.

"Don't worry. You gonna do good." The expression on K.T's face is hard to read. "Well, as good as a Channing reject can do, anyway." K.T.'s smirky look is back. She tucks her Prompt Script under one arm and stumps over to the light panel, then starts in on Jamal.

The sound of applause jolts me to my feet, heart pounding.

Mr. Smith's on stage, and he tells the audience, "Thank you for coming to spend a night with Mr. Shakespeare. This is an ambitious undertaking for our junior class, and a brave one. But here at Las Pulgas, we know a lot about bravery."

The audience applauds again.

261

K.T. and Jamal stop arguing and cluster with everyone else backstage, listening to our teacher.

Juan comes from the boys' dressing room and leans against the wall. He's let his beard grow the last two weeks—a special relaxation of the school rules for his role—which only makes him more annoying as far as I'm concerned. He catches my eye and I look away. I have to concentrate on what's coming in the next few hours. Juan Pacheco does not exist anymore. Only Othello counts. I have to think about the Moor, my lines and cues, and the blocking Mr. Smith planned so I'll move in the right direction at the right time. For the next two hours, I have to become Desdemona—poor, doomed, love-struck Des.

The introduction is almost over.

"And so why *Othello*?" Mr. Smith asks the audience. "At the heart of this play is a message for each of us—appreciate yourself for the person you are. Sometimes this is not an easy task. How often have any of us thought, 'I'm not smart. I'm not rich. I'm not pretty, handsome, strong, athletic?' Now pay attention to what Mr. Shakespeare has to say about a powerful man who has everything, except the ability to appreciate who he is. His tragic flaw allows jealousy to rule his better judgment. This will cost him the one person he loves most in the world, and it also will cost him his life."

The curtain parts in the middle as Mr. Smith returns backstage, leaving the applause to slowly fade behind him.

New sweat pops out on my forehead. Stage fright is like jumping into the deep end of a swimming pool and realizing there's no water. On the way down, you have just enough time to know landing is going to hurt like hell.

As I rub my damp palms on the red skirt, K.T. shakes her head at me. I look away, directly into Juan Pacheco's dark eyes. He winks and gives me that slow, sideways smile.

My mind goes blank, and it's as if I've never heard a single line of this play, never mind memorized it.

44

I'm shaking in the wings. My quivering knees have a lot to do about having to walk onstage with Chico for my first scene, and even more to do with what I have to say in the scene itself. My heart is pounding and my throat threatens to collapse. *Focus on Brabantio and your character. This has nothing to do with your real life or your real dad.*

"'Here comes the lady; let her witness it.'"

That's our cue. Chico looks at me, and then gives me a push, making my first step on stage look like I've tripped into the whole thing by accident.

"'My noble fa—'" I have to swallow or nothing else is coming out. "'—father,'" I close my eyes to stop them from stinging. When I open them, Pavan Gupta has such a pleading expression on his face that I hurry to say the rest. I have to get my lines out, before I can't. Juan cranes toward me, as if he's sending telepathic messages of support. Even Chico crosses his fingers.

In the wings, K.T. mouths the words along with me, and then rolls her eyes to heaven when I make it through the first part. But the hardest part is still ahead of me. I still

264

have to hear my father tell me he's through with me, and I still have to hear him tell everyone he doesn't want me in his home again. And I still have to say I don't want to be with him, either.

"Carlie love, you will always be my girl no matter what you do."

No matter if I . . . begged for you . . . to die and then hated you for leaving me?

As my heart gives up the truth I'd love to bury and forget, tears roll down my face and I stammer through those lines, looking out over the audience. I need to see Mom, but before I can find her, Juan takes my hand and pulls me toward the wings, saying his line. "' . . . we must obey the time.'"

Once I'm safely off stage I pull away. I have a break until the second act, and I need to sit alone in a quiet place.

I open the girls' dressing room door.

"You got through it," Juan says from behind me.

I nod, not trusting myself to say anything without losing it again. I so don't want to break down in front of Juan Pacheco.

"My first scene was the hardest one for me, too."

I nod again, and don't tell him that any other first scene wouldn't be a problem for me—only this one. I'm relieved that I'll never have to say those words again, and I duck quickly into the dressing room.

∽

When Act IV is almost over, I catch Nicolas midyawn. And then, when I open my mouth to say my lines, nothing comes out. The words have flown into outer space. Dolores goes blank-faced, her eyes switching back and forth, as if she's searching for a script pasted on a wall somewhere on the set.

It feels like an hour ticks its way around the auditorium clock dial, and uneasy bottoms shift in the metal seats. I pretend to look for something to hand to Emilia, praying it will cover the silence.

" 'Beshrew me if I would do such a wrong for the whole world.' " K.T. hisses my line at me from the wings.

I make up a transition line, then give the one Mr. Shakespeare wrote—the one I've known for weeks and forgot when it really counted. I'd begged Mr. Smith to change that word, beshrew. Nobody knows what it means. And now I owe K.T. *Merde.*

By the time Act V arrives, I'm the Moor's wife. Carlie Edmund doesn't exist. The bed chamber glows in an ominous crimson. Othello delivers his death sentence to Desdemona, and at the "knock-knock" joke part of the scene, I have no trouble remembering what I have to say.

As Juan leans over me, his hands clutching a crimson pillow, I plead one more time for my life. And then Othello says, "It is too late."

In rehearsal, he always covered my face, leaving me a little space to breathe, and my death scene moved along just as Shakespeare wrote it. But tonight, when I take a deep breath just in case Juan is too much into his part, he doesn't bring down the crimson death. Instead, he says that line again, as if I haven't heard it already, and kisses me. The Carlie Edmund I know seems to have gone on vacation, letting Desdemona respond. The kiss lasts longer and becomes deeper than the small peck in Act II that's given me fits for weeks, and suddenly I have pulses at points in my body that I never knew existed. Finally, he pushes the cushion onto my face.

Off stage, Dolores pounds on the prop door and shouts. "My lord, my lord! What, ho! My lord, my lord!"

The spell of Othello's last kiss is broken. Dolores always delivers these lines of Emilia's as if she's discovered a child doing something bad.

"Well done, Des," Juan whispers. "Great kiss."

I have no comeback. I'm dead. Well, almost. I have two more gaspy lines, which I hate because they clear Othello of murder. But tonight, when I say those words for the last time, I really do have to struggle for breath.

"Gotta go meet my destiny," he murmurs, his back to the audience.

Once Othello does himself in with the fake dagger, the curtain comes down and the audience applauds.

I've done it. When I look around, it's as if I'm standing in a whole different place; not the set for Othello, just a place behind a curtain with the sound of hands coming together.

The minor cast members file across the stage and take their places for the curtain call. The curtain rises and the applause becomes louder. Then Othello, holding my hand, sweeps us onto the stage along with Iago, who doesn't hold my hand. Together we bow low as the applause swells and most of the audience comes to their feet. Now I get why actors love what they do. Again, everyone bows from the waist, just like Mr. Smith trained us to do. The curtain falls, but then it swoops up again before anyone moves.

K.T's in control, and I pray she won't milk the audience by bringing up the curtain for a third time. But then Mr. Smith walks onstage and bows to more applause. He leaves and, to my great relief, takes the control from K.T. and the curtain falls for the last time.

It's over. Weeks of rehearsals, hours of memorizing lines, and now, at last, "the end." I'm relieved, yet as the cast members hug each other and go over the things that went wrong, I almost miss being Des.

K.T. hobbles over to me. "Not bad, Des. 'Course I could'a done better—like, no way would I blow my first scene, or forget that 'beshrew' line. I mean, come on, Des, beshrew ain't a word you can forget too easily."

"I owe you." I must sound sappy, because K.T. gives me her shifty-head move.

"Damn straight." She hops away and punches Dolores on the arm. "You did good, girl." I guess K.T. only holds certain grudges.

Keith crosses the stage, with Mom and Jeb following behind him.

She holds out a bouquet. "Not roses, but—" The flowers with a Las Pulgas Market sticker on the cellophane wrapper are a bit wilted, but I love them.

"Thanks, Mom," I tell her.

"Congratulations on an excellent job," Jeb says.

Keith shoves his hands in his pockets. "I thought you were a goner. Where's Juan? I'm thinking of hiring him to do some *real* smothering. You know, freeing up some bathroom time for myself in the morning."

"I'd laugh, but you're *so* not funny." I fake a punch at his middle just as Mr. Smith joins us.

"How quickly our star steps out of character." He turns to Mom, saying, "You must be proud of your daughter. I certainly am."

Mom's expression is dazzling. "Very much," she says, and puts her arm around my shoulders. "Oh, and this is Jeb Christopher, a friend."

Mr. Smith shakes Jeb's hand. "Jeb and I know each other quite well, and have for a very long time. You *must* be good friends, because I can never lure him into Las Pulgas."

"You don't come to the orchard anymore either, so we're even," Jeb says.

What other surprises does Mr. Smith have for me?

Mr. Smith says, "You're right. And I must change that—soon." He turns to Mom. "As you know, Mr. and Mrs. Pacheco are hosting a cast party. I'm already driving one of our cast members, so I'll be happy to see that Carlie arrives there and home, if that's agreeable with you, Mrs. Edmund."

"Carlie, is that okay?" Mom asks.

I nod.

"Then I will meet you at the side exit in half an hour." To Mom, Mr. Smith says, "It is a pleasure to have you in our community." He shakes Jeb's hand. "I'll come for a visit if you promise me stew like your dad used to make."

"Deal," Jeb says.

Mr. Smith makes his way to other clusters of families surrounding kids from the cast.

Mom watches him walk away, then says, "So that's *the* Mr. Smith. I understand what you mean. He's amazing." She hugs me again. "I'm so proud of you." She squeezes my hand. "See you later, at home."

After the three of them leave, Lena pokes her head through the curtain and, dragging Eric Peterson behind, pushes her way through the cast, family and friends. Nicolas Benz strolls after them, his blond hair glowing under the bright stage lights. He looks gorgeous. I'm glad he's my date.

"Hey, Des." Lena waves.

Somehow I don't like the sound of my nickname when she says it.

"Not bad," Lena says, eyeing me up and down. "You sure looked like Desdemona from the audience."

Implying I don't look like her now? "Thanks."

Her eyes dart around the backstage.

"Cool," Eric says.

"Very cool." Nicolas touches my arm, and suddenly I'm excited that he's taking me to the dance.

Juan comes out of the boys' dressing room, holding a towel. He's changed into his own clothes and has taken off the heavy make-up K.T. insisted he wear to add to his sinister look. Lena's eyes rest on him.

I'll be polite. "You know Lena from the Shack, Juan. This is her boyfriend, Eric, and this is Nicolas."

Nicolas doesn't put out his hand, but Eric does and Juan shakes it. "Glad you came to the play."

"Carlie, we have to go someplace to celebrate," Lena says.

"I can't. There's a cast party and I've already told people I'd go."

"You *have* to come with us." Lena twists her face into a Knudson pout. "We made *plans*, and you asked us to *be* here, so we *came* and—"

"Your friends can come to the party. My parents won't mind." Juan wipes the towel across his forehead. "They can follow one of us to the house."

The image of the hotel with the barred windows and the front yard of overturned shopping carts might just as well be projected on my face.

Juan shrugs. "It's up to you."

As he returns to the dressing room, Chico and Anthony come across the stage. They make a point of walking between Eric and Nicolas and bumping against them before they follow Juan inside and bang the dressing room door shut.

Nicolas backs away and looks quickly around at the clusters of students backstage, as if he's worried about being attacked by someone else.

"What was that about?" Eric asks.

"They're creeps. Don't take it personally." That sounds lame and much braver than I feel. We need to get out of here. Channing and Las Pulgas do not blend. "I have to change. It won't take me long. Lena, help me out of this." I point to my bodice.

Lena's at my heels as I enter the dressing room. "Okay, Carlie, tell me."

"Tell you what?"

"Evvverything." Lena clutches her chest.

"There's nothing to tell."

"Nothing about Juan? Come on. How come you're the keeper of secrets, all of a sudden? First Sean, now Othello."

"Sean's in New York. I told you he was going with someone."

The dressing room's empty. The other two have changed and left. Lena sits on a stool with her legs crossed, jiggling one foot. "So who's he dating?"

She's good at setting traps. And I'm equally good at spotting them by now.

"Got me. I never asked." I point to my bodice. "Can you undo this for me?"

Lena tugs at the laces. "So are you, like, seeing Othello?"

"Everyday." I slip out of the costume layers and hang them up, then take off the muslin gown and sponge the stage make-up from my face.

"You know what I mean."

I pull on a light sweater and brush out my hair. "We're not dating. We're not even friendly off stage."

"You sure looked friendly on stage. Did he really kiss you?"

"Come on, Lena. I don't want to talk about Othello anymore."

For weeks I've pictured how I'd feel after the performance, with no more rehearsals, especially no more pretending to love Juan or having to be close to Chico. But instead of being able to enjoy the night and the party, now I have to deal with more stress. My friends are about to enter the real Las Pulgas, the one I live in every single day. How am I going to explain Juan's home to this bunch?

By the time we come out, backstage is empty except for K.T., Jamal, and Mr. Smith, who are all on the other side of the stage by the light panel. We start toward the auditorium's side exit when Chico and Anthony step into the doorway. At their backs are the two scumbags who threatened me at the apartments last week.

Lena grasps Eric's arm and Nicolas dodges behind us.

Chico stands with his feet wide apart and his arms crossed, blocking our way out.

"What do you want *now*?" I don't add *Jerk*, but I might as well have. He knows that's what I intend from the way I ask the question.

Like a dog on attack, he's right in my face and fuming. It doesn't take much to bring Chico to a boil—something I should be getting used to.

He grabs my wrist, pulls me inches from his face and hisses, "Get them outta here." A speck of his spit lands on my arm.

I'm shaking, but it's more from humiliation and anger than fear. "If you don't want to be around them, you can leave. They're *my* friends."

"This is my territory. You got that?" Chico says with a snarl.

Then, from behind us, I hear Juan say, "Get away from her." Then he pushes between Chico and me, and backs Chico down the steps. I'm expecting another Las Pulgas fight, but Chico just strides off with his pack, as if he's won some battle. Anthony, being the class act that he is, flips us off as he follows them.

"Are you okay?" Juan asks.

No, I'm not. Lena's on the top step behind Eric, imitating a marble statue. Nicolas stares at me, as if I've sprouted snakes from my head.

"Welcome to Las Pulgas," I tell them.

"Chico isn't all of us, Carlie." Juan says as he starts to leave, but then he stops. "Sometimes a good face-off clears the air. *You* get that, don't you, Nic?" Then he turns and walks out toward the parking lot, his stride slow and confident.

"Well, who's brave enough to party with us in Las Pulgas?" I say, expecting Lena and Eric to run right to their car.

"You still want to go, Lena?" Eric asks.

She's staring after Juan and nods silently.

Eric glances toward the parking lot, then he shrugs his agreement.

Nicolas, his eyes still not meeting mine, waits as if he's deciding his entire future. "I, uh, have an early game tomorrow. My dad, we're . . . golfing, so I'll have to pass on the party tonight." He finally looks at me, but it's not an in-the-eye-look. It's more like he's spotted something next to my right ear.

I choke back what could come out as a feeble plea. "We'll miss you, Nicolas. Another time." I'm trying for that tone they call cavalier, but lead oozes into all my body cavities. I'll be lucky if I can pick up my feet enough to walk to the car now. I'm so humiliated.

Mr. Smith locks the auditorium door and comes toward us with K.T. and Dolores. "So, will you be following me?" Mr. Smith asks Eric, who has his car keys in one hand and his other arm still around Lena. "We'll be driving west, then south. Stay behind me and I'll take care not to lose you. Come, Dolores. Miss Edmund, K.T.?"

"I'm riding with Jamal." K.T. says and stumps her way across the parking lot as Mr. Smith marshals me toward his car. I *so* don't want to go to this party, but it's too late to bail now. Mom, Jeb and Keith are gone; I don't see the Tercel anywhere.

Juan is still in the parking lot, talking with Grits.

So who's he driving with?

"Juan? Do you need a ride tonight?" Mr. Smith asks.

"No, thanks," Juan says. He's standing next to a shiny new Camero, and when Grits takes off, Juan opens the driver's door and gets in. "My car's out of the shop, so I've got wheels again."

How many punches to the gut can I take tonight? The Las Pulgas scum have terrorized my friends. Nicolas peeled out of the parking lot and I'll probably never see him again, and Juan not only has a car, he has a new Camero. Can't anything around here make sense?

45

Scrunched down in the passenger seat, I haven't paid the slightest attention to where Mr. Smith's driving until we come to Escondido. This is the street with Juan's crummy hotel. Eric's classic Mustang is behind us and Lena's nestled next to him. My desire to disappear is so strong, I believe I might actually turn to dust and blow away. If I don't, disaster is about two minutes away. I go to twist my bracelet out of habitual anxiety—but it's gone. I feel around on my lap for it, and on the seat. And it's not on the floor. Somewhere between K.T's ridiculous costume check and now, I've lost my favorite possession. Can this night get any worse?

Mr. Smith passes the hotel, then turns right on the next street. *Where's he going?*

I start paying attention and gradually the neighborhood changes. Small aluminum-sided houses with cluttered yards give way to ranch-style homes and wide green lawns. As Mr. Smith drives up the winding road, I glimpse a sign— Barranca Canyon Road. That's where Lena said her mom's friend lives. We climb the hill and Las Pulgas switches from a congested, noisy city to a sparkling panorama of lights. Trees become a leafy canopy over our heads, and our headlights sweep across tall, gated entrances. Lights blink through trees from stately homes set far from the road, and Mr. Smith slows and turns into a driveway outlined by low lights. We sweep along a wide curve up to the impressive house at the top.

Dolores leans forward from the back seat. "Wow! That's so pretty."

"The Pachecos' home is quite beautiful, isn't it?" Mr. Smith stops the car in front of the high arches that frame the entrance. Before my brain catches up with my mouth, the passenger door opens.

"Hey, Des. Long time no see." It's Juan, and I can't move a muscle.

"Party's inside," he says and reaches for my arm as Dolores gets out and takes the steps to the front door.

"I don't need your help," I say. He's tricked me—he lied about where he lived, and probably laughed with his friends about how I gave him, the poor Mexican kid without a car, a ride in that beater of a Tercel. I swear, I'll go into this house and find a way to even the score with him for mocking me.

As I climb from the car, Lena and Eric join us beside Mr. Smith's car. I glance down the driveway in the dim hope that Nicolas might have changed his mind and followed Eric after all, but there are no other cars behind us. So in addition to being blindsided, I'm also dateless. Can this night get any more embarrassing?

Although Lena clings to Eric's arm, she never takes

her eyes off Juan. *Drool does not become you, Lena.* I avoid the three of them and follow Mr. Smith up the steps and into the house.

"Mr. Smith, this is such a pleasure," says a woman who greets us with a breathtaking, slightly sideways smile. Her ebony hair is smoothed tightly against her head and gleams under the entry lights.

"You must be the wonderful Desdemona." Juan's mother holds out her hand. "I'm so sorry I couldn't stay to congratulate you after the curtain calls, but I wanted to get back and be sure everything was ready here."

If I could just pry my jaw open, I'd come up with something charming to say to Mrs. Pacheco. I know how to act in someone's home—I've been to parties before, and Dad always said I was the best hostess in Channing. He used to have me answer the door, greet guests, get people situated. But here, all I can manage in reply is, "No problem." *Brilliant.*

Juan is suddenly beside his mother, and he's making introductions. "This is Lena Knudson and Eric Johnson, Mom. They're Carlie's friends from Channing."

Mr. Smith's my only hope now. I'll stick with him for the rest of the evening. I back away from Mrs. Pacheco and catch up to him, saying, "Thank you for the ride."

"My pleasure."

"You're a great driver."

"Thank you."

"And a great director, too."

"Carlie, dear," he says. "What is the matter? You remind me of one of those jumpy Tennessee Williams characters." He pats my shoulder and says, "Go and join your friends. Have a good time." Then he leaves me in the entry,

Suddenly I hear, "Yo, Des."

I whirl. "K.T?"

"Hey, who else?" She gives me that shifty-head move.

I can't believe the relief that floods through me. It's K.T.! Someone to talk to. "Am I glad to see you," I tell her.

"Whoa." K.T. holds out one hand like a traffic cop. "Don't go getting all cozy on me, now." She hops back on her rubber stump. "So's this your first time up here to the mansion? Mr. Juan hasn't introduced you to his family before?" K.T. transfers her weight onto her rubber heel, then says, "For a rich kid, he ain't bad, you know."

"Why didn't you tell me?"

"Tell you what?" K.T. does her shifty-head move again and folds her arms across her chest.

"About this!" I sweep my arms wide.

"Didn't think you was *in*-ter-ested." Then K.T. turns and hobbles into the living room, toward Jamal and Dolores.

I have no choice but to follow her. Lena's already cornered Juan. *So, who cares?* Definitely not me, but poor Eric's alone, leaning against a side table. It's easy to guess what's churning through his head.

I stroll over to him and say, "I guess Nicolas really meant it, when he said he wouldn't come along."

"Yeah, he had that early tee-off time with his dad." Eric glances over my shoulder at Lena and Juan.

I don't care about that, but I'm holding on to Eric. Lena can have Juan all to herself if she wants him.

279

"Want something to eat?" I ask.

Eric shrugs and follows me into the dining room, where a long table is covered with plates of sandwiches, fresh fruit, and a large glass container of chilled drinks. All we can manage is a lot of conversation about food.

Just as I'm out of witty comments, Lena appears and latches onto Eric's arm.

"I wondered where you disappeared to. There's dancing in the living room," she says as she grins at me and leads him away, passing Juan who walks toward me. He acts like he expects me to talk to him.

"Did you get something to drink?" he asks.

I'm ready to fire off several angry rounds and tell Juan Pacheco just what a jerk he is for letting me think he was a poor kid living in a dump with no car and having to work at Sam's to help his family.

"Come on," he says. "I'm thirsty." Juan takes my hand and pulls me behind him, grabs two sparkling waters from the ice and pushes open the swinging door into the kitchen. He unscrews one bottle and hands it to me. "Before you start screaming, let me say something."

My face stings with what I know have to be red blotches and I don't want to look at him. And I don't want him to look at me. My heart is pounding in my ears, and instead of yelling, I gulp water.

"You never asked me *why* I didn't have a car, and you never asked *why* I worked at Sam's. So I didn't tell you." He pulls out two stools from the center island. "Sit down, Carlie. Please."

I take him up on the offer. My legs are total rubber

from exhaustion after being on stage for hours, followed by the run-in with the track team low-lifes and Nicolas's hasty departure. On top of all that, discovering the truth about Juan has pretty much done me in.

"I did mislead you about the hotel and I was going to explain about it, but I never got the chance. And then you were here and it was too late. I knew you'd blow when you saw the house." He touches my arm but I jerk away.

"Okay. Here's the truth," he continues. "I work at Sam's to cover my car expenses—repairs, insurance, gas. That's my parents' deal with me. The mechanic lives at the hotel, and that night you gave me a ride, I went there to pay him for working on my car."

"You were making fun of me. You were hiding the truth at my expense—"

"No, really, Carlie. I wasn't doing that at all. But I guess I *did* want to make a point. And now that I see how upset you are, that point isn't important. I'd rather have you like me and not look like you're ready to rip my throat out."

"You're wrong, Juan Pacheco—about the point, that is. You wanted me to admit I was an uptight prejudiced Channing snob. That's a very important point—*for you*."

He sets his water on the marble island and says, "If you think it's important, then it is. Are you an uptight prejudiced Channing snob?"

The growl I've developed since leaving Channing is lurking at the back of my throat again. How can he ask me that question?! He doesn't know a thing about me.

"No. I'm someone who doesn't even have enough . . . money to buy a dress for a school dance. My mother has to

281

work at a—a—" I poke my finger in a direction that's supposed to be Las Pulgas. "—supermarket, and she studies nights and weekends to get her real estate license. My juvenile delinquent brother—" I take another gulp. "You know, my brother—the king of graffiti—is suspended and hates everyone in this world, especially me," I say, stabbing a finger at my chest. "And I'm the one who spends a lot of time wishing her life wasn't such a total mess. I live in the . . . slummiest apartment in this city because my dad . . . my dad . . . took so many months to die, and when the insurance didn't pay his medical bills, we had to . . . sell our house."

Juan reaches for me. But I slap his hand away.

"No," I say, wrapping my arms around myself. "My bedroom backs up to a couple from hell. Half the track team plays cat and mouse with me every time they see me, and I no longer have friends. I'm about as popular in school as, as a . . . cockroach. And I am totally a snob, because I refuse to let anyone from Channing see where I live now. I *am* uptight—because absolutely nothing—nothing is the way it should be, anymore. I *hate* my life. I hate *me*! The only person I'm prejudiced against is who I've turned into!"

I don't realize I'm crying until I finally shut up and Juan reaches for me again.

"Oh, Carlie. I'm so sorry. I didn't know."

But I stop him from pulling me close and tell him, "I don't want your pity!"

"That's not pity, and it's not what I meant. I'm sorry that I didn't know anything about you. I didn't bother to ask, and I was being a total jerk."

"I need to blow my nose," I reply. The humiliation just keeps coming, but Juan opens a drawer and hands me a tissue.

"Carlie, I like you a lot. And I totally apologize for misleading you, and for making assumptions about you."

Now I let him pull me close to him. I'm too tired to push away, and besides, my nose is running and I have to hold the tissue under it so I don't get snot on his sweater.

"Please give me another chance," he says into my hair. "I want you to trust me, to believe I'm someone who'll always be there for you—really."

I've believed that promise before, and when Dad couldn't keep it, my whole life fell apart. There's no way I'm ready to start believing that again, especially not from Juan.

I shove him away and tell him, "I need to leave."

46

I fasten the seat belt in Mr. Smith's dark sedan. Dolores gets in behind Mr. Smith, and Juan stands at the passenger door, his eyes riveted on me, no doubt willing me to look at him. Meanwhile, Lena and Eric walk to the Mustang; his hands are shoved in his pockets, and the distance between them is big enough to fit another person. My guess would be that third person is Juan Pacheco. *That's perfect. Lena and Juan will make a cute couple.*

Mr. Smith rolls down the passenger window and leans across to speak to Juan. "A pleasurable evening, Mr. Pacheco, and a wonderful performance. I don't believe I've commended you on your work yet. It's been a very full evening."

Juan smiles in that special way he shares with his mother. "I learned a lot doing that part—mostly, that I don't think I'll go into acting as a profession."

"Then you've already made a significant life decision! Until Monday," Mr. Smith says and starts the car, still keeping the window down.

"Goodnight, Carlie," Juan says.

Pivotal moment, my mind screams. *How I answer him will decide so much. I can look away and be a Channing Princess, or I can be Carlie Edmund saying goodnight to Juan Pacheco.*

I close the window and look straight ahead.

Before the sedan reaches the bottom of the driveway, I'm filled with regret, which travels from my head into my chest, and then drops into my stomach.

I glance back at the big house, where lights shine from every window, and where Juan remains standing, staring after us. I'll see him again. But when I do, nothing will be right between us.

I suddenly understand that I'm losing someone who's very important to me, and it's too late to do anything about it. This is another big moment in my life that I'm letting end badly, and somehow I don't think a phone call and an apology is going to work the way it did with Sean.

We drive without talking until Mr. Smith winds down Barranca Canyon Road and we're back to the Las Pulgas that I hate so much. I despise the clapboard houses and grit my teeth as we pass that hotel with its barred windows. The teacher stops in front of a modest home with a small front yard littered with plastic toys and two tricycles.

"Thanks, Mr. Smith," Dolores says as she gets out. She peers in the passenger side and waves at me.

I roll down the window. "Sorry I blew my lines in that scene, and thanks for not strangling me yourself, Dolores."

"Don't sweat it. You covered it up pretty good. So long, Des." She says, then hurries across to the house.

Once she's inside and the porch light goes dark, Mr. Smith pulls away.

I need to think about something besides returning to that apartment complex. "I meant it when I said you were a great director."

"Not great, but I've learned to provide adequate guidance to my actors over the years. I succeed because I am blessed with talented students."

"Like K.T?"

"K.T. is only one student I think is special; but, yes, she is talented."

There isn't that warning in Mr. Smith's comment, not like there was that first day, when he'd said, "I think you'll like this bunch, once you get to know them."

I *have* gotten to know them. I've managed to keep K.T. from beating me up, and I've even somehow built a shaky relationship with her. Dolores and Jamal don't exactly crave my company, but they do talk to me and what they say is nice, not snarky, and Pavan Gupta compliments me on my writing. But I don't want to think about Juan or the track team.

"Can I ask something?" I ask Mr. Smith. "It's kind of a nosy question."

He glances at me and says, "How nosy?"

"It's about Channing. Why did you leave?"

"I wasn't needed there anymore."

He's still the master of, as Dolores would say, innuendo—a good, but decent version of Iago. "I wasn't needed at Channing" really means "I'm needed a lot more in Las Pulgas."

I should know better than to ask my next question, but it's out before my brain censors it. "Aren't you sorry?" I ask.

286

Then the word *discretion* pops into my head, along with other memories of that first day in Mr. Smith's class; the class applauding when he entered, the way he encouraged K.T. to read Desdemona's part, and how the time passed quickly because I, Carlie Edmund from Channing, was enjoying Mr. Smith's English class in Las Pulgas.

"Do you remember what I said that day on the auditorium steps about taking the journey?" he asks me.

"Yes," I say.

"What I didn't say was that many journeys, often ones you didn't plan to make, take you to an unexpected destination that turns out to be exactly where you want to be."

I'm about to ask what he means exactly, but we're already at the apartment complex.

He slows the car next to the chain-link fence and stops at the back gate. "I'll add one more thing, since I'm in a philosophical mood and you don't seem to be completely satisfied with my answer. I chose Las Pulgas, Carlie. It didn't choose me. And what I do here is my life."

"Don't you have a fam . . . I'm sorry. I didn't mean—"

"Carlie, I'm an old bachelor with many wonderful children. So, yes, I have a family, a very large one." He opens his door. "And speaking of families, I believe your mother is waiting for you."

He walks me across the pool area and Mom's at the railing, waving. Next to her is the woman from # 147, leaning over the iron railing and blowing smoke into the air. *I don't believe it.*

"Mrs. Edmund, hello again," Mr. Smith says. "I trust we're not so late that you were concerned." We climb the steps and walk across the shaky, iron-railed balcony.

"Not at all," Mom says. "I needed some fresh air." Mom turns to include the smoking woman. "This is Georgia Callahan, our neighbor. Mr. Smith is Carlie's English teacher."

The woman flicks her cigarette over the balcony and shakes Mr. Smith's hand. "Pleased to meet you." Then she says to Mom, "Nice talking to you, Sarah." She walks to her door and steps inside, then pokes her head out again. "You stick to your guns. He needs an education if he wants out of this dump."

Mom blushes. "Sorry about all the shouting."

I can't be hearing this. My mom's apologizing to *that woman* for making noise? And what is this "stick to your guns" stuff? I must be more tired than I know. Nothing's making sense tonight.

"Please come in, Mr. Smith," Mom says. "I can make coffee."

"Our player is tired, but believe me, Mrs. Edmund, so is her director. It's time for me to go home, and it's absolutely time for me to get to sleep. May I take you up your offer another evening?"

"Of course. Thank you for seeing Carlie home."

"My pleasure," he tells her. Then to me, he says, "I'll see you in class on Monday."

Mom and I lean on the railing until he drives away.

"So," she says, when Mr. Smith's taillights disappear, "how was the evening? I can't tell from looking at you whether you had a good time—or not."

I don't answer.

"How bad was it?"

"If you don't count the jerks from the track team scaring Nicolas back to Channing before we even left the auditorium, and if you don't count their giving Lena a cheap slumming thrill, and if you don't count my being totally humiliated, you could say I had a super time."

"Oh, honey." She sighs and looks across the pool area. "My evening wasn't that good, either. You can now officially call me a shrew. I did lots of yelling earlier."

"Why? What happened?" I ask.

"Keith and I had a huge argument. He wants to drop out of school."

47

This is the first Sunday in weeks I don't have to grab my script and study lines. I don't take my chemistry book out and struggle to keep up with Doc, either. Today's a free day for me.

The phone rings as I push two pieces of bread into the toaster. When I answer it, I hope Sean's on the other end. But no.

"Hi, this is Nicolas," he says. He doesn't wait for me to say hello. He doesn't even have to tell me the reason for his call. And he doesn't even have to bother making up some lame excuse. I know he's calling to cancel our date to the Spring Fling.

"Carlie?"

"Yes," I reply. My voice is flat and dull, just like I feel.

He coughs; it's not a symptom of a cold, but rather one of nervous retreat. "I'm in kind of a bad spot," he says. "My mom . . . well she thinks . . . It's about the dance—" Another cough. "Lena's mom told her about . . . the—"

"Not a problem, Nicolas. I was about to call you to

290

back out of our date. I think I'm pretty much finished with Channing."

Why didn't I pick up the phone before he called? Cancel first? Keep some self-respect?

"Really, it's not me. Okay?"

"Sure. I understand. Goodbye, Nic." Nicolas Mr. Full of Himself Benz is out of my life. I jab the End button and toss the phone on the counter.

"Punishing the communications equipment this morning, are we?" Keith says at the refrigerator, reaching for the milk.

I snatch the milk carton from him and pour myself a glass. For the first time in weeks, I have time to catch up on the rest of my life and I have absolutely no life to catch up on. After I chug the milk down, I grab one piece of toast. Then, without buttering it, I slam my way back to my room.

I sag onto my bed, too exhausted to eat. I toss the toast into the wastebasket and take down my Jack-in-the-Box from the shelf. Crawling under the covers and pulling them over my head, I curl around the square metal box. I want to sleep; I need to sleep, and in the close dark space under the blankets, my breathing slows down. I pretend I'm in my Channing room, with the ocean sweeping in and out, in and . . .

Salt water breaks over my head and tumbles me onto the sand. I try to stand, but another wave knocks me down. Before I can get up from my knees, the sand is sucked out from under me and when I scream, the sound tastes bitter. Another wave lifts me and I'm tossed far from the shore, surrounded by a rising sea. Salt stings my eyes and burns my nose as I sink slowly below the surface into—

I bolt from the covers to sitting upright and choking. My cheeks are wet and my eyes really do sting. Returning Jack to his shelf, I pluck a handful of tissues from my desk drawer. I can't believe my clock reads almost noon; I've been asleep for over an hour.

The Très Elégant box pokes from under my bed, but I won't look inside.

I won't. Well, maybe just a peek.

Go ahead. Untie the ribbon. Remove the lid. Fold back the tissue. Just don't touch it.

Blotting my eyes with a tissue, then blowing my nose with another one, I lift the dress by its slender straps and hold it against me.

Get your act together, Carlie. You're not going to the dance. You're not wearing this perfectly perfect dress. There's nothing you can do about it.

I tuck all the pizazz back into its box and tie the ribbon. Once that's done, it's easier to think. I'll return the dress to Miss Lily, and then I'll run away and join some foreign army. I pat the Très Elégant box and go to get the car keys.

Mom's in the kitchen, rummaging through one of the still unpacked moving boxes. "Apple crepes sound good, don't they?" She says and pulls out her pastry cookbook. "I thought we'd enjoy them for dessert."

"Any kind of crepes sounds good. We haven't had those—"

The *click click* of the old stove clock marks off empty seconds of quiet.

"Since before your father got sick. I know." Mom flips to a slightly spotted page. "Well, that's about to change."

Seeing Mom with flour on her hands, her handheld electric beater ready and her measuring spoons lined up on the counter is like opening a special present.

"Can I have the car?" I ask. "I'm taking this—" I hold up the Très Elégant box. "—back."

"What?"

"NicOlas cancelled."

"Oh, Carlie, I'm so sorry. Isn't there someone—"

I shake my head. "I don't want to go." *I don't fit in there, anymore. This not fitting in is becoming a familiar feeling. Maybe I'll get used to it.*

She takes the car keys from her purse and presses them into my hand. "I know this doesn't help, but there *will* be other dances."

She's right; it doesn't help, but I hope it's true.

"We're eating at Jeb's tonight, so can you be back by four-thirty?"

I start to say, "Count me out," but she turns on the mixer and loses herself in making batter.

I guess if I want dinner, it'll have to be at Jeb's.

I tuck the Très Elégant box under one arm and sling my bag over the other shoulder.

At the mall, when I walk into *Tres Elegant*, Miss Lily is with a customer. I leave the dress and tell the sales woman I'll be back. I'm on my way past the accessory department when I hear my name called and I stop.

"It *is* you." Lena's holding three blue evening bags, and Paula, the exchange student from France, is next to her.

Lena's the last person on this planet I want to talk to right now, but there's no escaping. Smiling, I walk down the long line of couture handbags. "Have you found what you wanted?"

"I'm thinking this one." Lena holds up a small clutch with a blue bead fastener.

"Um, that's . . . pretty," I tell her.

Lena nudges Paula. "See, I told you."

Paula shrugs. "I am still not fond of it."

She has a lot better taste than Lena does. "But it'd be all right with her dress, don't you think?" I ask.

Paula's eyes cut to mine for a second, long enough to understand that we both feel the same way about Lena's Spring Fling dress.

Lena waves a clerk over. "Well, I don't care what anyone says. I'm buying it."

"Did your dress come from Paris?" I ask Paula. "Lena told me you ordered it."

"It came," she says.

"It's soooo beautiful, Carlie. You should come see it." Lena signs the credit card slip and picks up her small Très Elégant bag. "You know—since you won't be at the dance."

Kaboom! Everybody in Channing already knows that Nicolas dumped me. "Thanks, BFF. Very sweet of you to spread the word."

Lena tries for a shocked expression, but it doesn't work. Gossip-guilt is all over her face.

I turn my back on her and only speak to Paula. "I won't have time for a trip to Channing, but I'm sure your dress is a knockout. What color did you get?"

"Red," Paula says.

I rub one eye as if I have a speck of something in it. "Strapless?" I ask.

"But of course," she confirms.

"Carlie! Come—I am free for a short time and we must talk." Miss Lily wraps an arm around my waist. "What is this that my assistant is telling me?"

Without bothering to say goodbye to Lena and Paula, I let Miss Lily lead me away.

"You are returning my fabulous dress—before the dance?"

Leaving out the details of why my date cancelled and trying not to sound too pitiful, I explain, and then thank her, saying, "I really appreciate all you've done. You've been so kind, and I'm sorry—"

"No one feels so bad as I do. I wanted you to be beautiful and bring me many new customers," Miss Lily says. "But there will be another time. June, no? Prom?"

"Maybe." When carefully translated, that means not too likely.

"Oh, and, Carlie, Michael and Sean called yesterday. They will be back tomorrow."

"That's . . . that's great."

"I must go. Please come to see me. I will find you the perfect dress again. I promise." Miss Lily kisses me on both cheeks, then hurries to her next appointment.

I have nothing to do now except feel sorry for myself and try to keep from running into anyone else I know from Channing. Taking my time, I stroll along the main gallery, looking at my reflection in the wide display windows, wondering where the girl with the long black hair and jeans is headed. Is there even a chance one good thing could happen today?

I'm daydreaming about pizazzy dresses and Sean, and about how much my life sucks and— "*Ooof!*" I'm almost nose to nose with K.T.

"Whoa! Don't tell me I've almost run down the great writer, also known as the great Des!"

"K.T. What the—Are you always at this mall?"

"Ex-cuuse me?" K.T. says and puts her hands on her hips.

"Sorry—you just surprised me. I was . . . thinking."

"What about?"

"Gee, I don't know, suicide?" I suck in air. "Oh, K.T.— I didn't mean—"

"That's not funny." K.T.'s mockery vanishes and I see another K.T.—a younger one, a girl who might stammer or be afraid of the dark—but that only lasts for a second; then she's back to her usual, hostile Las Pulgas self. "You got it in your head to say somethin' to me? Huh?"

"No. I'm sorry—that slipped out."

"That's something you don't just let 'slip out.'" K.T. punches her words hard. Then she does her shifty-head thing. "So?" In one word, she demands an answer to her question.

"I was thinking that if I had a real life, I wouldn't have just returned the most beautiful dress I've ever put on. I'd be going to the dance Saturday night with a hot date, instead of—You fill in the blanks."

Why am I saying this to K.T.?

"The guy dumped you? You took back that—"

I look down so K.T can't see my watery eyes. "He did, and I did."

"Seems like you got what my grandma calls a case of the miseries."

"Actually, I think I've got several cases of them."

"Once you got the miseries, my grandma says you got to go on a long dark journey, before you come out on the other side."

"Gee, thanks for cheering me up, K.T. I feel a whole lot better now that we've talked."

"You don't have to thank me."

When I look over K.T's shoulder, Lena and Paula are headed our way. "Merde."

K.T. turns to look behind her. "Your Channing buds, huh?"

Lena makes a point of changing direction when she sees us, and she steers Paula away with her, leaning close to tell her something. Paula glances back. If Paula didn't know about the Las Pulgas "incident" before, she definitely does now.

"Guess I was wrong. They sure don't act like buds. Must be two of your miseries."

"Yes, they are." With K.T., the easiest way to make it through a conversation is to say it straight out.

"Looks like you be in for one long journey, girl. I'll catch you later, Des." She says this and hobbles away.

My desire for window-shopping evaporates so I slouch onto a bench, put my legs out and my head back, then stare at the domed mall ceiling.

Forget everything in your ruined life. Forget about Chico and Anthony waiting to pounce from every shadow. Forget about Nicolas and Lena and—

"So!"

"Yikes!" I jump to my feet, yanked from my gloomy thoughts by Grits, who's plunked himself down on the bench next to where I'd been sitting until he screamed in my ear.

"You move pretty fast," he says.

"Right. And now that you've shortened my life by a decade, what do you want?"

He tells me: "Since I finished my stint at Cal Works last weekend, I won't see Keith before school next week. So give him a message, okay? Tell him I'm working on damage control with Chico and some of the other butt-heads. You know, for when he comes back from suspension. Okay? Catch you later."

He hauls his long body off the bench and lopes through the mall, swatting fronds of each potted palm he passes.

48

I'm back to the apartment before four. That should make Mom feel like I'm cooperating when it comes to Jeb, and I am. I'm just not doing it with much enthusiasm.

As I climb the stairs to our apartment, angry voices come from behind a closed door. That's not unusual, but today they're not coming from # 147; they're coming from # 148—ours.

The front door practically bulges with tension as Keith shouts, "I told you, I'm not going back to that stupid school."

"Yes you will! You'll do exactly that, Keith. You're finishing this year and maybe the next one at Las Pulgas. We're Edmunds, and we don't quit."

Mom's using Dad's words. She's using him for support, just like she did when he could really show up and say, "Listen to your mother."

As if Mom's pushed a replay button, I'm back at one of the last grim days in the hospital. Dad, his eyes hard with pain and morphine, forces each word out. "I've always told you that Edmunds don't quit."

That day, I just stared out the window, and instead of letting him know I'd heard what he said, I watched the people outside—people who weren't dying. I wanted to be out there, with them, hurrying home for dinner, looking forward to my favorite TV program. I wished for all this to end, and I hated what I wished for.

"I'm choosing a different way," Dad said. "I'm not quitting." His breath came in short gasps. "But no more procedures."

The window reflected the room behind me: Mom at Dad's bed, Keith at the door, half in half out.

"No." Mom's words were muffled behind her fist. "Please. Please, don't give up."

When I faced the room again, Keith hadn't moved from the doorway, but he'd turned his back to us.

Dad had said one last thing to us as we'd left him that night: "I'm deeply sorry."

Now, so many months later, standing at the door of Apartment 148 and far from that hospital room, I know what his apology really meant. He was accepting his death and asking us to do the same. He was asking us not to . . . hate him for leaving.

He'd heard Mom beg him to stay. He'd seen Keith turn away. He'd seen me looking out the window, not wanting to be there in that room.

I sigh and push open the door to Apartment 148 and step inside. But Mom and Keith are too locked onto each other to notice I'm there. It's like I'm just one more ghost in the room.

"Your father would be so ashamed if he—"

"Don't trot out Dad," Keith yells. "He's dead. He doesn't count."

"You're hideous!" I scream. They notice me now, and I don't care if the whole apartment complex hears me. "Don't say that!"

Keith whirls on me, saying, "Cut the crap, Carlie. You hate him for dying and leaving us in this mess—just like I do. And you wanted it over too, only you're too Miss Perfect to admit it."

"Stop!" A sudden quiet throbs in the air, and I can almost hear Mom's interior dams crumble as her words pour out of her.

"I haven't—I . . . . Neither of you is angrier about your father's death than I am." She says this and covers her face with her hands, then sinks onto the couch as if her bones are melting. Her hands fall to her lap and she goes on. "Everyday I battle hating what has happened to us. Everyday I battle not resenting your dad, trying to hate the disease instead. He tried to stay with us—I wanted him to keep fighting, but he couldn't go on. He begged me to give him permission to stop the treatments. And I didn't!"

She pauses, then says, "But my lungs ached trying to breathe for him. I was so relieved . . . when it was over." The expression that has baffled me for months streaks across her face and is gone.

She's said exactly what I've been feeling—what I hadn't wanted to admit. She's shared feelings that I thought were mine alone.

When she's done talking, Mom leaves. It's more like she's vanished from sight rather than just walking down the hall to her room.

I expect Keith to rage at me again, but even he has no energy left for more screaming. He closes himself in his mole hole bedroom once more.

I sit at the kitchen table and put my head down on my arms. I think I understand how life works now. One minute you're alive; then, in the next one, you're not. One minute you love someone deeply; then you hate them. One minute you're safe; then you're in danger. Those swift, sudden endings and beginnings are linked forever. It's in these moments when you're shunted down a new path, a detour you'd never take if the world hadn't suddenly changed around you and forced you in a different direction.

"Carlie love. Remember that I said it's human to be angry about what's happened."

I remember, Dad.

I can almost feel a soft touch, the weight of down brushing across my shoulders.

49

Later, when Mom comes into the kitchen again, her eyes still show signs of crying. She strokes my hair and hugs me to her, asking, "Are you okay?"

I don't answer, but I hold her tighter, and that's enough of a yes.

She takes a covered bowl from the refrigerator and gets out her crepe pan. "Here," she says. "Take these to the car and I'll go get Keith."

"You mean we're still going to Jeb's?"

"He has dinner ready, and he has another guest he's invited especially for us. So, yes, we're still going."

I wait in the car for what seems like forever, especially with the car clock never budging from two forty-five. Finally the gate clangs shut behind Mom and Keith, and, while their expressions aren't happy, they aren't openly hostile, either. Maybe this afternoon opened some connecting doors for all of us. We've let out our guilt and our anger, and I hope those doors stay open.

When we arrive at the orchard house, Jeb greets us at

303

the door with a bottle of champagne in one hand. "You're just in time," he tells us.

We follow him into the kitchen, where he pops the cork and quickly fills three long-stemmed glasses. "Keith, pour some of this sparkling cider for you and Carlie." He pushes another bottle across the table and Keith pours our drinks.

"We need to toast our guest of honor, who's still outside exploring."

I'm wondering who the guest of honor might be when Mr. Smith, dressed in jeans, a Las Pulgas T-shirt and tennis shoes comes through the back door. "Mrs. Edmund! Carlie, Keith." He says, greeting us. Then, taking the champagne from Jeb, he lifts his glass along with everybody but me. I'm speechless and still recovering from seeing my elegant teacher dressed like—like a Jeb look-alike.

"To one of my oldest and best friends, Zacharia Smith," Jeb says.

Mr. Smith holds up his glass and clinks Jeb's. "It's been much too long."

"You're right on that score, considering you used to live here more than at your own house."

I look from one to the other of them. *How can Mr. Smith and Jeb Christopher be best friends?*

"You're letting my past loose in front of my student, Jeb." Mr. Smith says and looks at me. "Jeb's father was my probation officer—or you might say my guardian angel. He's the person I told you about, the one who saw a speck of decency underneath my well-cultivated bad behavior."

Jeb laughs and pats Mr. Smith on the shoulder. "He saw those specks in both of us, as I recall. I know this'll surprise all of you, since we're now what Las Pulgas considers upstanding citizens, but from the time we turned fourteen—"

"Ahem, make that eleven," Mr. Smith corrects him.

"Do we count swiping Mrs. Patterson's chickens?"

"What do you think?" Mr. Smith asks.

"Okay, then. Eleven. And when we were fourteen, we landed in juvie together. The sheriff had no sense of humor back then, either." Jeb leans against the kitchen counter and smiles at Mr. Smith.

It's obvious they shared something years ago, and they don't need more than a word or two to bring it back like it happened yesterday.

"It wasn't a hanging offense, but borrowing the sheriff's car wasn't much of a laughing matter." Mr. Smith shakes his head. "What we were thinking?"

Now Jeb laughs. "That we needed to get to the swimming pool to see those girls. *That's* what we were thinking." He sips from his glass. "My dad got ribbed about my arrest, even after he quit the department and bought this ranch. I never had even a slim chance of stepping outside the law again, either. He saw to that."

"I'm sure that's why he took me in, too. He was smart, putting us two wild lunatics in one cage, where he could keep an eye on both of us at the same time."

"Your mothers had to be made of steel." Mom's got that arched eyebrow look now, hearing these stories.

Jeb and Mr. Smith exchange quick glances, as if they're deciding how to respond. Finally, Mr. Smith says, "No mothers, Mrs. Edmund. That's what brought Jeb and me together in the first place. Two kids left early on with only their dads and a whole lot of anger."

"Oh, I'm so sorry. I—"

Keith's staring at his feet, and I'm hoping the conversation will keep going. What I've heard so far is totally amazing.

Jeb puts his half-full glass on the table. "Come on. Let's take a turn around the orchard before dark. Sarah? Are you up for a walk before dinner?"

Mom sets her crepe pan on a burner. "No, I can't right now. I have crepes to make. So please don't pester the pastry chef." As she adjusts the flame, the afternoon fades from her face. She smiles and says, "Try saying that three times."

Jeb laughs. "Okay. I give up. Keith, I'll show you what I've got in mind for your summer job. And Zach, I want you to see the trees I put in where the old barn used to be. Remember when you tried to fly off the roof? Had to tear it down before it collapsed." Jeb holds open the kitchen door and they head out.

"You'll never let me forget that flying stunt, will you?" Mr. Smith says.

"Nope," is all Jeb tells him.

Mr. Smith shakes his head. "I was young."

"Like my father told you, you should have known better, all the same."

From the window over the sink I watch the three of them cross the orchard and disappear around the barn. Keith is jabbering away, and Jeb points this way and that, just like a tour guide.

And who's that other cowboy next to them? What did Jeb do with Mr. Smith—the one good thing I found at Las Pulgas High?

"They seem to like each other," Mom says. Her batter sizzles as she tips the pan to spread it evenly.

"I guess you're talking about Keith and Jeb."

"Yes, but Mr. Smith, too. It's nice to have some men around, isn't it? It makes a difference for Keith."

"Jeb isn't Dad."

Mom flips a crepe from the pan. "No, he isn't, but that's not the point, Carlie. When Keith's with Jeb, I see my son the way he used to be. I'm counting on Jeb to help me get Keith to go back to school."

"So he's using Mr. Smith to make Keith cooperate?" I can't mask the acid in my reply.

"Yes, that's part of his plan."

"Some plan." I hate that we're already sniping at each other. But why can't she see that Jeb causes more problems than he solves?

"Stop," Mom says as she taps her spoon on the side of the pan. She removes the crepe pan from the heat and leaning against the counter, she rubs her temples.

"I want Keith back in that school. I want him to run cross country again, to come back to life the way he was, instead of letting anger chew up a little more of him every day. If it takes a hundred Jebs to help him, you're going to have to learn to accept every one of them."

Then Mom takes me in her arms, rocking me. I keep my eyes closed and let her hold me. I feel like a child—small, scared, and broken.

"I want my life back the way it was," I tell her.

"You can't have it back, Carlie. None of us can. We all need to move on." Mom tightens her arms around me, then holds me away from her so she can look into my eyes. "Your dad would tell us that same thing." She cups my chin in her hand. "And you know I'm right."

Yes. For months he's told me, and for months I haven't listened. I haven't wanted to hear it.

"Let's finish the crepes before those three characters come back."

I've seen Mom make crepes a hundred times, and one by one, the perfect French pancakes grow into a small stack, waiting for the diced apples already scenting Jeb's kitchen with cinnamon and sugar.

"Why don't you fill and roll these," Mom says as she sets the crepes on the table. "I'll start the dishes."

I finish the crepes and station myself at the kitchen window just as Mom stacks the last clean pan on the shelf. The three men come from behind the barn and stroll toward the house. Quicken trails behind them, sleek and fat, and clearly very happy.

At least your cat found a happy ending, Carlie.

Keith's talking, using his hands to punctuate his words. Mom's right. My brother *is* different when he's with Jeb— and I hate that. Why can't he be himself without this bossy interloper?

"It's time to move on, Carlie love."

Dad's voice is so close to my ear, I can feel the rush of air from his breath, like when I was small and he'd tuck me into bed. He'd whisper, "Sleep tight, Carlie love." Out of habit, I reach up and almost expect to touch his cheek. But there's only an empty space where he should be.

When the three men enter the kitchen, Jeb picks up his glass. Mr. Smith and Keith do the same. "To Keith's summer job."

Mom wipes her hands and finds her glass. She holds mine out to me, her eyes slightly moist and hopeful. *Please, Carlie*, her eyes ask. *Please.*

I take the sparkling cider and drink, but my toast is silent and different from theirs: *To moving on.*

Jeb sets his glass down and picks up an oven mitt. "Now, let's see if this dinner's ready. Everybody hungry?"

"I've been ready to eat since I first smelled that stew of yours," Mr. Smith says.

"Good. Carlie, you're in charge of setting the dining room table." Jeb opens the oven and lifts a large pot from inside.

Mom pulls out a drawer and counts out the flatware. When she gives it to me, she mouths, "Thank you."

At dinner I eat and listen to the conversation that goes back and forth across the table, as Mom, then Mr. Smith, then Jeb or Keith tell stories. My brother's become quite the talker and in a reversal of roles, I'm now the silent one.

"I was a new teacher—and somewhat arrogant." I look up at the sound of Mr. Smith's laughter.

"A lot arrogant, you mean," Jeb says.

"Indeed, but I love a challenge and so do you. Admit it! You were the one who took over Walsh Investments and turned it around, when even the Walsh family had given up on it."

"Walsh Investments?" That comes out of my mouth unexpectedly; I'd meant to say it only to myself.

Walsh Investments was a company my dad used to talk about as the financial success story of the decade. I try to picture Jeb Christopher in a suit and tie pointing to people seated around a large, shiny boardroom table, telling them what to do and how to do it.

"I never took the risk you did, Zach. Your job was on the line, but only my ego was in jeopardy. I never guaranteed the Walsh family anything." Jeb picks up the large serving dish of stew and asks, "Seconds?"

Keith serves himself another heaping bowlful. "So the other teachers at Channing got steamed just because your students' scores went up? That's nuts."

"Not steamed, exactly. More like unsettled," Mr. Smith says.

"Jealous is more accurate," Jeb tells him.

"Don't pay any attention to Mr. Christopher, here," Mr. Smith says. "The teachers were surprised, and they should've been. I was a bit surprised myself, in all honesty. But as Jeb said, I'd guaranteed that I'd bring those students up to grade-level or resign, so I had some scrambling to do before any of them started improving."

"What my modest friend hasn't told you," Jeb says, "is that he set up contests with cash rewards, made home visits every week, and took his kids on field trips—at his own expense. All to motivate them to do better in school."

"I didn't have much salary left that year," Mr. Smith chuckles. "And I took many a meal at this table to keep from starving."

"Those kids would have gone to hell and back again, not to let you down," Jeb says. "Every one of them scored in the 80's or 90's on those final tests. Three even made the honor roll in their junior year."

"That's when I decided there were probably more than just this handful of at-risk students out there who needed a boost, and they weren't going to school in Channing."

Mr. Smith lifts the serving dish from the center of the table and passes it across to me. For a moment he doesn't let go, and we hold that dish together, his eyes locked onto mine. "Las Pulgas had plenty of those kinds of students, so I came here to work with them."

The look he directs at me is one I've seen every time K.T. raises her hand, or whenever Chico reads one of his stories, or when Jamal recites an original poem. I can see that he thinks I'm like the other students in his class; he thinks I need a *boost*, too.

I take the dish and set it down, suddenly not very hungry anymore.

50

Of all my Las Pulgas Mondays, this one will have its own special place in my brain.

When Keith and I go through Mr. Icky's security stop, I'm so twitchy worrying about what my brother's going to be facing that I get sent to the wand guy for closer inspection. I want to stick close to Keith today, but he just brushes me off. Pulling the brim of his baseball cap down over his eyes, he silently disappears into the principal's office. His first official day back and he's acting like he's here for some kind of award, while I'm the one who feels sick.

And the assembly makes me feel even sicker. I'm closed in with hundreds of students, all with revenge against the Edmunds on their minds. The announcements take about fifteen minutes, then there's the prom committee report. Keith's waiting in the back corner by the exit, chewing on his thumb with his head down so I can't see his eyes.

When Bins steps onto the stage, I can almost taste the anger in the room. He takes the microphone and searches among the faces staring up at him. His eyes stop at each boy on the track team, and then he starts to speak.

"In the past month, we've had some incidents at Las Pulgas High that do not reflect well on our school."

Butts shift in their seats and K.T., who's sitting in front of me, jabs Big Teeth, who slaps at her without making contact. Someone kicks the back of my chair, but I keep my eyes facing forward and I don't move.

"So I'm giving fair warning to every student in this school." Bins pauses, looking at the spot where my brother stands. "One more fight, one more act of vandalism, and all athletic competitions, dances and clubs will be cancelled."

The tension ratchets up and a low buzz of voices travels around the room.

Bins holds up his hands and the buzzing subsides. "Now return to your classes. Have a great week, and I don't want to see *any* of you in my office for cutting or disruptive behavior the rest of the year. Got that?"

The student body shambles out the buzz picks up again all around me. I speedwalk to English, where my hot seat simmers under me every time Mr. Smith asks a question that he directs at me. Jamal leans in and whispers, "Told ya. That's the hot seat."

I scoot sideways, and in a low but threatening voice, tell him, "Jamal, if you say that one more time, I'm going to—to rip up your poetry book."

The wounded-puppy look he gives me makes me regret my nasty tone and I quickly say, "Not really—but just stop bugging me, okay?"

Between English and French, I slink along the hall to my locker, head down, making myself into as small a target as possible.

Get through today. Get through today. I repeat that thought like a mantra.

As I twirl the dial on my locker, a loud crash comes from the main entrance. A girl screams, and someone shouts, "Nail him!"

Everyone who was still in the hall now rushes in the direction of the commotion and to keep from being squashed against the lockers, I let the crowd sweep me along. Just before the security entrance everybody comes to a stop and I hear shouting.

"Get him, Chico!"

"Cream him!"

Pushing my way past to get a better look I see Keith and Chico, crouched and circling each other. Then Chico lunges and knocks Keith flat on his back. But before Chico can land a punch, Keith rolls out of the way and scrambles to his feet.

Chico whips off his jacket and lashes Keith across the face with it. Keith falls back, then swings a clenched fist and lands a solid punch to Chico's face and blood trickles from a cut below Chico's eye. Furious, he moves in close to grab Keith around the middle, then pins him against the wall. He slams Keith hard in the stomach and my brother crumples to the floor. Chico straddles him now, pounding his head and chest.

Screams and shouts surge through the crowd that's waiting for blood, and it's Anthony and the two scary scum-balls from that day by the pool who are yelling the loudest. I taste acid creeping up the back of my throat and I feel like I'm going to throw up.

Then, from somewhere inside, I hear, *"Carlie love, he's your brother. Take care of him."*

Before I think about how much pain I'm about to be in, I jump on Chico's back and hit him across the shoulders with Introduction to Chemistry.

The crowd is suddenly silent and I now finally understand the properties of a vacuum. Doc would be so proud.

Chico turns on me, crouched like an animal ready to spring and I try to remember the Aikido class I'd have taken more seriously if I'd had any clue that someday I'd be going to Las Pulgas High.

Redirect. That's the key. Don't oppose. But how?

We circle each other and I drop my weapon, keeping my hand out in front and open.

"You going to slap me to death, or what?" he smirks.

The snide look on his face makes me furious, but I remember that I have to keep calm. The key is to wait until he comes toward me. Then use his own force and weight against him.

He lunges and I catch his wrist, swing under his arm and pull, throwing him off balance and sending him head-first away from me. He's quick to recover and yanks free of my grip.

His fists are thick and I can almost feel the blow he's about to deliver to my head. I duck as he steps forward, but then suddenly he's on his knees. Somebody's tackled him. It's Juan! And then Grits jumps in, dragging Chico to his feet, pinning his arms behind him. Juan grabs Chico's shirt and pushes him against the wall. Jamal, Pavan and Doc surround him, and when Juan lets go, Chico raises his hands in surrender.

Keith, still gasping from the sucker punch in the gut, gets to his feet and shoves Grits to the side. "It's my fight! Not yours."

The shouts start again, but it's too late to finish the battle now that Mr. Bins and Mr. Icky push their way through the crowd. Mr. Bins steps between Chico and Keith.

"So is this settled?" He asks with his hands on his hips, like a referee.

I expect Bins to haul Keith off for more time at Juvie. But my brother surprises me.

"I was wrong!" Keith pants. "I'm . . . I'm sorry for what I did, and I'd like another chance."

As the crowd erupts in boos and catcalls, Grits puts two fingers between his teeth. His shrill whistle instantly stops all the commotion. It's almost like he's hit a mute button.

"Okay, you guys. I asked Keith to join the team this year, so shut the hell up about it."

"Like hell," Chico yells. "I'm not letting him on the team!"

Juan snaps around to face Chico with both fists clenched, and Chico takes a step back.

I'm surprised when Mr. Bins doesn't speak up. Instead, he seems to be waiting for Keith and Chico to finish their feud. The final bell's already rung, but half the student body is still here, crowded into this hallway.

K.T. stands next to Big Teeth, their arms flung across each other. Juan, his lips tight, is next to Doc. When our eyes meet, he looks at me questioningly, then he slowly crosses the space between us and asks, "Are you all right?"

I nod, because I'm shaking. And whatever bravery I had during the fight is all drained away. I want to tell him about Keith's shouted apology. "I—"

But then Mr. Smith pushes his way through the crowd and takes me by the arm, asking, "Are you hurt, Carlie?"

"Uh, no," I tell him.

Across from us Anthony and his two friends stand with their arms folded. Anthony's staring at me, but this time it's with curiosity, instead of his usual dark angry eyes. He glances at Juan, then back at me, before turning his attention to the main event.

Grits slowly walks inside the circle of grim-faced students surrounding Keith and Chico. "I don't know about the rest of you track guys, but I'm setting new records this year, and I'm planning on leaving those Channing scumbuckets in the dust."

The hallway explodes with applause.

"Keith said he made a mistake and he's sorry. You all too perfect to accept his apology?" Grits asks. "We need Keith. He's good. He'll help us whip Channing's butt." Grits holds up Keith's arm, as if he's a winner of a boxing match, and three of the track team guys push through the crowd of students to stand next to him. I expect Anthony to side with Chico, but he surprises me and takes a slow step to join Grits. Then his two surly friends fall in behind him, leaving Chico pushed into the background.

Keith's done it! He's crossed over that gigantic border from Channing to Las Pulgas. When he looks at me, he smiles. If he didn't have the dark bruise along his left jaw, his smile would be exactly as I remember it from a long time ago.

When I finally turn to say something to Juan, I can't. He's vanished.

51

Later that afternoon, I'm stretched across my bed with my Jack-in-the-Box on my chest, twirling the handle while escape fantasies play in my head. Suddenly I hear a loud, rhythmic knocking on the front door. I set Jack down on the bed and hurry to see who's at the door. When I peer through the peephole, I instantly understand why those knocks sounded so strange.

It's K.T., leaning against the iron railing.

I unlatch the door and crack it open.

"Hey, it's the girl what *whupped* that bad-ass Chico. How do you like that beat?" she asks, repeating it and holding up her fist.

"How did you —? What are you doing here?"

"I got my ways." K.T. pokes her nose around the door. "You're supposed to in-vite people in, when they come visiting. Don't you know that?"

I back up and K.T. stumps her way inside, as if she's inspecting the apartment before moving in. "Not bad. It's smaller than where I thought the great writer would live, but don't they live in teensy places called . . . what are they? Starts with a G."

"Garrets."

"Yeah, that's it." She spins around on her rubber heel. "So, where's your room?"

I point down the hall and K.T. doesn't wait for me to lead the way. She's already at the door to my bedroom.

"It's dark in here. How come the black curtain?" K.T. drops onto the bed. "Ouch!" She's up in a shot.

"Oh, gawd!" I retrieve Jack. Please don't let him be broken even more than he was.

"What you doin' with *that* in your bed?"

"Playing with it?"

K.T. starts to sit on the bed again, but stops halfway down. "You got anymore surprises in here?"

I risk my exasperated look, but K.T. ignores me and eases onto the covers. "So. About that ex-cep-tion-al story you wrote for English."

I'm double blinking, hearing her. "Did you say *exceptional*?" I ask.

"What's the problem? You think I don't know any big words?"

"No. I mean, yes!"

She crosses her arms and slaps me with her Las Pulgas stare.

"You're not exactly easy to know, K.T. I keep expecting you to bite my head off."

She waggles her foot and does that shifty-head move. "I just don't like snobs, is all."

First Juan with his Princess title, and now K.T. "But I'm not a *snob*!"

She's on her feet and in my face. "And I'm not *stupid!*"

"Okay. You're right. You're not, and I'm not."

Her eyes tense up into a squint, as if she's examining me closely for one glimmer of *snobiness*. "So what was that note about?"

"What note?" I ask, baffled.

"The one you wrote on my paper. You know, that stuff about acting tough not doin' the job, and that anger-guilt business." She crosses her arms and shifts her head again, waiting.

"I guess I just meant that no matter how tough you act—"

"Or stuck up?"

I clear my throat. "Right. Or that either. Yes—what's inside . . . still won't go away." Her wall is different from mine, but her reason for building hers is the same as mine. But whatever the reason we have them, our walls just don't work. Realizing this, I suddenly miss Juan, and wish I could rerun that night at the party. I'd say goodbye. I'd stop hiding behind my Princess wall.

But K.T. interrupts my train of thought. "You got something cold to drink?" she asks and walks around me, then goes into the kitchen. There, without hesitating, she opens the refrigerator. It's like she's already taken up residence.

"I'll get us some grape juice," I tell her.

K.T. sits at the table where Mom's books are scattered.

"Those are my Mom's. Go ahead and push them out of the way."

"Your mom. Where's she at?"

"Work. She's a cashier at Las Pulgas Market." I hand K.T. a glass of juice and sit across from her.

"Get out! I bet I seen her lots a times."

"Probably. She's there at least five days a week."

"What's your mom like?" K.T. asks, then tosses down her juice.

"Depends. When she's tired, she gets really cranky. How about your— I'm sorry. I—"

"Oh, stop already. So I don't have a mom. No secret about that. But I got a grandma. You got one of those?"

"No. My grandmothers both died before I was old enough to know them. Only my dad's father's still alive. But he lives in Florida and I never see him."

"So there you are. I got something you don't, and vice versa." Then K.T. gets up, saying, "I gotta go."

When she's outside, she tells me, "My cast comes off this week."

"That's great. Bet you'll be glad to be rid of that."

K.T. turns to leave, but then she stops and looks at me with her head tilted to the side. "You know, I got to thinking about that dress, and what you said about your date and all."

"Sorry about all that emotional stuff. I should be used to disappointments by now."

"I got a whole story I'm gonna write about dis-ap-point-ments. You can give me your comments on that one, too."

Great. Another rap poem. And yet, K.T. went to the trouble to find out where I live, she came to see me, and she hasn't even been nasty. Our relationship has moved from hostile, to cautious circling, to my sharing something personal with her. So I guess I can handle another of her rap poems.

"I just wanted to tell you the guy that dumped you is purely stupid."

"He's not exactly stupid, but he *is* a giant walking ego. I probably would have been bored by the second dance anyway." I'd like to believe that. But next Saturday, I'll be right here in this dumpy apartment. Alone, while my friends have a blast at the Spring Fling.

"Actually," I tell her, "the guy I really wanted to have ask me—Oh, well. That's not important anymore."

"So what're you doing next Saturday, since you're not going to that fancy dance?"

"I'm staying in bed all day and hide. What else?"

She rolls her eyes, then says, "That sounds great, but you wanna go to the mall, catch a movie with us instead?"

"Us?"

"Me and my girlfriends." K.T. looks at me as if I'm a disappointing pupil.

I didn't expect an invitation to join K.T and her crew. But then I never expected to see her turn up at my door, either, or that I'd answer with, "What time?"

"Meet us about noon at CineMall Corner."

Then K.T. swings away, pounding her rubber heel on the cement, as if she'd like to wear it down before she parts company with it.

52

The day after the fight, when I venture into my classes, I expect stares and more of those insect sounds at my back, and probably some really sweet comments about my butthead brother or the fight that this time *I* was a part of.

Chico's on suspension for three days, and nobody knows what'll happen to the track team. If Bins carries out his threat to shut down all school activities, Las Pulgas won't even be able to compete in the race against Channing next month.

Anthony slouches into English and for once, doesn't leer or threaten me with his eyes. K.T. plunks herself into her seat, doing some kind of serious rap in her head, but I might as well be a desk instead of sitting in one, because she doesn't give me her usual mouthy greeting. I wonder if I'm still invited to the movie on Saturday, or if she's changed her mind for some unknown reason, and if I should even ask.

Juan talks to Jamal and Pavan, then goes to his seat at the back of the room with nothing more than a glance in my direction. It's such a brief connection, it almost seems as if it didn't happen. Only the extra thud in my heart tells me that it did happen, and how important that tiny moment was to me.

This is so weird. Nobody's paying any attention to me and I can't be imagining it. Maybe I've become invisible? I've prayed for that, but now that I seem to have managed it, it doesn't feel very good. It's *almost* worse than being the center of attention. I totally thought my life would be easier after the track team accepted Keith's apology, but instead it's worse. Now it's like *I'm* the Edmund nobody seems to want around.

I reach down to finger my bracelet, forgetting for a second that it's gone. I thought maybe I'd left it in the dressing room after the play, but when I looked, it wasn't there. Nobody brought it to the lost and found when I checked in the office, either. I think about what K.T told me that day in the mall. "Once you got the miseries, my grandma says you got to go through a long dark journey before you come out the other side." I guess I can add one more misery to that trip.

⁓

The morning slides into noon, then into chemistry. For a change, Doc doesn't growl when he says, "Take notes." I'm excited that he even notices me. At least I haven't become invisible to him. While he's setting up the experiment, the teacher passes back our chemistry tests from last week. I give Doc the paper with the A at the top and wait, hoping I've at least passed.

"This is yours," Doc says and hands the paper back to me.

"Huh? I've aced a test? Omigod." Then, before I even think about what I'm doing, I throw my arms around his neck. "Doc, you're the best!" When I step back, his face is red and he's standing with one beaker in each hand, his eyes glazed. I've been learning a lot by watching and taking down whatever Doc tells me and I didn't even realize it.

"Okay," I say. "What are we doing today?" I pick up my pencil and wait for him to recover.

After class, I stash my books in my locker and start out the door to meet Mom. As I take the steps down, K.T.'s voice comes from behind me, calling, "Hey, Des, wait up!"

When I turn, she's barreling down the stairs after me. She *is* talking to me. *Why am I so relieved about that?* I can't answer that, but I do know that I'm suddenly not so lonely as I was this morning, when I thought she wasn't speaking to me.

"Take a look at this," she says and sticks her leg out. "I got it off during lunch."

Her cast is gone, and her leg looks like it's been in some kind of dark, underground storage unit for a really long time.

"It's skinny!" I tell her. "I think I'll wrap a cast around myself for a couple of months and see if that works. Dieting isn't working for me."

"You got a little self-image problem, girl." K.T. says. I'm used to her ridicule, but her jabs still irk me enough that she enjoys my reactions.

"So, you coming on Saturday, or what?" she asks me.

I'm still invited!

"Yeah, I am coming." I don't try to cover the eagerness in my answer. "Uh, K.T., were you mad at me this morning in class or something?"

"Say what?"

This is going to sound very dumb, but . . . "You and, uh, everybody else totally ignored me."

"Channing people get the looks and stares." She gives me her shifty-head move, then says, "Las Pulgas people don't."

She swaggers off to join her crew, and as usual, there's hugging and laughing, and K.T. holds out her skinny leg for all six girls to touch, just like it's some rare artifact.

I think she's told me I'm invisible now because I finally fit in here. Not being stared at is going to take some getting used to, though.

"Hey, Carlie," Keith calls as he jogs toward me. He's wearing a Las Pulgas track suit and a baseball cap.

He whips off his cap with a "Ta Da" flourish and I gasp. "When did you get the haircut?"

"Last night. I borrowed Jeb's electric clippers and did it myself. Not bad, huh?" He runs his hand over his head. "Tell Mom I got a ride with Grits after practice so she doesn't have to come back to pick me up. See you tonight."

I nearly forgot how he used to look before everything changed, and as he lopes off toward the track with his easy runner's stride, I realize how much I've missed the old Keith.

By Thursday night, Keith announces his best sprint time ever, and he's talking about the other guys on the track team as if he's run with them all year. He even says Anthony's a good runner. From my brother, that's a sign of major bonding. Even though Chico almost quit, Grits said he'd changed his mind. And, when he comes back from suspension, the team's going as a group to ask Bins to let them compete.

It looks like Keith's long dark journey is over and I'm happy for him. I'm glad for me, too. At least I won't have to do battle with a grumpy kid brother every day anymore, and our only fights are about who gets the bathroom first.

On Friday morning when I stumble out of my room, still half asleep but hoping to get in there before Keith locks himself inside for his wake-up shower, I find that I'm too late. I lean my forehead against the already locked door, listening to the sound of what I know is the last drop of hot water pouring over Keith's buzzed head.

Mom passes me in the hall and says, "He'll be a while."

"What else is new?" I tell her.

After I finally do get to shower, I dress and rush to grab breakfast. It's already seven-thirty and Keith and Mom are at the table. Juice, toast and hot cereal have blended into an inviting aroma.

Mom's dressed in her dark blue pants and cream sweater and already has her make-up on. She's pulled her hair back into a ponytail, the way she wore it in college. I seldom see her out of her Las Pulgas Market uniform, and it's been a long time since she's looked . . . I try to find the word. I guess it's *alive*.

I'm so used to seeing her slumped over the kitchen

table, exhausted and with her nose in a book that I take a moment to really look at her for the first time in what feels like forever.

"Where are your books?" I ask her.

"Gone," she says. "I took the last test and I passed. I'm done with the course and now all that's left is the state test. Come, honey. Sit down and have some breakfast." Mom puts a steamy bowl of oatmeal in front of me.

As I eat oatmeal and sip juice, Mom talks about tonight's dinner at Jeb's. She's bringing a salad and dessert, and Keith's running after school, then going to Jeb's to work on a couple of projects for him.

I know these two people from a long time ago, and I'm really glad to have them back. I'd like to be back the way I was, too. I think about Sean, who hasn't called, and wonder how he's doing at Channing. I don't expect to ever hear from Lena again, but that's okay with me. For an instant I think about Juan, too—another person who won't be making contact. I sigh and scrape up the last of my oatmeal.

The only thing I have to look forward to is tomorrow, when I meet K.T. and her friends at the movies.

Oh, well. At least it's something.

53

On Saturday around noon, as I hurry toward the Cine-Mall Corner, I spot K.T by the popcorn, waving her arms. "Hey, Super Des! Over here. Thought you weren't gonna make it."

"Sorry—Mom had to work today, so I had to drop her off at the market."

Big Teeth gives me a hard look, but then it softens into a grin. "You're one dangerous girl with a chemistry book."

"Better than with my Aikido moves, I guess," I tell her.

I buy my popcorn and Coke, and K.T., who knows the guy in charge of the almost-real butter dispenser, makes sure I get extra pumps, just like the rest of them. My popcorn box, like theirs, is totally soaked in yellow oil.

The pack of six girls romp their way into the movie theater and I follow, enjoying seeing them play almost as much as if I were part of it. K.T. waits for me at the door, and when I catch up, I'm swept into the gang's center. It feels exactly the way I imagined—like puppies falling against each other, shoving and sometimes catching the edge of a foot. It's a tangle of bodies used to hanging to-

330

gether. We jostle our way down the aisle to the center and follow K.T. single file until we come to some empty seats with two girls sitting in the middle of them.

"You gotta move over," K.T. tells them. "We got eight people here."

"Like, who are you?" one girl asks.

"I'm the one who's gonna kick some butt if I don't see you shifting two seats down, and I mean *now*."

I tuck my head down and look away, trying not to make eye contact with the girls. I'll never get used to K.T.'s in-your-face attitude, but it works. The girls get up and move to the opposite side of the theater.

"Thank you," K.T. says loudly to their backs.

I wonder if K.T. ever says *please* before she says *thank you*? I'm guessing no.

⌖

The movie they've chosen is not what I expected, and Reese Witherspoon is the last actress I'd have ever guessed K.T. or any of her group would want to see. But they're totally into this sappy romance. And I'm still not quite getting who these Las Pulgas people really are.

In the middle of the movie, K.T. leans into me. "You drink all your Coke?"

I shake my head.

"Can I have some?"

Do I have a choice?

She takes my Coke and slurps the last of it through my straw. Sharing is part of the deal here, so I'm—sharing.

She hands the cup back to me.

"Keep it, K.T. I've had plenty."

After the movie's over, the group's on their way to get pizza, but I can't go along. I've got to pick up my mom from work. Yet K.T. and company don't seem bothered that I'm bailing on the rest of our "date."

"See you Monday, Super Des," say Big Teeth, whose name I've found out is actually Marilee Lincoln.

"Yeah," I say. "I had fun today. See you Monday."

When K.T. *womps* me in the arm goodbye, I feel like I've passed another part of some Las Pulgas test.

As I make my way back to the Tercel, I realize that for the first time in almost forever, I've had a whole day—a good one—without thinking about Channing. It feels good.

When I pull up in front of the market, Mom's in front.

"Am I late?" I ask her.

"No. I just walked out the door," Mom says and slides into the passenger seat. I can hear how her tired body settles against the cheap material. "So how was your day in Las Pulgas?" she asks.

"Surprisingly excellent," I tell her.

She yawns and says, "Oh, I'm so glad."

And my mother really *is* glad I had fun while she was ringing up canned beans, bagging carrots, and making change. My mom loves me, and I need to go way back to when I promised to be a better daughter. I need to remember that she's the one who lost something major that I don't even have a clue about. We've both lost a lot, but it's different for each of us. Very different.

I haven't had time to think about the Spring Fling at all until I get home and finally close my bedroom door. The hurt I feel is more like a dull pain from a cut that's already healing, and I didn't expect that. I thought that by eight p.m., I'd be totally steeped in pain, but I'm not.

When I finally fall asleep, I dream about Quicken curled up on her pillow at the end of my bed. I dream about Sean and a pizazzy pink dress. And I dream of Juan, who calls me *Princess*. But in my dream, it sounds very, very nice.

54

I've marked off the last five days in May on my calendar. That's because today is our final day in Apartment 148. I tear the black sheet from my window and throw it in the trash. My bedroom in our new townhouse looks out onto the woods with walkways leading to a lake. A black sheet has no place in my new light and airy space, one without a wall I'll share with noisy neighbors.

The phone rings, and when I answer, it's Sean.

"Hey, beautiful girl."

"You haven't called in, like, forever. I was worried about you!"

"I've been buried, between tutoring in French and doing the last lap before graduation." He pauses a moment. "I . . . heard some gossip last month. But I don't do gossip, so I didn't call."

He knows about all of it: Nicolas—the dance—the dress.

"It's true," I tell him.

"How are you handling that?"

"Channing and Nicolas Benz are history."

"I *knew* you wouldn't fall apart."

"I started to, but then I changed my mind." We both laugh. "I have some good news, though," I tell him. "We're moving. You have to come see our new place."

"Sure, and I'd lend a packing experts' help, but there's no time."

"That's fine. I'll email my new address and you can come and help me unpack."

After Sean says goodbye, I get back to packing.

Unlike my first moving day, I have no problem sweeping my belongings into boxes, taping them carefully so I can carry them to Jeb's truck when he arrives. I can almost imagine winged feet taking me away from this awful place.

I pick up my Jack-in-the-Box and hold it for a minute; then I tuck it carefully into the corner of a box. Next I clear the top shelf of my closet, where the first item I pick up is my journal.

I swipe my hand across the cover and the gold letters, C.E., shine. I press it to my heart like a patient friend that's been waiting for me, waiting for me to open it again whenever I was ready. I search for a pen and sit at my desk. Then I turn to the page where I'd last written anything and run my fingers over the crossed out lines.

Sometimes bad things happen . . . even in Channing.

Below them I write, *June*.

I've put four letters on the page. It's only the month, but this time I'm not tempted to close the book or hide it away. Instead, I close my eyes and listen.

"Don't stop, Carlie love. Not now."

And then I write.

June 6,

Channing was a long time ago. I can't ever forget my life there. And I can't forget losing my dad and everything that's happened to us because he's gone. But the anger and guilt have to go. It's time to let my heart move on and let me accept where I am right now.

Slowly I close my journal on the first thing I've written there in months. Then I nestle it inside the packing box next to Jack.

There's a knock at the front door and I hurry to answer it because I know Jeb's here and the last stage of this exodus is about to start.

I yank open the door and there he stands, his wide brimmed cowboy hat shadowing his face. "Christopher Moving, at your service," he says with a flourish of his hand.

I step out of the way and he walks in, then asks, "How's your mom holding up?"

Actually, Mom's been super stressed lately. She just sold one house, has two more listed exclusively with her and, as of today, she has a sale pending on an apartment house. She's doing great and she's at the real estate office right now, dealing with some issue on one of those sales. Between all that and moving, she's snapping at Keith and me one minute, and giddy the next.

"She's tense," I say. "But I know she's excited about doing so well so soon after getting the job with that real estate company." I think about how Jeb's connections and his friends with property have helped Mom get on her feet and say, "Thanks a lot for helping her."

He takes off his hat and looks down at me. "I enjoy helping your mom. She's one courageous lady with two kids I happen to like."

"Huh?"

"Liking can be a one-way street for a while, Carlie. But not forever." He starts toward the door. "I'm heading over to the orchard to check on some work I'm having done there. So go ahead and load the truck with your boxes. If anything's too heavy, I'll take it for you. I'll be back as soon as I get my crew started on that back acre."

"Jeb."

He stops and waits.

"Thanks again. For being . . . for—"

"I get the message, Carlie. Oh, and I almost forgot. There's something waiting for you in the back of the truck. But don't be too long in coming out to get it."

After he's gone, I hurry to secure the last of the boxes with masking tape and label each one before I set them in the hall. Keith's using boxes to pack this time, so the contents of his mole hole line up next to mine.

We trudge across the balcony with arms loaded and cross the pool area toward Jeb's truck. But even before we pass through the gate, I hear the unmistakable yowl— Quicken! That's Siamese for "I'm really pissed off, and I want out, now!"

In the back of the truck, Jeb's left a cat carrier with Quicken inside it. There's even a note tied to the handle that says, "Thanks for the loan of your cat, Carlie. The mice have all been eaten or they've moved to less dangerous territory, but if any of them come back, I hope you'll let me borrow Quicken again. I'm sure she's going to love her new home."

I make sure she has water, and then I spend some time scratching her ears. "You're only going to be in that cage a bit little longer, okay?"

She stops yowling and makes a deep cat-stretch before parking herself in a corner of the carrier and staring out at me with a slow blink. I'm almost positive that means "Hurry it up!"

Keith and I make three more trips before we're finished loading the truck. On the last trip into the apartment, Georgia Callahan pops her head out from Apartment 147. "Got somethin' for you before you go." She holds a glittery key chain out to me. "Bought this in Reno last year. Thought we'd be movin' to a new place, one with some class. Not happening, so you take it."

She drops it into my hand and disappears inside her apartment, not waiting for me to thank her. From behind the closed door, I hear her yell, "Get up, you lazy bastard!" I won't miss that.

When Mom gets back, we cram the Tercel with the last small items and she hands me the keys. "Go ahead with this load, Carlie. Keith and I'll do the final clean up and go through the inspection with the manager. When Jeb comes, we'll meet you at the townhouse."

Then she picks up the cat carrier and hands it to me, smiling. "You should take Quicken with you so you can start getting her acquainted with the new place."

"Did you tell Jeb to give her back?"

"No. That was *his* idea. He knew you needed your cat,

and we both felt that since we'd be away from these apartments, she'd be safe, especially where we're going." Mom starts back through the gate but stops. "Oh, could you please stop at the market and pick up something cold to drink and some sandwiches? We'll need food for later." Mom hands me a crisp twenty-dollar bill and tells me, "Drive carefully."

∽

The familiar street leading out of town doesn't look so gloomy as it did when we first moved here, and the Las Pulgas Market doesn't seem so seedy, either. I roll the windows down halfway for Quicken and hurry inside. I select three chicken salad sandwiches from the deli section and pick up a six-pack of cold water. As I pass the dairy case, I grab a pound of butter. This time, I'm using every last ounce on Quicken's paws, if that's what it'll take to keep her settled in at our new home.

The checkout line has three people ahead of me, so I pick up a tabloid paper and thumb through it. Two-headed babies and space invaders never seem to be in short supply on their pages.

"I didn't think you'd read that stuff," someone says.

I look up and see Anthony standing next me. "I don't, usually," I tell him.

He takes the paper from my hand, reads the headline and hands it back to me. I pay for the food and get change, then put the tabloid back on the stand. As I leave, Anthony follows me out.

"I heard you're moving," he says.

"Yes," I tell him. *What does he want? All of Keith's issues are resolved. At least, that's what my brother tells me.* I unlock the driver's door and squeeze the grocery bag into a corner.

"This yours?" he asks, dangling my Sweet Sixteen bracelet in front of me.

"Where did you find it?" I gasp, then grab the gold chain, relieved to hold it in my hand again. I snap it around my wrist.

"Pacheco asked me to give it to you. He found it was on the floor where you and Chico had that run in."

Why couldn't Juan at least return my bracelet himself? It wouldn't have taken that much time or effort. But all I say is "Thanks."

Anthony doesn't leave, and I'm not sure what else I'm supposed to say.

Then he leans against the side of the Tercel. "You and Pacheco—are you through?"

"No," I tell him. "We're not." *We never even got started.* But I don't say this to Anthony, and by the time I realize what this conversation is really about, it's too late to try and avoid hurting his feelings.

The disappointment in his face is a surprise. He pushes away from the car, and as he walks back into the store, all he says is, "Just thought I'd ask."

Carlie, you are totally stupid sometimes. The guy you kept thinking was out to hit you, was really only trying to "hit on" you. Men are just too complicated. I really don't think I need them in my life.

The townhouse Mom's rented is on the other side of Las Pulgas, the Barranca Canyon side. To reach our new place, I have to take the road that Juan lives on. It winds up through the oaks, and in daylight, the views are beautiful— just like Lena's mom said. When I come to the Pacheco driveway, I glance toward the house in spite of vowing not to. Juan's Camero is at the top, right by the front door. I pull to the side of the road with the Tercel's motor idling.

Okay, Carlie. Let your heart move on. Let it help you accept that you like some things about Las Pulgas . . . even Juan Pacheco. Maybe especially Juan Pacheco.

I grip the wheel, panicking a little. *What if he slams the door in my face? What if he tells me to get lost? What if—*

"Don't imagine the worst, Carlie love. Always imagine the best."

I make a sharp right and drive the Tercel up behind the Camero. Juan's by his car, leaning over the hood with a polishing rag in his hand.

Now what do I do?

Juan comes to the driver's window and peers in at me. "Carlie?"

I crank the window down all the way, the pulses at my temples throbbing like tiny drums. "I wanted to—I appreciated that—. Thank you for finding my bracelet."

"Sure."

"We're moving."

Juan's expression is neutral and he doesn't ask me where I'm moving to or anything else.

341

I don't know what else to do, so I just keep babbling. "I guess you know my brother's on the track team. Bins has decided everyone's been punished enough, so he's not going to stop them from competing at the next meet. Las Pulgas is going to go up against Channing before the end of the school year."

"I heard," he says.

"Well, that's all I had—" Quicken gives out an impatient Siamese yowl. "Guess I have to go. My cat . . . she doesn't like being stuck in the carrier for long."

"That was some heavy-duty power move you made when Keith and Chico went at it. It took guts," Juan says.

Then why didn't you tell me that at the time?

"When you flipped Chico around by his arm, I thought, 'Damn, that Desdemona would have flattened Othello.' The play would have had a whole different ending if she'd been *you*."

I inhale his clean smell, thinking he'll give me that tantalizing sideways smile. But instead, he's looking out toward the road, not at me. He hasn't called me Princess even once.

I'd like to rewind to the night when Mr. Smith and I drove away from this house. I'd like to really say goodbye.

"Carlie love, you can't expect people to read your mind."

You've told me that before, Dad.

"Are you listening this time?"

"Juan. I need to say . . . I'm . . ."

Finally, he looks down at me. "You're what?"

You're not going to make this easy, are you?

"First, the party. I should have . . . Well, at the fight when you . . . I wanted . . ." *Why doesn't he jump in and say I understand or that's all right? Something.*

I square my shoulders and say, "Juan."

"Yes." He crosses his arms and waits.

"I'm trying to—*Merde*."

Now he does smile. He opens my door, takes my arm and helps me out of the car. "French," he says. "I'm beginning to appreciate that language."

"I'm trying to—"

"For a great writer, you sure have a hard time finding words sometimes."

"I'm mad. And when I'm mad, words don't come easily . . . or fast."

"I see," is all he says.

"Why didn't you give me my bracelet yourself, instead of sending it by messenger?"

"I thought you and Anthony were—"

"Were what?" I demand.

"Together."

"Where did you get that idea?" I ask.

"Chico said Anthony was asking you out," he tells me.

"How could you be so—"

"Dumb like Othello?" He pulls me to him and wraps me in his arms. "Jealousy, I guess."

I'm shaking my head.

"Besides, I like a little groveling. When it's done by a princess, it's a real turn-on."

I hit him once in the chest before he kisses me.

55

On her way to one of her Sunday afternoon Open Houses, Mom drops me at Sam's Shack so I can catch a ride home with Juan after work. Keith's with Grits at the track, which makes me the only Edmund with nothing to do. As I wave goodbye to Mom, for one wistful moment I think back to those endless hours of cramming Desdemona's lines into my head. But Mr. Smith's already dropped several hints about choosing a challenging Tennessee Williams play for the senior class fund-raiser next year, so it's only a temporary break.

"*Bonjour*, Carlie." Paula, the French exchange student, walks out of Sam's and comes up to me. "Are you going in to eat?"

"No, I'm just waiting for someone."

"Juan?"

I nod.

"He's talking to Lena." She says this with a snarky smile that shows me her teeth.

"I can wait." I glance at my watch, then at the door to Sam's. "So what's new at Channing?"

"The really big gossip is that Nicolas Benz was suspended from school for cheating. Now the debate team won't be able to go to the finals." Paula frowns and shrugs. "But did you know Eric broke up with Lena right after the Spring Fling?" Paula's French accent doesn't hide the implied warning about Lena's predatory interest Juan. Again I look toward the door.

Mr. Pacheco has exactly two minutes to get out here.

"You are dating Juan now?" Paula asks.

Of course I'm dating him and you know it, Paula.

"He's taking me to the prom," I tell her.

Juan Pacheco better come out that door this minute. And he'd better not have some kind of sappy look on his face, either. Miss Lily has already found me another pizazzy dress, and I swear, nobody's going to mess up this dance for me. Not Lena, and not Juan.

The door to Sam's pops open and Lena waves. "Sorry, Paula. I got to talking and—" She pretends she's just now seeing me. "Carlie!" she says.

Juan's behind her, and he doesn't look at all sappy as he comes toward me and puts his arm around me. "Ready, Super Des?"

Lena arches an eyebrow, but I'm not explaining what this new nickname means. It's none of her business. I follow Juan to his car, toss my sweater and bag into the back seat and settle into the passenger seat.

My new nickname is K.T's creation's. She was so impressed by my whacking Chico with my chemistry book and pulling that Aikido move, she wrote a special rap poem for me called *Super Des*. That made me the closest thing

Las Pulgas has had to a celebrity since Grits set the school cross-country record last year. But, like K.T keeps telling me, my fame is mostly because of her.

Juan takes the road that slopes up to my new home. After he pulls to a stop in front, he leans across and kisses me, then tells me, "I've been thinking about that all day."

"You must have, because it was perfect." I gather my things from the back seat. "Jeb said he'd have dinner ready about six, and you're invited. Mr. Smith's coming, too. Wait til you hear the stories he's been telling us about when he and Jeb were growing up. If it weren't for Jeb's dad, Mr. Smith definitely wouldn't be our teacher."

"I'll see you around five." He smiles his beautiful sideways smile, and I want it to be five right now. "We still have that vocabulary to go over, right?" he asks.

"Yes, we sure do." I climb out and wait until he pulls away. There is something I need to do today after all. I have to review my Spanish lesson from last week, and find those French CD's for Juan. We have a deal—he teaches me Spanish and I teach him French.

I'm barely inside and taking my CD's from the closet when the doorbell rings. I open the door to find Sean standing there holding a Jack-in-the-Box in his hands.

I throw my arms around him in a huge hug and say, "I've missed you."

"I had lots to take care of—finding an apartment for school, easing Mom out of her meltdown after she met Michael. You know—the usual." He presses his gift into my hands. "This is for you. It's not like the one your dad gave you, but—well I hope you like it."

The toy looks a little blurred, and so does Sean. I don't bother to wipe the tears away.

"I can't stay, Carlie, but I'll call you." He touches my face. "But I wanted to make you happy, not sad."

"I *am* happy. How could I not be, with a friend like you?"

He squeezes my arm and kisses my cheek. "Same here, beautiful girl. Save a few boxes for me to unpack. I'll come see you next week."

Once Sean drives away, I go to my room and put his gift on my bed. I take down my old Jack-in-the-Box that Keith repaired. I've taken it down and held it so many times these past weeks, but I haven't released Jack—not yet.

I wanted to be sure the miseries were behind me, that I'd finished the journey I started last year. I glance around me. My bedroom window doesn't face the ocean, but it's a pretty view of wooded paths and quiet spaces by ponds.

I'm not the popular Channing girl anymore, but from this distance, Channing doesn't glitter like it used to when I first moved to Las Pulgas. Now I fit in so much at Las Pulgas High, nobody even notices when I come into a room and I'm getting used to being invisible there. Mr. Smith was totally right that night after the party. My unexpected destination is exactly where I want to be.

I sit on my bed with both of my Jack-in-the-Boxes and slowly turn the handle on Dad's. The gears engage; Jack jumps from his metal box, his accordion body dancing free. Just like when I was four, with Dad sitting next to me, I laugh. Then I cry, and I hear my heart whisper...

"Carlie love. I'm sorry I couldn't stay with you."

You'll always be with me, Dad. Right here.
I touch my hand to my heart.